The Healing Time of Hickeys

KAREN RIVERS

DISCARD

POLESTAR
An Imprint of Raincoast Books

Polestar and Raincoast Books acknowledge the ongoing financial support of
the Government of Canada through The Canada Council for the Arts and the
Book Publishing Industry Development Program (BPIDP); and the Government
of British Columbia through the BC Arts Council.

Editor: Lynn Henry
Interior design: Ingrid Paulson
Typesetting: Tannice Goddard

NATIONAL LIBRARY OF CANADA CATALOGUING IN PUBLICATION DATA

Rivers, Karen, 1970–
   The healing time of hickeys / Karen Rivers.

   ISBN 1-55192-600-8

   I. Title.
PS8585.I8778H42 2003   jC813'.54   C2003-910387-0
PZ7.R5224He 2003

LIBRARY OF CONGRESS CONTROL NUMBER: 2003092545

Polestar / Raincoast Books   *In the United States:*
9050 Shaughnessy Street   Publishers Group West
Vancouver, British Columbia   1700 Fourth Street
Canada V6P 6E5   Berkeley, California
www.raincoast.com   94710

At Raincoast Books we are committed to protecting the environment and to
the responsible use of natural resources. We are acting on this commitment
by working with suppliers and printers to phase out our use of paper produced
from ancient forests. This book is one step towards that goal. It is printed on
100% ancient-forest-free paper (40% post-consumer recycled), processed
chlorine- and acid-free. It is printed with vegetable-based inks. For further
information, visit our website at www.raincoast.com. We are working with
Markets Initiative (www.oldgrowthfree.com) on this project.

Printed in Canada by Webcom.
10 9 8 7 6 5 4 3

To all of you who are wearing some sort of turtleneck or weird scarf or unusual neck-wrapping hairstyle or multiple layers of cover-up on their necks . . . and hoping that no one notices anything unusual. Trust me, it's not working.

CONTENTS

SEPTEMBER

Tuesday, September 3, 2002
or
The First Day of The Greatest Year of My Life (I Hope) . . .

MOOD	Anxious! Excited. Happy?
HAIR	Very, very, very, very bad.
HEALTH	So far, so good.
HOROSCOPE	Typical rubbish about travel, publishing, money and the like. No romance. Sigh.
JT SIGHTINGS	None yet, expect several.

Here's what I know: The first day back to school always sucks. This is a generalization, sure. But the thing with generalizations is that they are usually true. For some reason, I'm hoping this year will be an exception. Doesn't it seem only fair that just once in your life, you get a "first day back at school" that is the stuff dreams are made of? Please? (No, I don't know who I'm asking. God or the gods or the goddesses or the Fates or fate or the stars or anyone who's listening, I guess.) (Anyone who might be . . . well, omnipotent. Any deity will do.) (*NB*: If any actually exist.)

This is my last year for first days. (Unless I get into college, which I probably won't because my grades aren't as good as they have to be. And I'm taking auto-mechanics as my elective instead of something college, like Advanced Trigonometry.) My last first day ought to be picture-perfect, like the first day of school in the movies starring Molly Ringwald, circa 1984. (My dad collects movies. We have hundreds. Teen-queen movies from the eighties are my favourite right now, don't ask me why. I don't want you to think I'm a geek or anything.) You know the movies that I mean? The ones where everyone is happy and beautiful and even the ugly duckling is just someone like Cameron Diaz or Julia Stiles in a bad wig. And no one has bad breath, bad clothes, bad luck, belly fat, or bad teeth. No one has a panic attack and hyperventilates. No one faints in the girls' washroom, bruising her head on the sink on the way down because she skipped breakfast. (Not that this has happened to me. I'm just saying it's a possibility.)

No one does anything stupid.

It's eight a.m. and I have to leave in exactly fourteen minutes.

So here's the story so far: I meant to get up early (like at six) so I could do my hair. Being vain really isn't good for that eight-hours-of-sleep thing, but I slept through the alarm (which means I did actually get eight hours of sleep).

I don't really have time to write, but I need to do it so I don't forget. (Is v. important to document this, TGYML!)

Not that I have to explain that to you.

Because you *are* me. I am you.

What I mean is that I'm the only one who reads this. And to tell you the truth, I don't even read it. Maybe I will one day, when I'm old and have nothing better to do. (Hi, Future Me!)

So, school. First day. Last year. I want it to be perfect. But it won't be. I mean, who am I kidding?

Evidence That This Year Will Not Be Any More Perfect Than Any Previous Year:

1. Hair is truly horrible and can't be saved — both flat and lifeless, and frizzy (new conditioner is not the miracle it promised to be) and in no way is (a) blonde or (b) like Cameron's (even in a bad wig). (OK, maybe it's like a bad wig.)

2. Zit the size of boulder (OK, a small pebble) has sprouted on chin. Application of industrial strength cover-up makes zit look even larger and more infected than before. In fact, makes zit look like it's grown some kind of unusual fungus or mould. But cover-up can't be removed as zit is now glowing red like a beacon. And maybe no one will look at it very closely. By squinting and standing six feet from a mirror, zit looks more like delicate bump than infected pus-thing.

3. Weather is drab, damp, foggy (furthering bad hair situation) and making First Day of School Outfit seem like a bad (cold) choice. Will have to wear fugly (but warm)

jacket over the top.

4. Slept in (so did not have time to re-wash hair and get rid of all weird greasy-looking build-up from crap new conditioner that I'm never using again).

5. Tripped on stairs coming down to breakfast and fell on The Cat, who scratched me, out of some misguided attempt at revenge. Now have bleeding scratch on arm and possibly Cat Scratch Fever. I feel flushed. And nauseated. That can't be good. The good news is that The Cat seems unhurt.

Note to Self: Look up Cat Scratch Fever symptoms on internet at first opportunity.

8:18 a.m.
I'm nervous, and when I get nervous I get dizzy. This is possibly a symptom of a brain tumour or blood pressure problem (*Note to Self*: check later on internet). In order to feel less nervous, I dig my car key into my palm until it hurts, which theoretically distracts me.

There is no reason to be nervous, I tell myself. It's going to be the same as always.

Same school.

Same kids.

Same teachers.

Sigh. I have no idea why I spent hours (OK, minutes) doing my hair and choosing the right outfit, which is clearly wrong. I'm wearing jeans, Skechers and a T-shirt that says "Afternoon Delight" in glitter. And no jacket, even though I'm freezing cold.

I have no idea why I'm wearing this.

I should have worn a jacket.

When I put this outfit on at home, it seemed very I-don't-care-what-I'm-wearing-and-as-a-result-I-look-better-than-anyone-else-who-looks-like-they-are-trying-too-hard hot, but now I just feel like a hippie. Or a throwback to a seventies sitcom. Or just a jerk.

(*NB*: I spend large parts of my life trying not to be mistaken for a hippie. I mean, I shave my legs. I wear make-up. Afternoon Delight? What was I thinking?)

(It was supposed to be funny.)

Damn. I'm late.

8:25 a.m.

I admit it. I connected to the internet via my cell phone and checked my bookmarked source labelled "doctor." I can't help it. I *know* I'm a hypochondriac. How could I not know? Dad tells me all the time. "Haley," he says, shaking his head, "I don't know how I raised such a worry-wart. Hypochondria is a sickness, you know. Look it up."

My dad is a laugh riot. If by that, I mean he's not.

(from Medline)

Cat Scratch Disease

Cat scratch disease is an infectious illness caused by the bacteria *Bartonella*, believed to be transmitted by cat scratches, bites, or exposure to cat saliva. This leads to swelling of the lymph nodes (lymphadenopathy) near the site of the scratch or bite.

Symptoms
- A history of contact with a cat
- Papule or pustule at site of injury (inoculation), usually the first sign
- Swelling of the lymph nodes (adenopathy) occurs in the area near where the skin was infected (bitten, scratched, etc.)
- Fever in approximately one third of patients
- Fatigue
- Malaise
- Headache

Complications
- Parinaud's syndrome
- Encephalopathy
- Neuroretinitis
- Osteomyelitis

Uh oh.

9:45 a.m.
Thank God we're allowed to carry lap-top computers at school. Must get my thoughts down immediately in order to truly document this year, otherwise known as The Greatest Year of My Life. TGYML. (Which is pronounced in my head as "Tiggymul." Just so you know.)

9:49 a.m.
The story so far:
By the time I got to the school (late), I was sinking into a sea of insecurity, and possibly also afflicted with Cat Scratch Disease, brain tumour, and blood pressure issues,

with a nasty red mark in my palm from the key-gouging-to-prevent-dizziness. I walked through those familiar front doors into the red-tiled foyer and the smells washed over me and nearly choked me to death.

Every crummy thing that's ever happened to me at that school came back all at once. *This* is the setting for TGYML?

Ha.

It was just the same old school, same old hallways, same old people (albeit dressed better than usual) (and mostly with fresh haircuts), same old toxic fumes. I have no idea what they clean the floors with here, but it smells like no other chemical on earth. Probably something they buy in bulk from the Chemical Experiments Gone Wrong branch of the Cheapest Cleaner Company on Earth. It is, in fact, probably slowly poisoning us all. Or at least hatching tiny little cancers inside us that will spring up later, after graduation, when we're finally free.

And then kill us.

Not that I'm paranoid.

OK, I'm a little bit paranoid.

I think it's because I grew up in a house where everyone was smoking pot all the time. (*NB*: I don't smoke marijuana [or anything else, for that matter]. I've seen what it does to people, i.e., makes them idiots. Idiots who claim to not be idiots, who believe that they don't sound like the idiots that they sound like and don't act like the idiots they are acting like, who hold themselves up as evidence of how a lifetime of pot smoking has no negative effect. Which is ironic, seeing as how they are all idiots. I don't care what the studies say, it kills your brain cells, one by one. Until they are all gone. Eventually. Over time. Short-term memory loss? General dopiness? *Hello*, they don't call it "dope" for nothing.)

Think about it.

10:41 a.m.

I have spent all (OK, part) of this morning's wretched Welcome Back assembly (so far) staring at the blonde hairs at the nape of JT's neck. I can smell him. He smells like salt and sand and well, like summer. I know that sounds stupid, but it's true. He smells like he was just at the beach before he came to school. Come to think of it, he probably was. He lives in one of those houses down near the shore, where the rich people live. I love those places: houses with gates and long driveways and rock walls and pretty shrubs and matching curtains in all the windows. Matching cars in the driveway. Matching flowers in the gardens. Matching everything.

Where I wish I lived.

I specifically wish that I lived in his house. He lives in a place that is all glass and decks. It just oozes money. (Not that I think money is totally important, but it would be nice.) (Not that I'm interested in JT for his money, I'm not.) (OK, I believe money to be slightly important and a good thing in general, but not imperative to happiness.)

At any rate, I'm after JT solely for his looks.

Ha. That's a joke.

Seriously, I think I love him. How do you know when you're in love?

I have taken in big lungfuls of him. So much so that

I got slightly light-headed and dizzy (possibly hyper-ventilated, but recovered by breathing into my purse in lieu of a paper bag). (*Note to Self*: clean purse, something bad-smelling has spilled in there). Below the smell of salt and sand on JT is the slightly cleaner smell of soap and hair gel. Sexy. He's obviously just got his hair cut (like everyone else) because I could see a line of white, untanned skin around the edges of his scalp. Every once in a while, he reached back and scratched. I could hear the scritch-scritch. It made me weak in the knees, or it would have done if I hadn't been sitting down.

Random Observations About JT Made
During Incredibly Long Assembly:

1. His nails aren't the cleanest in the world, by which I mean they are revoltingly filthy. All kinds of disgusting things can fester behind your nails. But for some reason, his don't gross me out. Probably because I'm crazy. I must be crazy. His nails are really gross.

2. He has big hands. And as Kiki would say, *you know what that means*. I'm sure *she* knows what that means. More about Kiki later.

3. He smells good.

4. He can't sit still for longer than five minutes and does not seem to notice when he smashes other people's shins with his bony elbows. Not that I mind.

5. He smells good.

6. He has no idea that I exist.

7. Oh God, I think I love him.

8. He smells good.

About Kiki:

Kiki is my best friend, or one of my two best friends. She is, to say the least, not shy. She is the opposite of shy, whatever that may be. Aggressive? Outgoing? Hysterical?

But not. I mean, you wouldn't know it to look at her, but she's the sweetest, kindest person alive. She's so nice, you feel like there must be a catch.

If there is, I don't know what it is. Yet. I've only known her for five years. Maybe she's got a secret, evil personality that comes out at night. I don't think so, though. If she does, I'd be really surprised.

Kiki doesn't have a boyfriend right now, but trust me, that's rare. She's decided to go through twelfth grade as a single, free-wheeling, independent girl. She doesn't want her memories of high school linked to any one guy in particular. Honestly, that sounds like the slow crazy madness of someone afflicted with some sort of mercury poisoning or perhaps syphilis. (Not that she has these things, which are both pretty rare). She'd rather have her memories of high school linked to loneliness and despair?

All of my memories of school are already linked to JT.

Examples of Memories Linked to JT:

1. ninth grade, first day — first day I saw JT. He was wearing a rugby shirt with navy blue and red stripes and was wearing braces. He made braces look good, much like Tom Cruise.
2. tenth grade, gym class, late November — JT was my partner for square dance lessons for two entire weeks. He had to talk to me at least fourteen times. (OK,

exactly 14 times). His hands were not even slightly sweaty and I stepped on his toes. Fourteen times!

3. eleventh grade, last day of school — JT wrote in my yearbook "It was grate to get to know you better this year, yor a cool chick." Me! A cool chick! (OK, he can't spell. But is that really important in the big picture?) I wouldn't let anyone else sign that page.

11:17 a.m.

The longest assembly in the history of humanity (TLAHH) (pronounced: tuh-LAH), continues.

Kiki is drawing cartoons of the principal on the back of her schedule, and I'm trying to type with the screen turned down so no one can see what I am typing. (Not that they care.)

I've named my laptop JT jr, but Junior for short. (I wouldn't want people to think I was crazy, naming my computer after a person who has all but ignored me for the better part of three years.) (That would be embarrassing.)

TLAHH has gone on so long that Junior's battery is going to die. Furthermore, Junior is burning my lap. Junior gets very hot when left running for a long time.

11:28 a.m.

Junior's battery is dea

5:00 p.m.

First day of school recap!

Was it good? I wouldn't go that far.

Was it bad? No.

I guess it was . . . OK.

TLAHH went on until noon, when we were finally freed for lunch. If by "freed" I mean "allowed to leave the gym." We aren't allowed to leave the school grounds at lunch. It's a very strict sort of place is Sacred Heart High, otherwise known as SHH! (because that's what they are constantly telling us to do). (Its strict rules do not stop us from leaving school altogether and not coming back, but that's another story.)

But back to the assembly, because I have more to say about it.

Here's what happened, in a nutshell. (What does that expression mean?) Mr. Pork Butt droned on and on and Kiki drew and I tried to type but then Junior died. (He really doesn't have much battery power.) I'd buy a new battery if I had any money whatsoever, which I don't. (*Note to Self*: Get a job.)

If you hadn't noticed, I'm slightly jealous of Kiki. Never mind that she's beautiful. Did I mention that? And also tall and thin and has amazing clothes. And good posture. As if that's not enough, she's smart. And athletic. And also, a very talented artist.

I, on the other hand, am a shabby hunchback who can fall over at the slightest provocation. I dress from thrift stores and am short and not terribly thin and not always very nice. I draw one line on a piece of paper and then become paralyzed with doubt and have to erase it.

Kiki and I are opposites. Black and white. Yin and yang.

I like watching her draw, though, which is good as there was really nothing else to do, except watch the back of JT's head and inspect his nails for possible worm-like activity.

When Kiki is drawing, it's the only time that she seems to disappear into what she's doing. In other words, it's the only time that she stops fidgeting with her hair and being beautiful. Seriously, she's beautiful like it's a full-time job, only she doesn't work at it. She just is.

It drives me crazy.

Kiki drew an extremely life-like sketch of the Mr. Dork Mutt. (OK, his name is Dick Borklud. Why a person with a name like this would opt to be a high school principal, I'll never know. He's just begging to be ridiculed.)

"Ha ha ha ha ha," I burst out laughing. Loudly. She'd drawn him as a giant Dick. Literally. A very, er, accurate one.

Not that I'd know how accurate it was, would I? (She would, though. She's very mature for her age. Last year, she dated the same guy all year. He was a senior. I don't know for sure, but I'm guessing that . . . anyway. Let's just say that she'd know what phallic things looked like.)

My outburst caused everyone to turn and look at me, including JT, which made me blush with the heat of a thousand suns. (I blush easily.) (A horrible sort of blush that starts on my chest and creeps up my neck and cheeks like the tide coming in or something.) So I hid my head and pretended to listen as Mr. Pork Gut yammered on. And on.

And on.

At some point, I think there was inspirational music, and I use the word "inspirational" pretty generously. I contemplated sticking something sharp in my ear or faking a seizure just so I could get permission to leave. You wouldn't catch Molly Ringwald starring in THIS film, that's for sure. Where are the wacky antics? The handsome misfits? Judd Nelson? I hate to sound shallow, but a large percentage of the student body at this school is slightly sub-attractive. (I'm including myself in that, totally, by the way.)

By 11:30, I was starting to cramp up. You can develop clots, you know, from sitting motionless for extended periods of time. It's very dangerous. People have died. It happens all the time on airplanes, and really, there is no difference between sitting on bleachers for three hours and sitting on a cushioned airplane seat. (Except the obvious differences: the airplane seat is more comfortable and presumably a flight ends with an interesting destination, whereas these bleaches are hard, narrow slats of wood and this assembly is going to end with . . . lunch.) I shifted around, trying to get the blood flowing. OK, I perhaps kicked my legs slightly, causing my foot to brush against on JT's back.

Aaaah.

"What the hell are you doing?" Jules asked loudly, smirking. (Jules is my other best friend. More about Jules later.)

"Nothing," I hissed. "Shhhhh."

"It looks like you're trying to do some sort of yoga," she drawled. "Don't hurt yourself."

Sometimes, I think Jules has issues.

"Blah blah blah," said Mr. Dick. "Blah blah blah blah."

Luckily, at this point, the microphone cut out, allowing us to have a break from the monotonous drone of his voice, if nothing else. JT stretched. I only mention this because his hand banged against Junior and he said, "Ouch, sorry," without turning his head. At that moment, the microphone got fixed and a giant squeal of feedback made us all shriek and cover our ears, ruining my first JT Moment of the year.

I sat back and thought dark thoughts about Mr. Borklud, who was obviously invested in destroying my relationship with JT before it could even start.

"Sorry," he chirped cheerfully. (In many ways, Mr. Borklud resembles a large, brown bird of some sort). "As I was saying, this year is shaping up to be the best of your lives! Blah blah blah . . ."

"Idiot," mumbled Jules. "What do you know?"

"Shh!" I said, out of habit.

"This is NOT going to be the best year of MY life," she said, with no small amount of hostility.

"Me neither," I agreed. On one level, I'd really hate to think it was all downhill after this. And yet . . . I don't know. TGYML! Maybe I should change it to TGYMLSF (The Greatest Year of My Life . . . So Far). I wonder if grade 12 was the best year of Mr. Borklud's life. It probably was the last time he had hair, come to think of it, so probably it was his favourite. He's likely spent every year since reminiscing about high school and how great it was. What else would drive a person to become a high school principal?

"Shh!" said Kiki, flipping her paper over and starting a new sketch.

I groaned. Honestly, my butt was killing me. You'd think I had enough cushioning to prevent butt-bruising, but I didn't. I adjusted, nearly dropping Junior through the benches. I grabbed him just in time.

"Shh!" said Jules.

"I didn't say anything," I said, glaring at her. She stared straight ahead. Her perfect, blonde, straight, frizzless hair formed a curtain between me and her. I fought the urge to mess it up.

I mean, really. Too much perfection is bad for a person, especially in the case of Jules.

Finally, after forever, Mr. Borklud raised his hand in a kind of victory salute. It looked like a finale of sorts. The entire mass of pimply people lined up on the bleachers groaned collectively but also clapped (because they thought he was finally finished). Granted, I'm sure none of them were listening to any of his speech, but rather staring off into space and fantasizing about how much better their lives (or this day) would be if they were (a) thinner, or (b) had better hair, or (c) had better skin. It's all about looks. Let's face it. Later, it might be about brains. But in high school?

Come on.

I myself was thinking, *I wonder how many of us have a crush on JT?* All the girls, I'm sure. And at least some of the boys.

(I hate the word "crush." When I say it, even in my head, I picture myself as a puffy, sweaty, red-faced giant, literally crushing an ant-sized JT under my bulging, swollen giant's feet.)

Further Observations About JT Made
During Interminable Assembly:

1. He has black ink marks on his fingers. Why? What has he been writing?
2. He scratches his head a LOT. I hope this doesn't mean he has lice. Or scabies.
3. The five freckles on his left arm could be all joined together to make the shape of a ... bagel? Donut? Something round. Sort of. (The freckles should be checked for signs of sun damage, i.e. Skin Cancer.)
4. He has a tattoo on his back that was peeking out the collar of his shirt. It's black. I wonder if it hurt. I have no tattoos because I read somewhere that tattoo ink could cause melanoma, which I'm sure you know can be fatal.

I contemplated JT for a while and made every effort to not listen to Student Council President Bruce Bartelson take the mike from Mr. Dick Wad. (Apparently, TLAHH was not over, but just moving to the next exciting segment: the Student Council Speeches!) Bruce Bartelson is hard to ignore at the best of times, and was nearly impossible to tune out when he had a mike in his hand. He shouted and danced and basically screamed the school song in a hysterical chant. (I think he may be on drugs. More about that later.)

I wish I had a crush (ugh!) on someone easier, or at least less obvious. Like Dylan, the guy with the glasses and the stutter who was sitting next to me. He smelled like bratwurst.

But he probably wouldn't go for me either.

I wish I wasn't such a dork.

I wish I had better hair, a better body (or at least 10 pounds less of this one), and whiter teeth.

I wish I was as beautiful as Kiki or Jules. Why are they friends with me? I have a theory that they only hang out with me because the fact that I'm ugly makes them seem all the more beautiful. And me uglier. (More on this theory later.)

Also, I laugh at their jokes.

Secretly, I think they don't even like me. But that could be the paranoia creeping in again.

"TLAHH is never ending," I whispered to Jules, sighing heavily and dropping my head onto her shoulder.

"Get off," she hissed. Further evidence that she hates me.

At that moment, JT and his two friends got up (there's no love lost between JT and Bruce Bartelson since the second grade when JT accidentally shoved BB off the climbing ladder in the gym and BB broke his arm in three places, and JT had to get a paper route to pay for BB's medical bills). They noisily pushed their way to the end of the bleachers and disappeared. I waited about five minutes (or 30 seconds), and then I snuck out to "use the washroom." (I realize this makes me look like a stalker, but I'm not. Really.) This drew a great deal of attention to me, as I dropped (a) my purse and (b) my pile of schedules and assorted junk and (c) Junior. And then had to stop and pick everything up.

Bruce even stopped talking (though how he heard the commotion over the screech of his own voice, I'll never know) and everyone stopped doing what they were doing (i.e. Not Listening) and stared at me. Seriously. I froze. And blushed.

Finally, I managed to get my armful of stuff together and mumbled "Sorry" and the kids started talking and laughing. I could hear Mr. Cork Butt yelling as the door slammed behind me. My face was probably the colour of a pomegranate. This is not a good look for me, as you can imagine.

I used the washroom out of guilt after that. Even though I didn't need to go. There was no sign of JT and his pals. So there was no point to any of the drama. But a girl can't help trying, right? I knew I should go back into the assembly, but first I decided to make some use of this free time to just pop really quickly into the library to use the computer, where I would have access to the entire medical knowledge of the whole World Wide Web, and not just the one site bookmarked on my cell phone.

Kiki and Jules say that my obsession with my health

will prevent me from getting a boyfriend. What do they know? I just like to stay on top of these things. I mean, you never know when things might go wrong that you need to be aware of. The human body is very fragile! Honestly, you can die just walking down the street: a bubble in your brain can burst (aneurysm!) and down you go. Game over.

No warning.

I just sort of want to know what to expect. Any boy worth anything would understand that.

I am The Girl Who Has Never Actually Had A Boyfriend. I haven't figured out exactly why. Am I ugly? Not really. Fat? Nope, not totally. Boring? No. Well, maybe. Honestly, I have no idea. But I just don't think I'm repulsive. It's just never happened. There is no explanation.

Unless I am repulsive.

Do repulsive people know that they are repulsive?

Or maybe, as Kiki and Jules also regularly point out, I won't meet anyone until I stop obsessing about JT. But what do they know? JT is like my hobby, for goodness sake.

It was a bit tricky sneaking into the library. I had to take my shoes off as the floor is made of these big flat tiles that echo and squeak with every footstep. The librarian, Ms. Dorchester, was reading a book (good for her for avoiding TLAHH), so I had to kind of slide by at waist height in my socks to get to the computer bay.

Luckily, she couldn't see the computers from her desk.

(from Web MD)

cat-scratch disease (fever)

Miller-Keane Medical Dictionary, 2000

A benign, subacute, regional lymphadenitis resulting from a scratch or bite of a cat or a scratch from a surface contaminated by a cat. The causative agent is the bacterium *Bartonella henselae*.

Various organisms, including viruses, rickettsiae, and chlamydiae, have been suspected as etiologic agents. Although the disease has traditionally been considered to be nonbacterial in origin, evidence has implicated a gram-negative, silver-staining bacillus as the causative agent. Cats thought to be associated with human infection show no signs of illness, and probably act only as vectors of the disease, conveying the causative agent on claws or teeth.

In half the cases, after several days there is a persistent sore at the site of the scratch, and fever and other symptoms of infection may develop. There is also swelling of the lymph nodes draining the infected part.

In milder cases, the symptoms soon disappear, with no aftereffects. Sometimes the attack is more serious and the glands may require surgical incision and drainage. Occasionally meningoencephalitis is a serious complication. The disease is generally mild and lasts for about 2 weeks. In rare cases, it may persist for a period of up to 2 years.

No specific remedy exists for cat-scratch disease, although certain antibiotics appear to shorten its course.

The main treatment consists simply of keeping the patient as comfortable as possible. The disease can, however, usually be prevented by avoiding cat scratches or bites or by thoroughly washing and disinfecting any wound that does occur.

Avoid cat scratches!

What excellent advice.

Well, too late for that. *Are* my lymph nodes swollen? Where exactly are my lymph nodes? There certainly is a persistent sore at the site of the scratch.

Two years is a long time to have Cat Scratch Fever. Rare=me. If someone's going to get it, I am.

Damn the Cat! Vector of the diseases, indeed.

I also checked my e-mail. (None.)

Being in the library wasn't as exciting as I'd hoped and I had a crazy thought that JT was probably back at the assembly and I could be staring longingly at the back of his head instead of lurking in the library with excessively cold feet. (Those tiles get very cold.) This is when I learned an important lesson, that I share with you (Future Me, otherwise known as FM):

Next time you sneak out of assembly early to investigate symptoms of Cat Scratch Fever, do NOT stop at vending machine for Diet Coke on the way back. In fact, do not go back at all, for any reason, unless it is an actual emergency, although I can't think of an example of what such an emergency might be.

I got back right when everyone was standing up to leave, so naturally I tried to make my way back to where I was so that (a) I could find Kiki & Jules and (b) so that I could see JT for a few more minutes (or seconds).

But here's where things started going badly. For one thing, it's hard to climb up bleachers when everyone else is climbing down them, particularly with an armful of stuff. So when I tried to get back to where I was, I accidentally (read: "totally on purpose") fell (lurched) into JT. It was a good plan. Only I missed completely and just kind of stumbled, like someone with a serious drinking problem who had just downed a twenty-sixer of gin in the washroom. And I dropped my Diet Coke. No one would have noticed if not for the fact that it blew up.

Yes, *blew up*.

Exploded, really. (Who knew this could even happen?) And subsequently sprayed out all over my jeans, and also into the hair and clothing of many people in the immediate vicinity. Jules being one of them.

She was all, "What the *hell*?" And then she started laughing really loudly so that people (i.e., JT) gathered around.

And laughed.

Hi, I'm a laughingstock! Laugh at me!

I laughed, too. Sort of. To keep from crying, basically.

"Klutz!" shrieked Jules, running her hands through her perfect, waist-length blonde hair, which may or may not have been sprayed with Diet Coke, but certainly looked none the worse for wear.

About Jules:
Jules drives me crazy. I love her, but I also completely hate her. (I have a love-hate relationship with many, many

people.) I'm leaning more towards hate than love right now. This could be temporary. As my dad says, "We all have our ups and downs!" Which means we fight like cats and dogs and then we make up because we can't think of a reason not to be friends. We've been friends since birth, practically. Well, not since birth, but since the ballet-toddler class my dad took me to when I was four. (Later I found out that he paid my teacher with marijuana. More on this later, I can't talk about it right now.) (Oh, but I used to love that teacher. I thought she was so perfect. I dreamed that she would fall in love with my dad and marry him and make him . . . well, normal. Ha. THAT didn't happen. As soon as she left town, I quit ballet. I wasn't any good at it anyway.) (I loved the shoes, though. Those pink slippers with the ribbons. Those were great.)

Long story short, I got to be friends with Jules out of the deal. Somehow. I don't know why she would have picked me to be friends with, clumsy lumpy me with the mousy hair. But you know how they say you pick your friends but not your relatives? She's more like a relative, like the sister I never had. The perfect, pretty, dancer sister with the handsome, perfect boyfriend and the fairly perfect life. Not that I'm jealous.

OK, I am. Totally jealous.

It's probably a bad thing to have friends that I'm madly jealous of, most of the time. But really, I could probably be jealous of anyone, given the chance.

About Me:
I'm Haley, by the way, which you (Future Me), obviously

already know. But I feel like I should introduce myself. Just in case something happens to me, like maybe I get hit by a golf ball square in the temple and I die. Or maybe I fall into a frozen lake and lie in a coma for years, and the only key to who I am lies in this laptop computer.

You never know.

Anyway, I'm Haley Andromeda Harmony. (The Haley was clearly a compromise name: My dad wanted to call me Andromeda. He's a hippie, so that's no big shock. Yes, he "chose" the last name "Harmony" because it was more in sync with his aura. His first last name was Schwartz. More on him later.)

And this (ta da!) is my diary, I guess, or the story of TGYML. I sort of wish it was the written-down sort of diary, and not the typed-on-Junior variety. There's something really cool about little blank books of paper that you can write in, but I can't hand-write nearly so fast as I can type. I can type fast. I'm kind of proud of that, because let's face it, there are only about three things that I'm really good at, and typing is one of them. I got the idea for doing this from that movie Bridget Jones' Diary, which was a great movie, by the way.

But I'm not Bridget Jones, so don't get your hopes up. I mean, she ended up with Colin Firth in the end, right? I'm not going to end up with anyone. At least, I doubt it. I'm like a Boyfriend-free Zone. I'm warning you now, so you don't get your hopes up. Also, she's English (Bridget Jones, that is). The English are just naturally funnier and more charming than everyone else.

Anyway, I love all things British, if by *that* I mean that I love Prince William, Ewan MacGregor, The Beatles and old Duran Duran records. And British curse words: *sod off*, and *bloody hell*, for example.

We couldn't be any further from England if we tried. I'm sure that if you took a globe and measured the distance with a piece of string, that this would be the furthest point from England in the world. And my life would be the furthest thing from Bridget's ever imaginable. Let me explain.

OK, I'm not sure that I can explain. But I'll try.

It starts with my dad.

About Dad:

My dad is a hippie. I wish that he wasn't, but he is. There's nothing I can do about it. He's old to be a dad. I mean, he was 20 in the 60s. Which means that he's sixty-ish now. He's an artist, but he never paints anything. Or he hasn't for a long time. I wish he'd start again, but I can't make him. I can't make him do anything.

He's the parent, right?

I'm just the kid.

Anyway, "hippie" doesn't even begin to describe him. I'm not even sure how to start. I mean, he's the smartest person that I know, but also the dumbest, if that makes sense. Like he'll spend the morning sitting in the garden reading Stephen Hawking's book about the universe and then he'll spend the afternoon on the couch watching cartoons and Judge Judy. I bet that if my dad took an I.Q. test, he'd score off the charts. But at the same time, he's the stupidest man in the world. Or maybe just the worst dad. I love him, I do.

OK, I should just get to it. My dad gets by without having a job and without taking a nickel from the government. And our basement is chock full of leafy green plants. Get it? He sells it, I guess. I mean, I know he does, I just try *not* to know about it. I avoid going downstairs, he doesn't talk about it, and I pretend it doesn't exist.

I know this is screwed up. It's just the way it is.

Kiki and Jules are the only people I've ever told about it. They think I should sell at school, like that would make me popular. But me? I don't want to be a *pusher*. (Do people even use that word anymore?) Seriously? A DRUG DEALER.

Me?

I don't think so.

I mean, it sounds more dramatic than it is. It's not like Dad is skulking around in airports, dropping packages into unsuspecting tourists' baggage. I think he just sells to his friends, or maybe they aren't his friends at all, but people who come to him for his supply. It's not like he ever really leaves the house (and I use the word "house" pretty loosely here. It's more like a multi-storey shack.) Seeing as he's home all day, every day, you'd think he could do some of the stuff other fathers do: slap up some siding or repaint the front steps. Where we live though, I guess it doesn't matter. There are WAY too many hippies in this neighbourhood. You wouldn't believe it. It's like Haight-Ashbury circa 1970 (as featured in movies like

Hair: The Musical), and trust me, only the kids-of-hippies
(and movie buffs) know anything about *that* place.

So, the marijuana. It's not a big deal. There aren't guns
or violence or wild police chases or anything. People
are pretty laid back about pot here, even the police. It's
herbal.

Right?

I should make him stop selling the drugs. I bet that I
could, if I wanted to. If I begged and pleaded and had a
hysterical fit about it. But what else is he going to do? I
mean, we have to pay the rent, right? And a girl's clothes
don't just fly off the hangers and into her life. And food.
OK, we grow some food in the backyard, but not that
much. Not enough to live on. Not enough to buy my dad
all the steaks he craves. (I know what you're thinking:
What kind of hippie eats steaks? It's a good question. I'm
a vegetarian myself.)

This year, I'm going to get a job.

I am.

Note to Self: Type up resumé and get work. (But what
would I put on it? It's not like I've ever done anything.)

I'm thinking of maybe trying to save up some money
for college. Ha. As if I'm good enough/smart enough/
worthy enough to get in. I don't even know what I'd
study, if I did. English? What do people do with English
degrees? Maybe I should take Marine Biology. Or
Astronomy. I like the stars. I know most of the constellations. Outside my window last night, I could see the Big

Dipper and Cassiopeia. I know which one Libra is, and Gemini (I'm a Gemini).

I probably *should* be a lawyer. One of these days, my dad will probably need one. Or maybe I'll be a cop. (I don't see it though. The uniforms are fugly.)

But I was talking about my dad. My dad's biggest reason for living seems to be to fight for the legalization of marijuana. If he smoked less marijuana, he'd probably do more to further the cause. Instead, he talks about it and then doesn't go to the rallies because he can't be bothered. The only thing he actually works hard at is the pot production in the basement. It's really impressive and almost pretty. He uses hydroponics and the plants are strong and green and healthy. We get our power from solar panels and wind generators in the back yard, which is more of a field that we don't weed very often. I try to grow organic vegetables there. (Do you have any idea what's in the vegetables you buy in the grocery store? I'll tell you what: chemicals.) The point is that "they" (the Big Evil Ones!) can't see our power consumption. Sometimes, we *sell* power back to the power company. That's got to be a good thing, right?

But to tell you the truth, I wake up in a cold sweat wondering what will happen if/when we/he gets caught. If/when the police suddenly start to care about marijuana and turn their attention to grow-ops in houses. And take him away. I guess I'd go into Foster Care. I started school early for some reason (because I'm a genius, or so my dad says, or maybe because I was a genius when I was five. Don't get excited. I'm pretty good at IQ tests, that's all), so I'm only sixteen. Foster care until I was eighteen, I guess, and then out on the streets? Or Foster Care until I finished the twelfth grade and then college.

College is the answer. It's my ticket out of here, my ticket to normalcy, to a white-bread life of normal problems and normal fears and big glass houses like JT's or totally suburban homes like Kiki's. Something different than this.

Sometimes, I just get tired of being the grown up, you know?

I'd rather not think about it. I'd rather think about other things. Like my hair, for example, which is right now just past my shoulders and stick-straight and brown. I like it straight. It takes about an hour with a straightening iron to get it as smooth as I need it to be, but it's worth it.

Or my teeth, which are straight, thanks to the efforts of Dr. X and Dr. Y, my two orthodontists who fought constantly over the best method of bracing them and eventually, after I had the braces for less than a year, Dr. X pulled them off my teeth while Dr. Y was away in Las Vegas. Dr. Y had wanted them to stay on for two years. At the time, I was fascinated with the relationship between Dr. X and Dr. Y. Did they fight over all their patients? Were they a couple? Was this some kind of couple-fight? I'm still kind of mad about it. The end of that story is that my teeth moved back to being slightly crooked and seeing as how I can't get them fixed without the aid of the crazy Dr. X and Dr. Y, I've decided to whiten them to the point of ridiculousness so that people won't notice they are crooked.

Overall, my life is OK. I know I don't make it sound that

way, but I'm pretty happy.

I'd be totally happy if I had JT.

JT Cooper. Even his name is cool. Who is named JT? If I were to go by my initials, I'd be HA. Needless to say, that won't be happening anytime soon.

To be honest, I'm always thinking about JT, in the back of my mind. Sort of like a sweater balled up in the back of my closet. (If JT was a sweater and my mind was a closet, that is.) He's been scrunched up in there since the ninth grade. Who has time to think about other stuff when your mind is full of JT and hair straightening techniques and tooth bleaching options?

I don't know if I told you this, but I'm a bit obsessive. It's probably a phase. Maybe I'll grow out of it.

Maybe not.

▶ ▶ ▶

Wednesday, September 4
2:17 a.m.
I can't sleep.

3:15 a.m.
Still can't sleep. Recharging Junior.

My horoscope for tomorrow says, "Watch for falling items." THAT'S a horoscope? That something might fall on me? Like what? A piano?

4:02 a.m.
Slept for a bit and had a dream about a frog the size of a Volkswagen falling on my head and crushing me to death.

I'm going to look horrible tomorrow.

6:37 a.m.
Uggghhhhhhhhhhhhhhhh.

9:52 a.m.
Was late for school this morning, but luckily found Kiki
and Jules out smoking in the parking lot, also late.

"Hey," said Jules punching me in the arm. Affection-
ately (I think).

"Smoke?" said Kiki, offering me the pack.

"No," I said. "I don't smoke. Did you know that more
people die from —?"

"Oh, stuff it," said Kiki. "Besides, you're more likely to
get skin cancer. Nice peeling nose, by the way."

She was right, my nose was peeling. But through no
fault of my own. OK, it was totally my fault. But it
was also JT's fault for getting a job in the summer that
involved being at the beach a lot. As a result, I also had to
be at the beach a lot. So naturally, being "fair" (if by "fair,"
I mean "completely pallid"), I happened to get one or two
sunburns over the course of July and August. Kiki was
with me, but of course she doesn't burn, being fortunate
enough to have her dad's complexion. (Her dad is African-
American). If my dad was African-American, I'm sure
I would not have inherited his beautiful skin. I'm the
kind of person who is doomed to inherit the least-good-
qualities of both parents.

I scratched my nose.

"Don't scratch," advised Jules, through a veil of smoke.

"It looks like you have leprosy or something."

"Gee, thanks," I said.

"You really have to let go of this thing with JT," observed Kiki. "Especially if it's affecting your . . . er, nose."

"I don't have a thing for JT," I said, haughtily.

The bell rang, indicating that we'd already missed the first class. I made a small move to go towards the school. I couldn't remember what my second class was meant to be. It was a bit like being in one of those dreams where you know you have to go somewhere, but you can't remember where and you haven't written it down. Also, I still felt half-asleep.

Jules and Kiki were laughing hysterically. Clutching at each other. Really, it was very over the top. "Don't have a thing for JT!" gasped Jules, when she pulled herself together.

"That IS funny," said Kiki, wiping her eyes.

"I have to go," I snarled and marched into the school, whereupon I was immediately swept up into the traffic. It's very hard to break out of the current unless you know where you are going, and as I didn't really know, I just allowed myself to be swept into a classroom. Quite probably not the class I was supposed to be in, but I'd work that out later. The room was full of familiar people (thankfully NOT JT) and I figured I could get away with it. Right away, I found a desk at the back and began staring out the window to contemplate how TGYML was going so far.

And then I had a revelation.

I spend WAY too much time thinking about JT.

"Hmmmf," I said out loud. Which caused the teacher to pause in what he was saying and to say, "Yes, Miss . . .?"

"Harmony," I said.

"Your name is Harmony?" the teacher asked.

"Yes," I said. "I mean, no. My name is Haley. Haley Harmony."

"Oh," he said. He looked confused. I felt a bit sorry for him. He was obviously new and didn't look much older than we were.

"It's OK," I said.

"Oh," he said, looking even more flustered. Finally, he went back to what he was talking about, which was something to do with ancient Greece. I was sure I was not taking any sort of history class, so I really ought to have moved, but I couldn't be bothered. It was very restful in this classroom and I was a bit dizzy from not sleeping. I went right back to thinking about JT.

Over the summer, I spent a bit of time (read: two entire months) hanging out at the beach and tanning (which I'm totally opposed to, what with the risk of skin cancer and premature aging and all the other horrors of sun-exposure) just so I could stare at JT while he worked (this is possibly worth dying for).

JT had the greatest summer job of all time this year — a gig at a local radio station where he trolled the beach all day giving away movie tickets and sodas and radio-station crap and tickets to concerts and Frisbees. Mostly to gorgeous, bikini-clad girls, obviously. Most of whom went out with him later. I saw them in his jeep, riding around downtown. This isn't that big a place. You see everyone, all the time. Even when you aren't looking.

And I was looking. Not always, but sometimes.

I mean, I wanted to know what he was up to. And who he was with. I guess I'm kind of a sucker for punishment.

I even wore a bikini but I probably shouldn't have. For one thing, I got such a bad burn on my stomach that I was sick for a week with sunstroke. Also, I had to lie fairly still the whole time because I'm not at my best when I'm nearly naked. It makes me feel strange and frozen, like I can't walk properly or like everyone is staring at me. (Which they probably are.)

I looked around the room. People were generally writing things down. These are people, I thought darkly, who are going to college.

"Can I borrow a piece of paper?" I asked the person sitting behind me, a boy I vaguely recognized from last year.

"Uh," he said, and ripped one out of his notebook.

I dug around in my purse for a pen and began my list.

Goals for Grade 12:
1. Boyfriend — get one.
2. Teeth — whiter.
3. Hair — better.
4. Hips — smaller.
5. Mood — more positive.
6. Health — exercise more, stop reading WebMD, Medline, Dr. Koop, Intellihealth, Merck, etc. online.
7. Boobs — bigger? Can boobs get bigger via exercise? Find out.
8. School — study more, get into college, graduate.

9. Job — get one, i.e. one that doesn't involve police raids and baggies of dried leaves and old hippies eating ice-cream right out of the container.

After that, I was stuck. Luckily, the bell went and I managed to get to my locker to pull out my schedule. I'd just spent my study period in someone else's class.

"Great," I said to no one in particular.

Random Observations Made During Lunch So I Can
Look Busy While Wondering Where Jules and Kiki Are
and Why They Didn't Wait For Me:

- JT's locker is ten feet away from mine. I'll see him every day. I really have to get some better clothes.
- Jules and Kiki are clearly mad at me for some reason: figure out why.
- One hour of sleep is not enough.
- Junior is my best friend, in the way that some people's best friends are their dogs. The fact that my best friend is a lap-top computer and RL (real life) best friends do not look for me at lunch on the second day back at school is a very alarming sign.
- JT half-nodded to me when I yelled "Hey, JT!" at him in a much louder voice than I'd intended, indicating that he at least knows who I am.
- Am going to make a point of stopping thinking about JT and starting to think about things such as what class I'm supposed to be attending and whether strips work better than that paint-stuff to enhance tooth whiteness.

- Lymph nodes are not swollen. Possibly do not have Cat Scratch Disease, but did not feed The Cat special treats before leaving for school as I usually do, to punish him for possibly killing me at some later date.

Making that list wastes only ten minutes of what is proving to be an interminable lunch hour. I just got up and walked around, hoping to catch sight of Kiki and Jules and now I give up. I like making lists.

Outfits I would Buy (If I Had Any Money) That Would Make Me More Attractive to JT:

1. Short, belly-button revealing tops (*Note to Self:* must do more sit-ups to flatten belly and allow for short, belly-button revealing tops).
2. Padded bras? To enforce illusion of curviness.
3. Casual sportswear in the style of casual, fun girls who regularly participate in sports and might, at any moment, be participating in a sport and have to be dressed for it at all times. (He seems to like athletic girls.)
4. Short skirts to show off long, tanned legs. *Note to Self:* get proper tan (— fake?), work out (!) and get muscles in legs.
5. Expensive, brandname clothes to boost self-esteem. High self-esteem = More attractive demeanour. So while JT might not have a clue about what brand-name clothes are, better brand-name clothes will equal general improvement that will attract JT.

2:00 p.m.
*Notes taken in Afternoon Homeroom while Teacher
Tries to Manufacture Interest in Getting Us to Run
for The Student Council:*

Reasons why I hate JT:

He's a jock. I hate jocks.

He's a player. I hate players.

He's seeing someone. (He's always seeing someone.)
(*Note to Self:* find out *who* and work voodoo magic to
end their relationship.)

He doesn't know I exist.

He smiles at Jules in the hallways.

He would never ever ever go out with me.

Reasons why I love JT:

He's tall, blonde, and gorgeous.

When he smiles, his eyes crinkle up at the corners.

Habit?

He smells good.

Uh, he's tall, blonde, and gorgeous.

Oh, dear. Should have paid closer attention to the goings-
on in Homeroom. Somehow I've been voted on to the
Student Council. How did this happen? Was I running for
Student Council? I *hate* school activities, especially school
activities that mean I have to participate in things.

I *loathe* participating.

I despise it.

In an attempt to ward off a panic attack, I just replayed
the entire class in my head. Unfortunately, I wasn't paying

any attention at all and really have no idea what happened. I remember roll call. I said, "here!" at some point. I borrowed a piece of paper from the girl next to me. I borrowed a pen from the boy in front of me. I played tic-tac-toe with the girl I borrowed the paper from. I stared out the window. I honestly do not remember suggesting that I wanted to be on the Student Council. I do remember raising and lowering my arm several times but I thought we were voting for something unimportant, such as whether or not having a soda machine in the foyer was the root of all evil.

Craptacular.

Isn't there usually some kind of speech involved with running for Student Council? I'm my Division Rep. I don't want to be Division Rep. There are fifty sodding (British swear words!) divisions, so that means there are fifty Division Reps. Maybe no one will notice if I never go to a meeting.

Haley Harmony, Div Rep, it says on the board. Oh, help. I'm just not Student Council material.

Apparently it can't be undone. (Meaning "no one else wants to do it either.") Oh God. This sucks. How do these things happen to me? How?

I never liked Bruce Bartelson.

If only JT were Student Council president. That would make it OK. I immediately begin daydreaming about JT being Student Council President and me being . . . I don't know. Division Rep Supreme. And us talking urgently about the state of the school gym or whether stilettos should be allowed to be worn during school dances.

This is definitely sub-good.

But I guess I'll have to live with it, won't I?

3:02 p.m.

Just spent half an hour lying on the grass outside the school where other, more athletic students, were running around in matching shorts being sporty and generally annoying.

"I can't be on the Student Council," I moaned, leaning back in the grass. It was a nice day. The kind of day that made you (OK, me) wish that it was still summer and I was still burning on the beach and catching glimpses of JT, the Sun God.

"You made your bed," said Jules unsympathetically.

"I wasn't paying attention!" I protested.

"Uh huh," said Kiki. "Like you ever do."

"I do so," I said.

"Do not," she said. I should mention that Kiki is basically a straight-A student, not because she ever works, but because she's just naturally smart.

"Do so," I said, sticking out my tongue.

"Girls, girls," drawled Jules. "Let's not look dorky. Look at who's coming our way."

For a second, my heart jumped into my throat, and then I realized that the "who's coming our way" was not anyone interesting.

"Blech," I said. "He's a teacher."

"So?" Jules challenged, raising her eyebrows.

"So," said Kiki with exaggerated slowness. "Off limits, girl. That's 'so', OK?"

"Pffft," said Jules. "I need cigarettes."

"Don't look at me," I said, closing my eyes and letting the sun warm up my face.

"I'm only looking at you because you're going to burn your burn," said Jules. "You don't learn fast, do you?"

"Fast enough to know that smoking is going to kill you," I said.

"Gah," said Kiki, giving Jules a cigarette. "Don't start."

"Fine," I said. "I wasn't going to."

"Good," she said. "I'm tired of hearing that same old lecture."

"It's not always the same," I said.

"Yes, it is," she said.

"Not," I said.

"Stop it!" said Jules. "It IS always the same! Want to hear it? Here's what it sounds like." She stood up and made a weird slumping pose.

"Is that supposed to be me?" I said. "That looks nothing like me."

"Shh!" she said, clearing her throat and affecting a weird pseudo-British accent. ("I don't have a weird pseudo-British accent," I interrupted. "Yes, you do," she said.)

"There are a hundred reasons not to smoke. For one thing, it yellows the teeth. For another, cancer. Hello? Cancer? You don't seem to think it will happen to you, do you? I'm not like that. I just assume it *will* happen to me. Also, it's expensive. And have you seen the pictures on the cigarette cartons? Seriously, I would quit just so that I never had to look at those. And hellllooooo [she waved her arms around dramatically], YOU ARE PROBABLY

KILLING ME WITH SECOND-HAND SMOKE!"

Kiki burst out laughing.

"That's not funny," I said, my face burning (from rage, not from the sun). Jules can be totally a bitch sometimes. "Besides," I said, stiffly. "I don't care if you smoke. And die."

Jules blew a smoke ring at me. "Don't sweat it, sweetie. You know we love you."

"Right," I said. "Sure." To tell you the truth, I wasn't really feeling the love.

She hugged me. I pushed her away. "You stink," I said.

"Can we stop talking about this?" Kiki said.

"If you quit, we'll never talk about it again," I point out.

"Oh, give it a rest," said Jules.

We lay there for a few minutes, on the grassy hill that overlooks the track. Apart from the overly enthused athletes, people had gone home already. Except us. And a few people in the parking lot behind us. I could hear music and conversation. I was half-asleep, really. I hate not sleeping. It really messes me up. No one said anything for a few minutes. Then, before I knew it, we were back into it again.

Same old script, same old responses:

Kiki: Smoking keeps us thin. (Kiki is rail thin, for the most part, as is Jules.)

Jules: Yes, thin.

Me: I thought you were supposed to be an athlete. Besides, I'm thin. Well, sort of.

Kiki: You're flat-chested. It's not the same thing. (Kiki has huge boobs, by the way. She's like Pamela bloody Anderson.)

Me: Yes, it is.
Jules: Can't we ever talk about anything else?

I got up suddenly, practically falling over. I saw stars for a second. Sometimes that happens to me when I stand up to fast. (I have very low blood pressure.) "I have to go," I said.

"What's wrong?" Kiki asks.

"What?" I say. "I don't know what you're talking about."

"You're moony," Jules says. "It must be JT. He'll never go for you. You're not his type."

"Argh," I say. "Aren't you supposed to be my friend? I thought you were supposed to butter me up and make me feel better about myself."

"No," Jules says. "It's our job to keep you in touch with reality."

She blew smoke at me and waved at someone over my shoulder. I turned to look.

And guess who it was?

Obviously: JT.

In a school of 800 people, most of whom have gone home, who else would it be? And to make it worse, he smiled back. At Jules.

Why didn't he smile at me? Me? I was the one who was standing up, after all.

(Jules has great teeth. Why are her teeth so white? She smokes. Technically, my teeth should be whiter. Obviously, he's drawn to her superior dentistry.)

There's something you should know about Jules. She's a great girl. But — and it's a big "but" — she hates it when a boy is interested in someone who is not . . . Jules.

"So Jules, how's Danny?" I asked pointedly.

"Oh, he's great," she said quickly. "He's really great." But that's all she said. Kiki latched on to it right away.

"Trouble in Paradise?" she said, wiggling her eyebrows at me.

"No," said Jules. "Nothing like that. I don't want to talk about it."

"Oh, come on," I said. "Who else are you going to talk to?"

"Nope," she said. "Not going to talk about it."

And that was that. I mean, when Jules really doesn't want to talk about something, she won't. I'm not like that. I'll tell everyone anything. If they ask. (Not that they ask very often.) (You know how in friendships there's always a listener and a talker? With Jules, I'm definitely a listener. I don't think she's asked me anything about me since . . . well, I can't remember.) I was kind of annoyed after this, to tell you the truth. I mean, I hope she and Danny don't break up. I really really hope it.

Please, I said in my head. Don't let them break up. Then I added a bunch of names, just in case. God, Allah, the Fates. (You never really know who to address these things to, do you?)

They can't break up. Because then JT would be fair-game, and I'd definitely lose against Jules.

Note to Self: Do not confide anything relating to crushes to best friends ever again for any reason whatsoever.

Evening

I slammed into the house at around 5:30. I needed a nap, stat, and was in no mood for Dad and his weirdness. I was exhausted. (What is it about school that is so exhausting? It's not like we do anything there.) Of course, I only had an hour's sleep last night. But I'm young, I should be able to cope with that.

On the other hand, maybe I'm exhausted due to the Cat Scratch Fever. My arm still definitely hurts. I glared at The Cat as I walked by. The Cat was curled up asleep in the sunny splash of light in the front window without a care in the world. Waiting for the next innocent victim to walk by so that he could infect them with Cat Scratch Disease, no doubt.

"You should have to go to school," I told him. "As punishment. Or better yet, give everyone there Cat Scratch Fever. Shut the place down."

I swear he rolled his eyes at me. Typical. He'd fit right in. Sometimes, The Cat reminds me of Jules.

"Vector of disease!" I hissed at him. Nothing.

I wished I could lie down on the floor next to him and sleep and wake up to find that this is all a dream and that TGYML has not started yet, that I'm two days into a year that is shaping up to be FFTGYML (Far From The Greatest Year of My Life). I sat down on the floor, which was slightly sticky. The problem with wood floors is that you have to sweep them quite often, and also that they aren't very comfortable to lie down on after a long day. I lay there for a few minutes and stared at the wall. On the wall, there is a portrait that my dad painted of me when I was about five. I really loved that painting. It was probably the last thing he did paint, come to think of it. I turned my head and contemplated the dust bunnies under the sofa.

Notable Things That Happened Today:
1. Stupid Student Council thing.
2. Jules attempted to steal JT.
3. Met all my "new" teachers. (That was joyous. Like I hadn't already met them last year. It's just the same old motley bunch of unhappy looking adults who look like they can't imagine which wrong turn led them to Sacred Heart School. I can totally understand. I mean, who would want to be stuck there, day in and day out, forever? At least we, as students can see the light at the end of the tunnel. I mean, we have college to look forward to. Where at least some of us will probably get degrees in teaching and end up back at Sacred Hell, slogging through the same blood red hallways and chemical fumes to the same crappy classrooms, year after year.) Oh God. Someone shoot me. Please.

Positive things about today:
1. JT is in four of my classes, which is unbelievably lucky. If nothing else, that will make for an interesting year. I can stare at the back of his head. Must remember to make sure to sit behind him to avoid swivelling head to look behind me all semester.
   Oh, JT.

Not so positive things about today:
1. Am tired. Hungry. And house is a mess.

I dragged myself off the floor.

"Dad!" I yelled, walking into the kitchen. He wasn't there, but he had been. There was an open pitcher of orange juice and a half bowl of cereal left on the counter. And a dish of what might have been congealed eggs on the stove. I hate eggs. The sight of eggs makes me gag.

"DAD!"

I finally found him in the TV room, lying on the couch, smoking and watching Oprah. (He loves Tivo in a sick sort of way as it allows him to watch ALL the daytime shows well into the evening.) It was a Dr. Phil day. If Dr. Phil could see my dad, he'd drop dead on the spot. My dad is hopeless. He was tossed from the sixties into the twenty-first century, completely unaware that things have changed and that it's not terribly cool to be a past 60-year-old man with waist-length hair, no job, a Harley and a grow-op in the basement.

At least not when you are supposed to be a father.

He was wearing a shirt that said, "Here today, Gone to Maui" (where, for the record, he's never actually been). His pants were frayed and obnoxious. I looked closer and saw they were actually pyjamas. Plaid. Flannel.

"Earth to Dad," I said. "Come in, Dad."

"What?" he said.

"You're hopeless," I told him.

"Hopelessly devoted to you, maybe," he said. Or sang. (He can sing all the songs from Grease. This is part of the benefit of having a huge movie collection and no JOB).

"Huh," I snorted, flopping down on the couch and pulling The Cat (who is stupidly attached to me considering that he so recently attempted to kill me) onto my lap. (The cat has no name, by the way. He's just The Cat.) "Being able to sing all the songs from every movie you have ever seen is not a skill, you know."

"Aw," he said. "How's my gorgeous girl's first day of school? Tell your old dad all about it. How's JT? And the girls? Better yet, let's order take-out to celebrate. No cooking for my princess on her first day of twelfth grade."

"Dad," I said, patiently. "Yesterday was the first day."

"I know," he said. "But today was the first REAL day. The first first day doesn't count."

"Uh huh," I said. I suspected that he didn't know yesterday was the first day, but it doesn't matter. I'm used to this. Really, it doesn't bother me. (Are other people's fathers like this?)

Just then, the Cat coughed up a hairball on my lap.

"Great," I said, pushing him off and flicking the disgusting hairball onto the ground to clean up later.

Sometimes I wonder if I'd trade my dad (The Dad!) in for a more normal variety of father. A guy who wore a suit and sold computers and had no interest in my life. Or something.

Nah.

He belched. "Dad!" I said. "That's disgusting." I sat back to watch Dr. Phil and re-evaluate. Dad scratched his butt with the remote control. Yes, I'd definitely trade him in.

No.

Yes.

OK, well, it's not like it's an option.

We dialed out for food (vegetarian curry, my favourite, a huge concession because my dad likes to eat meat and lots of it. But he ate it gamely, and almost seemed to like it).

And then we just talked and hung until 10:00 at night. We were both so stuffed it was disgusting. I could see my waistband getting tighter and my belly spilling over the top.

"Ugh," I said, pinching it and lying back on the couch to stare at Dr. Phil, who was paused on the screen, where he'd been for about three hours. Dr. Phil is probably a great dad, I thought. For a second, I imagined my dad being on TV doling out advice, but that fantasy didn't get very far. I just couldn't picture it.

I dragged myself to my feet, leaving my dad sleeping on the couch with a half-finished carton of noodles resting on his chest. I couldn't be bothered to clean up. It's time he learned to clean up his own mess.

The thing with my dad is that no matter how annoying he is, you just can't help but love him. Or his way of just being. Just living. And always being happy. He never worries. I worry. A lot. (To the point of total craziness, really.) I wish I could be more like him. OK, OK. There's a lot of stuff there that you have to overlook. But it could be worse. He could be mean. Kiki's father is mean. And Jules' father is a dead-beat who only visits on major holidays. Of the three of us, I definitely drew the long straw. Or the short straw. I never understood that expression, anyway.

11:45 p.m.
So it wasn't a great day, but at least I wasn't crushed by a falling piano. Or a giant frog.

That's something, anyway.

Thursday, September 5

MOOD	Fair
HAIR	Moderate to Flat
HEALTH	Possibly dying of CS fever.
HOROSCOPE	Today is the kind of day you hope for! (It is? Good!) Relationships with family members can cause problems. (No kidding). Friends will offer good advice. Travel is possible.
JT SIGHTINGS	5

9:45 a.m.
Terrible news. JT has exchanged words with Jules. She claims that he said, "Hi" and that she said, "How's it going?" and that he said, "Great."

How dare she?

Jules is clearly a bitch and I shall no longer speak to her for any reason.

3:14 p.m.
Have tentatively forgiven Jules as I need to borrow clothes

from her for party this weekend. But have not really forgiven her, because as we were walking away from Auto
Mechanics class (taking this class was my idea, and was a
stroke of genius as Jules and I are the only girls in the class
and as a result, all the boys want to help us with the tools.
OK, they want to help her, not me, but they help me
because I am usually standing in the way), she said, "I'm
thinking that in my last year of school, I don't really want
to be attached to just one guy, you know? Like, maybe
Kiki's right."

"No," I said. "I don't know. She isn't right. Danny's a
great guy and you should not break up with him under
any circumstances."

She regarded me coldly. "What do you know?" she said.
"It's not like you've ever had a boyfriend."

Hate Jules.

6:52 p.m.

Me: (sitting in back "garden" talking to Kiki on cordless
phone) I think Jules hates me.

Kiki: She doesn't hate *you*, she hates everyone.

Me: Then she must hate me, if she hates everyone.
Unless I'm no one.

Kiki: She doesn't hate you. She loves you.

Me: No, she doesn't.

Kiki: Yes, she does. Guess what?

Me: What?

Kiki: My mom's friend is going to read my cards. Want to
come over?

Me: Yes, but I can't.

Kiki: Why not?

Me: I don't know.

Kiki: Are you mad at me because you think Jules hates
       you?

Me: No.

Kiki: OK, I have to go.

I hung up the phone and made patterns in the dry earth
with my sneaker. I actually would have liked to have my
tarot cards read. I'm sure I would have drawn the Death
Card and the reader would have said, "Oh, that just means
change, not death" and I would then have become totally
convinced I was going to die, and then I would probably
have died.

I wonder if Jules would cry at my funeral if I died.

She'd probably show up only to flirt with JT.

Hmmm. I wonder if JT would come to my funeral if
I died.

I thought about this as I half-heartedly watered my
organic tomatoes. They weren't doing that well. It was
Dad's job to remember to turn on the sprinkler in the
morning as we're only allowed to use sprinklers for
approximately one hour every morning. (Something to
do with reservoir depletion.) He always forgets.

I sprayed water into the cracked ground the plants were
coming from and it just ran off, like the ground was made
of clay. For some reason, this made me want to cry.

This is the best year of my life, I told the plant. And it
fell over. I guess a desiccated tomato plant can't stand up
to much water pressure or personal sharing. I propped it

back up again and spent a half hour randomly spraying around the garden until it all looked dampish. •

I love the smell of wet ground. I know this is weird.

Things I Love the Smell of:
1. JT's neck.
2. The ground after it rains.
3. The beach.
4. All the usual things, like roses.
5. Erasers.
6. Pencil shavings.
7. Curry.
8. My new shampoo (smells like grapefruit!)
9. Leather.
10. Clean laundry.

Things I Hate the Smell of:
1. Cigarette smoke.
2. Marijuana.
3. The inside of the house (stale) (*Note to Self*: Buy Febreze).
4. Bad breath.
5. Gasoline.
6. Licorice.
7. Popcorn.

Did I mention how great JT smells?

He doesn't smoke. Thank God (goddess/the Fates/Buddha/etc).

► ► ►

Saturday, September 7

MOOD	Anxious! Excited. Happy?
HAIR	Doesn't matter as will change soon.
HEALTH	Dizzy, tired. Possible lymph node swelling
HOROSCOPE	Change in appearance will bring positive news! Be careful of promises made to friends. Trust yourself to make choices that scare you.
JT SIGHTINGS	0

9:00 a.m.
It was raining when I woke up.
   And I was late.

Choices:
1. Go back to sleep.
2. Get out of bed and go to hair appointment.
3. Neither.

9:02 a.m.
I dove out of bed, threw on some clothes (khaki pants, grey tank top, Skechers) and ran. It takes fifteen minutes to walk. I was sure I could run in five.

   I actually like to run. Running reminds me of being a kid. When do you stop running for fun and start running for exercise? That's what I want to know. You don't see adults suddenly sprinting down the sidewalk just because it feels good. I don't get it. It's like as you get older, you hold yourself stiller and stiller until you stop moving altogether.

It's sad, really.

I liked the feeling of my feet hitting the pavement. Hard. OK, so it was a little jarring on the knees. Usually (OK, once in a while) (a long while), I run on trails and stuff. I do. Well, I just started running again. Last week.

Kiki and I are supposedly training for a mini-marathon.

But don't laugh, it's not until the spring. We have lots of time. The point is, running is fun.

Or not.

OK, I hate running. I admit it. My knees were killing me, I could hardly breathe, and I wasn't nearly there. I had to stop on the corner and bend double to try to catch my breath.

The thing is that I *want* to like running. I like the idea of it. I do.

"Gah," I said.

"Are you OK?" a little old lady stopped in front of me, peering up from underneath a hugely ugly orange umbrella.

"Yes!" I said, cheerfully. (Lying through my teeth.) I started to run again. I got about ten feet before I was gripped with horrible cramps that were foreshadowing instant cardiac death if I continued.

I walked the rest of the way.

I was on my way to get my hair done as a "favour" from a friend of my dad's. "Friend of my dad's" usually equals "complete disaster," but Dad swore the guy wasn't a complete waste-case or a freak. (Of course, he also swore that he watered the organic vegetable patch, and we all know how that turned out.) From the outside, the hair place looked relatively normal.

Well, it was clean anyway.

9:15 a.m.

I slogged into the salon, panting and sweating.

No one was there. So I sat down and read hair magazines. "Read" is not exactly the right word. "Looked at pictures," would be more accurate. (Also, I read the Astrology columns. It amused me hugely that hair magazines have horoscopes and that they were all related to hair. Sadly, the magazines were all hopelessly out of date. My hair-o-scope for June 1998 suggested that I invest in a good deep conditioner. I tried to remember what my hair looked like in June 1998, and I think it probably looked exactly as it looks now. Well, deep conditioner is always a good suggestion.

I flipped through the glossy (and somewhat sticky) pages and tried to guess why anyone would torture their hair in this manner. There was not one decent looking haircut in the bunch. These things were hair *sculptures*. They were hair *horrors*. There was enough hairspray in them to single-handedly deplete the ozone layer. These poor girls definitely could have used deep conditioners once they washed all the junk out of their hair, no matter what their sign.

Very quickly, I started to get bored.

Half an hour later, there was some crashing in the back room and a guy emerged wearing red bike shorts and an orange and green spandex shirt and a bike helmet that was half-crushed on one side. He did not say, "Sorry,

I'm half an hour late!" Or "I hope you haven't been waiting long!"

Or anything for that matter.

The half-hour wait should have been a red flag. (At least it gave me a chance to catch my breath, which was good, but five minutes would have been plenty.) But the way he didn't actually talk should have been more of a red flag.

Look, Haley, red flags everywhere!

(Revelation! I spend most of my life noticing red flags and then ignoring them. Why is this? *Note to Self*: if ever in therapy, ask therapist to investigate this problem more deeply.)

Instead of greeting me (and he seemed totally unfazed to see me sitting there by myself. I could have stolen everything in sight!) he silently handed me a cup of coffee. I don't actually drink coffee, but that's OK. (Coffee yellows the teeth and makes me jittery). It gave me something to hold on to while we talked. And by "we talked," I mean "while he ran his hands through my hair and flipped it this way and that in an obnoxious way."

"I just want a trim," I ventured.

"Shh," he said.

"That's funny," I said, "That's what we . . ."

"Shhh!" he said, this time so loudly and emphatically that he spat all over my left cheek.

I shhhh'd.

Oh, well, I thought. He seemed like a take-charge kind of person. And confidence is good. Right?

He actually had good hair. Or he might have had, if he didn't have helmet head. OK, his hair was completely plastered to his scalp with sweat and impossible to assess reasonably.

I trusted him. He seemed, uh, well. OK, I didn't trust him. I should have got out of the chair and run.

But I didn't. Because I'm too polite.

"Right," he said. "We'll cut this off and brighten you up a bit, shall we?"

He had a Scottish accent. I loved that. I love all accents. Of course, it was probably totally fake. He's probably never left this town.

"OK," I said, "I trust you."

"Shh," he said.

It occurs to me that I spend a lot of my life being shhh'd by other people.

9:45 a.m.

What was I thinking? There was nothing wrong with my hair. It was long. It was straight. I could work with it.

Things I could do with my hair when it was long (i.e., One Hour Ago):

1. Ponytail.
2. Braid.
3. French braid.
4. Wind it around a pencil to create weirdly interesting bun-type thing.
5. Hide behind it.
6. French twist (why do the French have so many hair-styles named after them? You don't get a Canadian Braid or a Swiss Bun).

7. Librarian bun.
8. Random up-dos created with clips and pins to look sex- ily messy and tousled.
9. Nothing.

9:47 a.m.
Isn't it traditional to actually wet someone's hair before you cut it? Were those even proper hair-cutting scissors? And why were his hands shaking like that?

9:49 a.m.
My hair was mostly on the floor. I couldn't breathe. It was possible that I was choking to death on noxious clouds of hairspray, or that I was having a heart attack. Either way, it was clear that I was a goner. I looked around for a paper bag to breathe into but there obviously wasn't one. I took a deep breath and held it.

There was a mountain of hair under the chair. A thick carpeting of hair. A *conflagration* of hair. I couldn't look. I refused to look. I was going to be sick. I was going to pass out. Whose idea was it to let one of my dad's pothead clients NEAR MY HEAD WITH SCISSORS? This was a terrible idea. I blame my horoscope (not my hair-o-scope). "A change in appearance" can only mean a hair cut, right? How could the stars be so wrong?

I'm not going to look at myself in a mirror ever again.

9:49½ a.m.
I looked.

9:51 a.m.

Cleverly pretended to need to use the washroom (urgently!) and called Kiki on my cell from the tiny pink bathroom in back of the salon. On a side note, it was awkward to try to pee while wearing a knee length vinyl cape. I felt like an escapee from some kind of facility for the mentally impaired. Or a super-hero. (This is why you never see super-heroes eating or drinking anything. How DOES Spiderman get out of that suit?)

Still, I felt obligated to use the toilet since I'd made such a big deal of it. Someone had actually made a toilet-paper cozy out of a Cher doll and someone else (probably the Mute Monster out there) had chosen to display it. The bathroom was horrifying. But not as horrifying as my actual hair.

Or lack of hair, as the case may be.

Kiki wasn't home.

Called Jules out of desperation, although Jules isn't really the "friend in need" type.

Jules promised that she would be on her way, stat. Or so she said.

10:01 a.m.

Allowed fake-accented pseudo-artiste cycling mute hair-demon to convince me that my hair was going to become (somehow) cute and chunky in the style of Meg Ryan's in "You've Got Mail" (when her hair was at its peak) once colour was applied.

Him: This will be great. You'll look cute. Like that what's-
     her-name in that movie that what's-it was in.

Me: (Made strangled gasping noise of agreement.)

Him: (Lapsed back into silence.)

10:45 a.m.

Jules did not show up and hair was now completely covered with tin foil and scalp was beginning to burn and
itch. I could probably have received radio transmissions
with all this foil. (I never understood how that worked,
come to think of it. I mean, I've heard people say that they
get radio stations through their fillings, but how? If they
open their mouths, can other people hear it? Honestly, I
haven't got a clue.)

To make matters worse (like there could be a "worse"),
I inadvertently drank the whole cup of coffee in an effort
to not look in the mirror. At which point I began shaking,
sweating, and palpitating. Probably, I thought, I'll have a
heart attack and die and this will be the last hair cut I ever
get. I closed my eyes. If I couldn't see what had happened,
I could pretend that I was still sleeping and that I'd never
made this terrible, awful, irreversible decision to get my
hair cut right at the beginning of my last year of high
school.

12:14 p.m.

My hair was totally gone. The hair that I had left was
blonde. If by "blonde," I mean "coppery orange colour
found in nature only in the inner flesh of a mango." Help?

This was a situation of the direst importance. My legs
felt funny and weak. I wondered if perhaps the stress
had caused me to have a stroke. I was quivering on the

sidewalk outside, contemplating dialing 9-1-1, when Jules rolled up. With red eyes and a huge attitude.

"I love it," she said dubiously, in her voice that means "I'm lying." She touched my hair like it might be made of some new fabric. I swear it almost broke.

"It suits you," she said sunnily, in her "still lying" voice.

"Thanks," I said through gritted teeth. I felt like crying. To make it worse, I over-tipped the silent hair weirdo with all the money in my purse. I have no idea why. I just wanted to make him feel better, although he apparently didn't feel badly.

As soon as we got into the car (Jules' car, naturally, is both Nice and New), Jules burst into tears. At first I thought it was because my hair was too fugly for words. Then I realized that she didn't (a) care about my hair (of course not) and (b) want to talk about my hair. So in my role of supportive best friend since childhood, I listened as she told me that she and Danny had broken up.

"No!" I exclaimed in true horror.

"Yes," she said, turning to look at me and allowing a tear to escape from her perfect blue eye. (OK, from behind her fake blue contact lens.)

"What happened?" I said wildly. "Can you kiss and make up?"

"I don't think so," she said. "No."

"Why?" I said. "He loves you! Also, he's perfect. And everyone is so jealous of you." (She loves thinking everyone wants to be in her place.)

"He doesn't love me," she said, smoking furiously.

"Don't smoke in the car," I said.

"It's MY CAR," she yelled.

"Sorry," I said, opening my window. It was freezing cold and wet outside. How does the weather know when school has gone back? Last week at this time, we were at the beach.

"Don't you want to know what happened?" she asked.

"Oh, sorry," I said, attempting to concentrate. I scratched my head, which was unnervingly itchy. Probably, all my hair was about to flee from my scalp. But this was about Jules, not about me, never mind that it was the worst day of my life, to date.

"Tell me," I said, with exaggerated patience.

"I can't," she said. And then, this was the weird part. Because she really started crying. Blubbering and sobbing. Snot bubbling out of her nose.

"Pull over!" I said, alarmed as the car began to weave around.

So she did. And then she told me. She caught Danny KISSING HER MOTHER IN THE KITCHEN. I'm not making this up. Danny. Jules' Mother. Kissing.

In the kitchen.

I guess this is what happens when you date college boys? Not that I'd have to worry about that, as I have no mother. I'd only have to worry about my father selling them pot and turning them into idiots.

Or that they were using me to get closer to their pot supply.

"What am I going to do?" Jules sobbed.

I patted her on the arm. I really had no advice. After all, I have never had a boyfriend. She (of all people) knew that. I mean, really.

"Maybe they were . . . uh," I said.

"What?" she said.

"Rehearsing a play?" I said.

"Honestly," she said scathingly, straightening up and twisting the mirror around to look at her red, puffy eyes. "You're so naïve."

"Sure," I said. "Whatever."

I just let her talk. The gist of it was that Jules is not speaking to either Danny or her mother, although she did throw a glass jug of orange juice at her mother (her mother caught it and the glass didn't break but orange juice got all over her new white Michael Stars T-shirt) and Jules is now officially grounded-with-a-capital-G. (Which, considering the circumstances, does seem a little unfair.) And she snuck out to meet me. "Because you needed me," she sniffed. "I couldn't let you down." (Or because she needed me? I'm guessing it was the latter. But I'll let it go, this time.)

I tried to make comforting sounds, but all I kept thinking was KISSING HER MOTHER! IN THE KITCHEN! Was there tongue? Or was it just a kiss-on-the-cheek greeting kind of kiss? I couldn't ask, because I'm slightly afraid she would throw something at me or drive us both off the road. (I'd hate to die with bad hair.) A real kiss? It was so absurd, it was almost funny.

Let me try to explain: Danny is short. Jules' mother is tall. Danny is, well, stocky. Jules' mother used to be a lingerie model. Danny has, um, acne. Jules' mother does NOT. Jules' mother is obsessively clean. Danny is most certainly NOT.

I just couldn't picture it, and yet couldn't stop trying. It's like when you get a song stuck in your head, only in this case, I had an image stuck in my head. No matter how hard I tried, it was funny. But I could sense that this was not the right time to laugh.

Actually, there might never be a right time to laugh about this. Jules and Danny have been dating forever. Or at least since last Christmas, which is also a long time, if you think about it.

I hiccoughed back an uncontrolled giggle and looked out the open window. Jules turned the stereo on, still smoking like a fiend, and ignored me.

I'd never really thought too much about Jules' mother, but she is (a) young for a mother and (b) pretty. In a Sela Ward kind of way. I guess having a father and no mother is better than the reverse. Imagine having to compete with your own mother for dates? Although, isn't there some kind of law about kissing minors? Is Danny a minor? I guess he isn't. I guess he's 19.

"Is Danny nineteen?" I asked.

Jules stared at me like I was a monkey who has just dropped down from a tree and begun talking. "Yes," she said, witheringly.

"OK then," I said. "Sorry."

"Let's go shopping," Jules said, smoking an entire cigarette in what looked like one drag. (She didn't even cough. She must have lungs of steel. Perhaps Jules isn't even human, perhaps she's half-human, half-machine.)

"Uh," I said. "I'm broke." As in, "I just gave all my money to the hair guy as a tip."

"We'll go to the thrift store," she said. "You like the thrift store."

I don't exactly LIKE the thrift store, but I do buy lots of stuff there. I don't have very much spare money lying around. And sometimes you can find good stuff. I bought a pair of Seven jeans there for $2 and sold them on E-bay for $103.50. Jules, on the other hand, hates the thrift store. She claims she'd rather shoplift half-decent stuff than pay for someone else's old crap. Her wanting to go there made no sense. I stared at her.

"Sure," I said slowly, waiting for the catch. "Um, are you sure you want to?"

"Yes," she said. "We need to find you a new . . . sweater. To go with that new hair."

Gee, and I thought she didn't care. I mentally took back what I'd said about Jules. She's a good friend. She's just . . . flighty. And ever-so-slightly self-centered. But in all fairness. Danny! Her mother! I'd be self-centered, too.

"Besides," she said. "I have some items. To sell to them."

"Items?" I said, dumbly.

Our tires squealed as we jerked to a stop outside the store. (Jules thinks she can drive stick, but she has a bit of trouble with timing the clutch.)

"Items," she said. "Stuff." And with that, she produced from the trunk of her car a giant green garbage bag stuffed to bursting with what could only be her mother's clothes.

"Ha ha," I laughed merrily, mentally calculating the E-bay value of her mother's designer clothes. "Isn't that Grand Theft?"

"Doesn't your dad sell drugs?" she said.

"Right," I said, not laughing. "OK then."

We went into the thrift store. On the plus side, I scored a great black wraparound Donna Karan sweater from the bag before she dumped the lot on the counter. On the down side, Jules was crying again and I couldn't seem to make her stop. She cried all through the process of cataloguing the clothes in the consignment book, which took forever. Baby elephants have been born in less time. I was starving, and beginning to get light-headed. (I am slightly hypoglycemic.) The clerk didn't pay the slightest bit of attention to the tears plopping down on her carefully inked list, or to me repeatedly saying that I was starving. There was a plate of danishes behind her. Were they all for her? It was all I could do not to leap over the counter and steal one. Instead, I patted Jules reassuringly on the shoulder a few times.

I have to admit that after about half an hour of that, I felt more like slapping her in the face. She sniffed daintily and continued to drip her tears all over everyone as though she was doing us a favour. Prettily. Who looks pretty when they are crying?

Jules, that's who.

Where was Kiki when you needed her?

"I'm not going to the party tonight," said Jules, dropping me off. "You go without me. Kiki's away, by the way."

"Away?" I said. But she'd already gone. I hoped she'd drive into the ditch, but she missed it by an inch and a half.

Great.

Summary:

- Best Friend Kiki is "away" and didn't tell me.
- Best Friend Jules is "crazy" and Grounded.
- Can't go to party by myself.
- Hair looks like electrocuted clown wig.

Monday, September 9

MOOD	Depressed. Suicidal. Catatonic.
HAIR	Don't want to talk about it.
HEALTH	Who cares?
HOROSCOPE	You will receive good news in the mail! An authority figure will surprise you today.
JT SIGHTINGS	2

Early morning, too early to care about time

I wandered into school and bumped smack into JT.

"JT," I said, grinning weirdly.

"Hi," he said. And laughed and walked away.

I froze, and relived the moment in my head ten times in a row. I tried to breathe normally. This was supposed to be a good day. Didn't my horoscope promise a good day?

I've forgotten. I've forgotten everything, such as "how

to walk" and "how to talk."

To recap:

JT Cooper said "Hi!"

JT said "Hi!" to ME.

But why did he laugh? Probably at my hair.

Note to Self: Kill self.

Or at least buy wig.

8:04 a.m.

I found Kiki sitting on the floor, leaning on our lockers, grinning away happily. Wearing a (tight) T-shirt that said "Hard Rock Café, Maui."

"Where did you get that?" I said suspiciously. I know Kiki well enough to know pretty much everything in her wardrobe.

"Maui," she said. "The Hard Rock Café. And I have to tell you, I'm really tired."

"Why?" I said.

Then she told me. She spent the weekend in Hawaii. Yes, Hawaii. How is that possible? The weekend? Who does that?

(*Mood update*: insanely jealous, even more massively depressed than before.)

"Hawaii," I said, sliding down my locker and sitting next to her. The floors were newly waxed, and while not exactly shiny, they were sure slippery. I scraped my nail across the tile and got a scraping of white crud. Ew.

Kiki smelled like Hawaii, even over the gross stench of the floor cleaner.

"Hawaii," she repeated. "I brought you a present." She dumped a lei of flowers around my neck. "Now you've been lei'd. Laid, get it?"

"What?" I said, sneezing three times in a row. (I always sneeze in threes. You never want to sneeze in even numbers. It's bad luck.) "How? Why?"

"It's a joke," she said. "Lei'd. It's a lei. Get it?"

"No, no," I said. "I mean, yes. I get it. I meant, Hawaii: how, why, when?"

"Oh," she said. "I met this girl. Some friend of my sister works on the airline. They get to take free trips. She invited my sister but she couldn't go. So I went. It was great. You should have been there. What did you guys do?"

"Hawaii?" I repeated. "God, I've always wanted to go to Hawaii. Who is this girl?"

"It wasn't that big of a deal," Kiki said flipping her hair (which was in a million little braids and looked fantastic). "Do you like it?" she said. "I got it done on the beach."

Other Things I Used to Be Able To Do
With My Hair Before Cutting It:
1. Have it put into a million braids on the beach in Hawaii.

"It's, uh," I said. "You look great."

"What did I miss?" she said. "Your hair looks . . . cute, by the way. The colour makes your teeth look whiter. Or something."

"Oh, thanks," I said. (It does? Really? Must check in the bathroom at the next opportunity.) But first . . . "You did miss a thing or two," I said.

And then I told her about Jules, who was conspicuously absent from school.

And that's when we hatched The Plan. The Second Weekend Back At School Beach Party To Cheer Jules Up Plan. (In my head, this is actually The Plan To Seduce JT At A Party Or At Least Get Him Drunk And Get Him To Kiss Me. But I would never say that out loud.)

"Are you going to invite JT?" Kiki said.

"No!" I said. "I mean, it's not like we'll issue invites, right? We'll just tell people. Er, word will get around. I suppose he might be there."

"Give it up," she said. "You can do better. He's an idiot."

"No he isn't!" I said. I fight the urge to tell her about this morning's encounter.

"Is so," she said, knowingly.

"Blargh," I said, to end the conversation.

"That's not a word," she said. "What does that mean anyway?"

"Nothing," I shrugged. "It's just a sound."

"Don't be weird," she said.

"Fine," I said. I wondered if I'd ever have friends who actually appear to LIKE or ACCEPT me. I glared at her.

"Don't be mad," she said.

"I'm not," I said.

"Good," she said.

And then the fire alarm went off.

Things to Do When the Fire Alarm Goes Off:
1. Go to locker and immediately get all important personal belongings, such as Junior. And bagged lunch (may be

outside for a long time and possibly will get hungry.
2. Continue to stand in the hallway until teachers run by, flapping their arms, and screeching, "Get out right now!"
3. Run for your life. (Seems like a lot of work.)
4. Place bets on who pulled the fire alarm and why.
5. Go outside into the freezing cold (OK, it's 63 degrees, but still) and stand shivering while your friends blow smoke in your face and the fire trucks finally arrive and declare the whole thing a childish prank while delivering a stern warning on why-you-should-never-pull-the-fire-alarm-unless-there-is-an-actual-fire.

5:47 p.m.
"Dad," I said impatiently when I got home. "DAD!"

"What, honey?" he said, looking up from his book.

"I asked you if I could have some money to buy some stuff for school."

"What kind of stuff?"

"Um, books?"

"I thought the school provided books. Isn't that what our taxes go towards paying?" He put down his book (The Bible) and warmed to his subject. "Education is a right! Not something you should have to subsidize —"

"OK, Dad," I interrupted. "I meant, for 'clothes.' I need some new clothes. Please?"

"Nope," he said.

"Nope?" I repeated.

"Nope," he said.

"Great," I said. "Perfect."

"You could always get a job," he said mildly, returning to his book, his feet up on the table. (Please note, his socks were unmatched and one had a picture of a dog in a tam knitted into the side.)

"So could you," I said as nastily as I could muster.

"How was school?" he said.

"Please," I said, storming out of the room as well as I could in sock feet. "Don't pretend to care!" I yelled from the kitchen.

"I hope you aren't making that horrible tofu thing again," he said.

"I like tofu," I said. And proceeded to start chopping. Honestly, if the man wants steak, maybe he should do the cooking. Or the cleaning. Or ANYTHING ELSE AROUND HERE.

"You know I love you, honey," he said from the doorway behind me. I could feel his big, sad, brown, hippie eyes on my back. But I didn't turn around. Honestly, sometimes it is very difficult to have such a half-baked father.

Things I would Talk About with my Mother if I had One:
1. JT.
2. My day at school.
3. The future.
4. My friends and why they hate me.
5. My hair, and how it's ruined.
6. Her.

"Did you change your hair?" Dad asked, gnawing on a hunk of raw carrot.

"Yes, Dad," I said. "Two days ago. Thanks for noticing."

"You're so beautiful," he said. "I don't know how an ugly old fool like me could possibly have fathered a kid like you."

OK, so when he says stuff like that, it's so hard to hate him.

▶ ▶ ▶

Thursday, September 12

MOOD	Edgy
HAIR	Still there, still orange, still horrid
HEALTH	Not actively dying
HOROSCOPE	Today represents a change in planetary alignment that will affect you for the next twelve years and will teach you many valuable lessons. Try to pay attention.
JT SIGHTINGS	16 (!)

It didn't take long for the rumour to start swirling through the school. It always amazes me how quickly these things happen. So TSWBASBP (The Second Week Back At School Beach Party) (pronounced TuhSwabAsp) was a well-known thing. Everyone was talking about it. OK, not everyone, but enough people that I kind of felt like it might happen.

I was nervous. And excited.

After all, maybe this party would mark the true beginning of TGYML. Maybe the first week back at school was a bit of a dry run and didn't count towards the overall superiority of the year. I doodled in the margin of my notebook while Ms. Phil discussed the right and wrong way to level off flour in a measuring cup. I don't know why I decided to take Home Ec. It was a big mistake.

I took it because I knew JT was taking it.

JT was not in my Home Ec class. Who knew that so many students would sign up for it that it would be split into three classes?

I nudged Kiki with my elbow. She grinned at me, and held up a list she was writing in her planner. "The Plan," she whispered.

"Have you talked to Jules?" I asked. I had tried to call Jules a whole bunch of times. OK, once. Her mother had said she wasn't home. And she wasn't at school, either.

"Yes," she said, leaning her head closer to me. She still had her hair in braids and they shone in the light. How does she wash those things? I made a mental note to ask her later.

"MISS HARMONY AND MISS ANDREWS!" yelled Ms. Phil. "Perhaps you would like to come up here and demonstrate to the class how to separate an egg."

"Yes," I said. "Sure."

Kiki glowered at me. "Not really, Ms. Phil," she said. "We're sorry, it won't happen again."

"Fine," said Ms. Phil. "But please pay attention."

I was kind of disappointed, because I'm actually very good at separating eggs. I can do it with one hand. I've had lots of practice. My dad likes omelets. I don't eat eggs myself, of course. Think about what eggs ARE. Would you eat those? Seriously? Very disgusting.

In fact, the smell of cooking eggs makes me gag.

Kiki shoved her day-timer onto my desk. "The Plan!" I whispered.

Now that it was written down, it seemed like a real adventure. We'd go rescue Jules from her tower and force her to have fun. Hmmm. Also sounded risky and implausible. But the most important thing was that we had A Plan.

Possible Imagined Scenarios for TSWBASBP
(The Second Weekend Back At School Beach Party):

1. JT doesn't show up.
2. JT does show up, but with someone else.
3. I don't show up.
4. We both show up, but he ignores me, as usual.
5. Neither of us show up.
6. No one shows up.
7. Everyone shows up, we're both there, but don't see each other.
8. We do see each other, fall into each other's arms, and kiss.
9. We do see each other, I trip and fall into the fire, and have to be air-lifted to a hospital in a different city to treat my wounds.
10. We do see each other, he trips and falls into the fire, and dies.
11. We see each other and he pushes me into the fire.
12. We all show up, and he runs off with Jules.
13. Jules refuses to come.
14. Jules has run away and isn't there when we go to rescue her.

15. Jules comes, but sulks through the whole evening.
16. A natural disaster (earthquake? tidal wave?) occurs and
    the party is swept into the sea and never seen again.
    Better yet, a natural disaster occurs, the party is swept
    into the sea, JT and I manage to survive by clinging to a
    floating log, get swept to deserted island, where we
    must live out the rest of our lives alone and . . .
    Hmmm. That's a good one.

▶ ▶ ▶

Friday, September 13

MOOD	Happy / Nervous / Excited
HAIR	Moderately OK, considering.
HEALTH	No symptoms of anything.
HOROSCOPE	You may alienate those closest to you. Your temper will flare. Try to get some exercise.
JT SIGHTINGS	2

9:19 a.m.
Slept in, was late for school, AND
managed to acquire the following:

1. A bruise on my left knee and left elbow (fell while running to the bus).
2. A detention (was caught sneaking into class by
   Mr. Pork Butt).
3. A new "friend" (odd boy who smells like sausage has
   attached himself to me as needed "partner" in class that
   I was late for. Everyone else had a partner already so will
   be forced to spend weeks and weeks writing a "debate"

with geek, who, while I'm sure is very nice, will ruin my social status.) "Friend" now has my phone number and promised to call this weekend. Oh, joy. Tried to alienate him with my fearsome temper, but he was not dissuaded, and patted me on the arm as though I needed comforting.

4. A discolouration on my front teeth. If by "discoloura-tion," I mean that repeated use of Crest Whitestrips and Colgate whitening gel have caused alarming trans-parency to appear around edges of teeth. Are teeth disintegrating?

5. A bad mood.

Saturday, September 14

MOOD	VERY EXCITED!
HAIR	Needs work.
HEALTH	Blood Pressure — high!
HOROSCOPE	Something you have been waiting your whole life for will happen.
JT SIGHTINGS	None yet, expect at least ONE.

9:30 a.m.
Good things about tonight:

1. TSWBASBP (i.e. Plan to Seduce JT) is coming to-gether. Leg and arm bruise are covered with cover-up. Weather is perfect. It's like mid-summer, I swear. Hot and dry. Yippee!

2. Am wearing Kiki's new dark rinse jean jacket over Jules

black tank-top with white sketch of a hand on it, which I love for no good reason except that she looks good in it, so ergo, I must look good in it. And Juicy Couture pants bought at thrift store for $5 (probably formerly Jules' mom's).

3. My hair has settled into new style. If by that I mean I don't necessarily want to kill myself every time I look in the mirror.

4. Courtesy of Jules, have new PROFESSIONAL STRENGTH tooth whitening strips which must be better than the regular strength ones and perhaps will fix the transparency problem with my teeth. Jules bought them with the money she got from the consignment of her mother's clothes at the thrift store. (Suspect this is some kind of present to win me back as she knows she needs friends, even ugly weird friends without boyfriends. ESPECIALLY ugly weird friends without boyfriends.)

5. Kiki has her mom's car for tonight.

6. JT will be at party tonight.

7. Will have opportunity to flirt with JT at party tonight.

8. Am determined to at least get JT to talk to me at party tonight. Or fall in love with me. Either one.

Bad things about tonight:

1. Jules is still grounded, but as guest of honour at Second Weekend Back At School Beach Party To Cheer Jules Up, we have to get her there. This will involve drama and intrigue.

2. Jules is still in an evil mood re: Danny. And her mother.

Furthermore, everyone at school seems to know about it and this makes Jules believe that "everyone is laughing at her." When, in fact, they are more shocked than anything. And interested in knowing what Jules' mother looks like. OK, some of them are laughing.

3. Have a million homework assignments to do this weekend and have so far done zero of them, including my part of mock "debate" with class geek. Geek is sure to demand it from me bright and early Sunday morning.

4. Was forced to invite some dorky people from Student Council meeting on Friday after school to party because accidentally mentioned it to someone and then couldn't tell them not to come. Am worried that I will be associated with these people and will lose my semi-cool status. Am worried that no one will show up anyway. Am worried that party will be busted and I will be arrested as resident drug dealer and taken to jail. Am worried that JT will show up with someone else and ignore me all night. Am worried that someone will drug my drink and I'll get ill and have to go to the hospital. Am generally worried.

OK. I took a deep breath and held my breath until I couldn't stand it and then I let it out. Which made me light-headed. (Why do I do things like that?)

I just looked at the clock. 9:49 a.m.

Kiki is on her way over and we are going to go for a run before the party. Great! I love running. OK, I hate running. I love the *idea* of running. I plan to begin loving to run as soon as I get into better shape and am able to run further without collapsing, and/or throwing up. (Truth be told, I only agreed to do it so that I could casually drop into conversation how Kiki and I were just on a run before the party and people might mistake me for a cool, sporty, athletic-type person. And by "people," I mean JT.)

Two hours later
Dear Junior:
Am exhausted, red-faced and sweating even though we finished our run an hour ago and I've already had a shower. My body refuses to stop thinking it's running. Heart is racing. Face is red and blotchy.
    Please help.
Love,
Out-of-Shape Girl

Note to Self: Do not go on run before going to social event
    where looks matter.

Important additional note: Kiki did not even get slightly
    flushed while running. Secretly hate Kiki and her
    superior, athletic genes.

"Running," Dad said, shaking his head and inspecting my ruddy cheeks. "Honestly, when I was your age . . ."

    "Dad," I said, "When you were my age you were probably at Woodstock splashing around in the mud. Let's agree that 'when you were my age' is not a good way for you to set examples for me."

"I didn't go to Woodstock," he said defensively.

"Fine," I said. "Whatever."

"Actually," he said, "When I was your age . . ." Then he kind of drifted off and stared into space. (Don't be alarmed, this happens to him quite often. He's the poster child for why smoking marijuana day in and day out for thirty-five-plus years is bad for your brain.)

We have a budgie bird (The Bird) that has no cage. (Dad does not believe in imprisoning animals, which is The Bird's bad luck as The Cat would be more than happy to imprison The Bird in his mouth.) And just then The Bird flew into the room, landed on Dad's shoulder and started pecking at his beard. (Everything The Bird does looks like a cry for help to me, but maybe I'm just projecting.) The Bird is blue, with a yellow head. Neither of us knows if it's a boy bird or a girl bird. Is there some way to tell? We both watched The Bird for a minute and then I remembered that Dad had started to say something.

"Dad, WHAT?" I said.

"Forget it," he said. "It's not important. But you should take a shower or something before your party. You're all red and sweaty."

Gee, thanks, I thought. "I already *did*," I said.

But then I took another shower. I mean, you can never be too clean, right?

Later (no watch)
The plan to rescue Jules from her house backfired horribly.

Horribly.

You can't even imagine.

It started out OK. I mean, everything was on track. We got to Jules' house without any problem. The weather was pretty nice and everything was shaping up. We had a car and (reasonably) good hair. OK, Kiki had perfect hair (still in perfect, miniscule braids, not even slightly frizzy or falling out) and mine didn't look as terrible as it could considering its alarming colour and bizarre shagginess.

I called Jules on my cell and she came to the window, and kind of pressed her nose against the glass, goofing around. Which was a positive sign. Like maybe she was in a good mood. (Trust me, you don't want to be around Jules when she's not in a good mood. Jules in a bad mood is, well, *evil*, for lack of a better word). She disappeared for a few minutes, and we waited.

Finally, she climbed out the window (granted this was awkward as it was one of those push-open windows and she really had to stuff herself through the opening — thankfully, she's as thin as a piece of paper so this really wasn't an issue) and appeared on the roof. Which was great, except for the fact that the roof is this really sloped red-tile stuff (we always said her house looked like it was built in the style of Colombian drug lords, which isn't funny considering what my dad does for a living and the fact we live in a shabby lump of a house and she lives in a stylin' mansion and her dad is not involved in drugs in any way, as far as I know).

And she was wearing heels.

Not heels, exactly. Not like stilettos or anything. But wedge-slides with heels on them. They weren't high. But I guess the were high enough, and they had no grip because they were those wooden ones with the hard, slippery soles. Actually, come to think of it, they were really stupid shoes to wear to a beach party.

Or to climb off a roof.

Next thing I know, Jules kind of flew through the air. It was graceful (naturally), in an oh-no-she's-falling-and-we-can't-catch-her kind of way. (Could you really ever catch anyone who is falling off a roof? Think about it. Best Case Scenario would be that they were saved by squishing you completely. And frankly, Jules and I aren't such good friends that I'd want her to squish me in her stupid shoes.) Luckily, I didn't have to, because she kind of caught herself. So in the midst of her Grand Escape, she ended up dangling off the eaves, which she had to hold on to for dear life. Kiki and I were killing ourselves laughing. It was really very funny. I laughed so hard that I thought I'd given myself a hernia, it hurt that much. I had to hold on to the vines on the trellis to keep myself from falling to the ground and rolling around in hysterics. Kiki started to climb up the trellis (to save Jules, I think) and I followed, because I guess I'm a follower. I don't know why, really. I was laughing still, and it was hard to think straight.

I don't know how her mom didn't hear us. (Her mom does drink a bit too much, or so Jules says. Maybe she'd already passed out. In which case, we should have just used the door.) At one point, Kiki was literally screaming with laughter. That was when Jules was apparently safe, but flailing and trying to keep her shoes on at the same time. She was dangling just above us like a bug, arms and legs akimbo, shoes hanging off her toes. Whisper-screaming "Help! Help!"

Finally, the gutter broke and she passed us on the way down, grabbing at my sweater. I pulled away. I mean, I didn't want her to wreck my clothes. Besides, the ground wasn't that far off, and if I'd let her pull me down, too, the trellis would have broken for sure and we would have been caught.

She landed laughing, in that laugh that says, "I'm laughing, but this might not be very funny and any second now, I might just fly into a horrible rage."

She probably won't be laughing tomorrow when she thinks about it, I thought as I climbed down (carefully) to see if she was really OK. As I got closer, I could tell that she wasn't. Her arm was at a really gross angle. I almost fainted.

It was definitely broken. I could tell just from looking. Jules is going to be some pissed off when the shock wears off, I thought. (I happen to know that sometimes when you injure yourself really badly, it takes a few minutes to really feel the pain.) I guessed she wasn't there yet, as she was still giggling.

I've never broken any of my bones. At least, not that I can remember. I can only remember things that happened after the first grade. (My life before I started school is a complete blur. I have no idea why this is. One day, I'll spend a fortune on psychiatric help and find out. Not that I really want to know. My mom left when I started school. It doesn't take a medical degree to understand why I've blocked out all my time with her.)

OK, this is an aside to the story, I know it is. But I just want to say that my mom was a bitch. She must have been. Or else, why did she leave?

Anyway. Enough about that.

In the car on the way to the hospital (Jules wouldn't let us take her inside to get her mom's help, although she's probably right when she said her mom wouldn't be any help anyway) Jules started to cry. In the usual way, which is to say, she still looked pretty. But I guessed it did hurt, after all. I kind of patted her on her good arm supportively. I didn't really know what else to do, and I am her friend. Being supportive during tragedies is the least that I could do. Besides, I'm sure she'd have done the same for me.

Maybe.

We ended up in the emergency room. (I hate the smell of hospitals. Why do hospitals always smell so appalling? They make the school smell positively pretty. That antiseptic, sick smell made me dizzy. I had to put my head between my knees so as to avoid fainting.)

Jules got her arm put into a cast. Somehow (I have no idea how), she convinced the doctor to call *my* dad instead of calling *her* mom. As she was doing this, I was concentrating on breathing deeply (but not hyperventilating) so as not to get sick myself. I wonder how many people get sick just from setting foot in a hospital. Probably, quite a few.

The doctor was capital-h Hot (tall, dark and handsome, if slightly buck-toothed and, well, zitty — do doctors get acne? This seems wrong to me). Jules was flirting like crazy (and coincidentally, she stopped crying). She's seriously unstoppable. It's like she thinks this is ER, the TV show, and the doctor is George Clooney. Or better yet, Noah Wylie. (Yum. Noah.) Put anyone male and under the age of fifty in the room, and she pulls out all the stops.

Really, it's disgusting.

Lucky for her (and me), my dad didn't answer the phone (I'm sure he was very busy sleeping in front of the TV or nurturing Mary Jane, i.e., The Love of His Life). The doctor was so distracted by Jules' overwhelming beauty (he was getting a little flustered and the emergency room was getting fairly busy) that he didn't call anyone else.

Jules is so freaking pretty, it makes me want to stick pens in my eyes. Why do some people get all the looks? She has amazing skin. Perfect teeth. Great hair. A dancer's body. And what do I have? Freckles. Slightly crooked teeth. Belly fat.

Oh, crap.

Anyway, she actually made the doctor blush. (Which in turn made me blush. I'm very suggestible. Don't faint in front of me, because over I'll go. Same with yawning. And the hiccups.)

Finally even Kiki got sick of it and pointedly said, "We should go, then, as we have important high school events to attend."

"What?" said Jules.

"Yes," said Kiki. "You know. High school stuff." I swear, she was trying to look even younger than she is so the doctor would feel like an idiot. I'm sure he did. I mean, I kind of felt like a fool too, to tell you the truth.

Jules huffed and got off the table. She shook the guy's hand. "It was very nice to meet you," she said formally. "And thank you for saving my life."

"He hardly saved your life," I pointed out. "You broke your arm."

"People can die from broken arms," she snapped. "You're the one who told me that."

Which is true. I mean, it is possible that when you break a bone, you can get a tiny blood clot, and if you are unlucky or if your number is up, it can float along into your lungs, and then bam. Game Over. Thank you for playing.

"I guess," I said sullenly. "At any rate, we're late for this HIGH SCHOOL thing."

"Fine," she said.

And we left.

Jules hadn't mentioned Danny and her mom at all. I mean, sure she'd been busy with falling off the roof and breaking her arm. Maybe it was a good sign that she hadn't mentioned it. Maybe she was getting past it.

(Or that it wasn't true to begin with? This is a mean thought that I stuff back down again as soon as I have it.) (I'm sure it's true.) (People don't make up stuff about their college-aged boyfriends kissing their mothers.)

Maybe she was just over it, I thought. Though I seriously doubted that I ever would *ever* get over such a thing, if it happened to me. Which it couldn't, as my life is missing the important players in that drama, i.e., the boyfriend. And the mother.

Later still.
By the time we got out of there, we were seriously late for the party. Not that it mattered. I mean, only the losers show up at a beach party early, right?

Right.

And we aren't losers. (At least, Kiki and Jules aren't. I'm possibly only cool-by-association.)

2:00 a.m., in bed. On bed. Can't get undressed.
Dear Jumklnior:
Am never drinking again. Have hiccups. Uh-oh. And bed spins. Not good. Feel like getting up to throw up but can't be bothered. Oh nooooo. Must sleep. Stop moving around so I can . . .

Ugh.

Remind me to fjklsjk;aswe
Love,
Hslru

▶ ▶ ▶

Sunday, September 15

MOOD	Too ill to have any mood.
HAIR	Hair is ill.
HEALTH	Extremely ill.
HOROSCOPE	Too ill to get paper which is miles away at bottom of driveway.
JT SIGHTINGS	Absolutely too ill to care.

Sometime in the morning, very bright, can't find watch.
(From MDAdvice.com)

Symptoms
Headache after excessive alcohol consumption. Nausea
or vomiting.

Possible Problems
"Hangover." (Why do inverted quotes imply "it's your
fault and we don't care?")

What To Do
Use a non-prescription pain reliever.

Huh. What do they know? Of course, there are other
possibilities:

Symptoms
Severe headache that worsens when bending head
forward. Eyes sensitive to light. Lethargy. Confusion. No
recent head injury.

Possible Problems
Bleeding in membrane.

What To Do
Call doctor now. See Subarachnoid Hemorrhage. See
Brain or Epidural Abscess.

Noonish.
Dear Junior:
Possibly have Subarachnoid Hemorrhage. Am going to
die.
Love,
Doomed Girl

3:17 p.m. (found old watch)

TSWBASBP (TCJU) or What I
Can Remember About Last Night:

There was a path down to the lagoon through the woods.
When I say "path," I'm using the term loosely. It was
more like a break in the trees where you could walk with
only occasional uncalled-for attacks from protruding
stumps, branches and aggressive, prickly shrubs. And
of course it wasn't lit, so we had to see our way with
lighters. Which was fun, to a point. But as a result, we all
got burns on our thumbs from trying to keep them lit.
(Stupid child-proof lighters). Or at least, I did. (I press on
it now, and it hurts. It's a weird kind of hurt, though. It's
almost like when you get a sore in your mouth and you
can't keep your tongue away from it.)

(Ouch.)

OK, back to the party. The shrubs and trees were attack-
ing us and Jules had black streaks on her cast from the
smoke. (It's possible that a couple of the branches got
slightly charred on the way past.) It all seemed wrong at
the time. The path, that is. Like we'd taken a wrong turn.
But none of us were bright enough to look for other
options. It turns out there was a road that took you right
up to the beach and all you had to do was walk down
some stairs.

Go figure.

By the time we got there, it was close to 11:30. The
party was really going, if by "going," I mean there were
a lot of people sitting around drunkenly shivering on
blankets, or just plunked down in the sand.

The music was loud. The nice thing about the beach we chose is that it's in the middle of nowhere, so people didn't complain about noise, unlike the usual beach party, which features partygoers dumping alcohol into the ocean and the police telling people to pack it up and slapping fines on everyone for lighting a controlled fire.

I love beach parties. Or maybe I just love the idea of beach parties. (The reality involves sand fleas and an overwhelming smell of campfire smoke. I don't know what it is about me, but I'm like a smoke magnet. Wherever I sit in relation to the fire is where the wind turns so as to blow smoke all over me.)

So there we were, at the party, smoke blowing all over me and into my eyes and suffocating me and big hunks of burning ash leaping in my direction as though the gods or the Fates or whoever is in charge were trying to send me a message saying, "Move away from the fire, stat."

This was nothing like the parties you see in movies like *Risky Business* or *Van Wilder* (*Hello*, Ryan Reynolds? Yum.) where everyone is happily swinging from chandeliers in designer clothes. People at our party looked downright depressed. And cold. And unhappy. And mean. I had to fight the urge to say, "Buck up, campers!" (For one thing, "buck" is not a word that should ever be used for any reason.) But it was there, in my head, like a song with lyrics you can't stop repeating.

In my experience, come to think of it, most "parties" consist of a bunch of people sitting around waiting for something to happen. And that "something" is usually that someone throws up or passes out and everyone buries them in sand or undresses them or writes on their face with lipstick or indelible ink. In the summer, I went to a party and there was a guy there with a goatee. As he was passing out, he said, "Whatever you do, don't shave off my beard."

So we shaved his legs, painted his nails, and neatly plucked one brow clean away.

OK, I never said we were mature.

At this party, I guess we happened. By being late, I mean, we got lots of attention. Jules had a cast, so naturally she immediately became the center of the universe and everyone swirled around her like little stars in her galaxy.

It was a little sickening.

But who doesn't love to write on someone else's cast? Jules was a good sport about it, which was surprising considering she doesn't like to be touched. I guess cast-writing doesn't classify as "touching." She glowed and whimpered dramatically, as though the pain was intolerable (maybe it was) but she was a brave little soldier who would get through.

Ha.

I swear to God, if she flipped her hair one more time, I would have flicked a spark at it just to see it go up in flames. She just sat there and let herself be adored. Flip, flip, flip.

I was generally ignored. I mean, I'm used to that. And it's not like I have any hair left to flip. Eventually, I wandered out of the path of the smoke and set about building a sandcastle at the high-tide line. I used to build great sandcastles when I was a kid and we went to the beach. That's the nice thing about hippie parents: the summers are spent hanging out at beaches and eating food cooked over an open fire and building sandcastles (entire sand villages, really) because you have all the time in the world.

Hippies don't actually ever have to go anywhere.

It was harder to build the castle than I remembered. Of course, I didn't have a bucket, which would have helped. And building sandcastles alone isn't so much fun. Suddenly, I was hit with a vague memory of building a sandcastle and standing on it and having the tide come in around my feet and thinking I was going to be trapped in the middle of the sea, on top of that castle, forever.

There was a woman in that memory. I froze for a minute and then got myself a drink.

Dad has no pictures of Mom anywhere. I don't remember what she looks like.

Or perhaps I do, but I choose not to.

OK, back to the Party-Like Event.

Everyone was there.

And by "everyone," I mean JT.

And this is what happened:

. . .

. . .

No, I can't tell you. I'm too embarrassed. But let's just say that "Hey, JT, how's it going?" is not an opening line I'll use again. Because he fully ignored me. Fully. Like, he looked over my head and started talking to someone behind me.

Maybe he was drunk.

Or maybe he's just an asshole.

So in an effort not to look at him or speak to him or even appear to care about him, I plunked myself down next to the first person that I didn't know. And we talked.

OK, by "talked," I mean "kissed."

Hi, my name is Haley Andromeda Harmony, and I'm a slut. It was so Not Me, I still can't believe it. I'm not totally sure what happened. I keep trying to remember the details. But all I can recall is talking to this guy (cute-ish stranger) and flirting (giggling) and having some beer and then . . .

I got the hiccups.

I always do when I drink, which is why I'm not much of a drinker. They aren't charming, cute hiccups either. They are big, serious hiccups that sound like my stomach is trying to crawl out through my throat in the style of the alien that bursts out of peoples' guts in that Sigourney Weaver movie. Pretty! And then the Cute-ish Stranger tried to plug my nose. He said that was the cure for it.

It was very hard to carry on a conversation with his fingers on my nose. My poor, burned, peeling nose.

Then he said, "The best cure for the hiccups is kissing." And so I kissed him.

Me.

That is SO not like me.

That's how I came to spend the whole party kissing a cute-ish strange guy I'd never seen before. I don't even know his name. It was fun.

Or was it?

I'm not totally sure that I didn't do it just because I thought it would make a funny story later. Funny. Ha.

I guess it was, but more in a "what a loser I am" way than in a "I'd like to see him again" way.

Ideally, I'd like him to disappear from the planet Earth.

What was I thinking? I'm so embarrassed. Humiliated! Jules said something like, "Nice tongue action, face sucker!" when she left. Ugh.

Dear Junior:
Had humiliating experience at party and am too embarrassed to ever leave home again. Will become reclusive, pot-smoking hippie. Will miss you, as reclusive, pot-smoking hippies do not use lap-top computers.

Think I will just go back to sleep after putting in a new set of tooth-whitening strips. I might as well accomplish something while I'm sleeping off this hangover.
Love,
Reclusive Pot-Smoking (OK, not) Hippie Girl

Things I Won't Accomplish While Sleeping For An Entire Day:
1. English Essay about "What I Did on My Summer Vacation." Teachers still seriously assign stuff like this? Why? Do people actually DO things on summer vacation? Other than work, or look for work, or fantasize about how great their last year of school is going to be? (I would have worked, had I been able to get a job.) (I looked for work. Really, I did.) I lay on the beach. That would make a great essay, no?
2. Helping Dad repaint the upstairs bathroom. It's his Project of the Day. Which implies that he actually has

Daily Projects when the last time he did a Project was 1998 when he painted the downstairs bathroom. Sort of. Part of it, anyway. He's really going after it this time, probably because he knows it's driving me crazy. If he keeps scraping the walls like he's doing, I'm going to kill him and then the bathroom won't be an issue.

3. Calling Jules to find out how her arm is. She and Kiki disappeared quite early, come to think of it. I got a ride home with the Cute-ish Stranger. He was driving a mini-van. A mini-van! Who drives a VAN? Soccer moms, that's who. Soccer moms and FREAKS. I'm an ass. I make bad choices. I am a colossal idiot.

   At least I didn't, you know. Do It. (Am I the only person in the twelfth grade in any school in North America who still thinks of this as a big thing?) (Probably.)

4. Four hundred math questions that I can't begin to understand. Why do I need to know how fast a train would go in order to drop a bomb on a car travelling west at 10 miles an hour on the highway? Do they want us to all grow up to be terrorists? How does this apply to real life? That's what I want to know.

5. Looking at College Catalogues that Dad stole from the library. I don't know why he can't check things out like a normal person. I don't even know what normal is any more.

7:08 p.m.

Slept through the forty-two phone calls that Dad claims I got during the day. And when I woke up the second time,

I drank four huge glasses of water that made my head feel marginally better. (Did you know that the reason why you get a hangover after drinking is that your brain actually shrinks? You have to re-inflate it with water. I wonder what would happen if you didn't. If you drank a lot of alcohol, would your brain just continually shrink and shrink until it atrophied to the size of a peanut?)

Note to Self: Research this possibility on the internet.

There is something to be said for sleeping all day. I had the best sleep. Apart from the headache. And the fact that I could barely move my legs. When I first woke up, I thought perhaps I had suffered a small stroke, or worse: a massive stroke. Or a spinal hemorrhage. And that I was paralyzed from the waist down. Then I remembered that Kiki and I went for a run before the party.

I may never walk again.

My body clearly does not approve of "running" as an activity.

I didn't really feel like calling anyone back. I was sort of (read: "completely") too embarrassed to talk to anyone about the Cute-ish Stranger.

On the plus side, he must have thought my hair looked OK. At least the new hair didn't completely act as a Total Boy Repeller. Maybe it's OK, after all. I was checking it out in the mirror (and it didn't look too bad if I squinted and didn't turn on the lights) (especially considering I've been sleeping on it for 14 hours), when suddenly an URGENT SITUATION came to my attention.

My knees buckled. I sat down on the toilet seat and put my head between my knees. Which, for the record, made me excessively dizzy. (I guess my brain hadn't rehydrated yet.)

I stood up and looked again, and then called Kiki, stat.

Me: Kiki, help.

Kiki: Oh, hey. What's up?

Me: Oh My God, Oh My God, Oh My God.

Kiki: I thought you didn't believe in God.

Me: I'll start right now if He can help me out of this.

Kiki: (laughing) What?

Me: (pausing for dramatic effect and/or hyperventilating) I have four giant hickeys on my neck. It looks like I got attacked by a large vampire bat. Or worse. Like I have a terrible skin disease. A contagious, terrible skin disease. I'm going to kill myself. I have no other choice. I can never go to school again.

Kiki: Ha ha ha! Who was that guy?

Me: I have no idea. It's not funny.

Kiki: You could wear a turtleneck. Ha ha ha. Are you hyperventilating?

Me: No. I mean, yes. I don't know. You have to stop laughing. It's serious.

Kiki: Ha ha ha.

Me: I'll use concealor?

Kiki: That won't work. It will make it look worse. Are you going to call him?

Me: I don't know . . . No. Of course not. He's disgusting. I think . . .

Kiki: You didn't think so last night. Ooops, hang on, that's
       my call-waiting.
Me: Sure.

    . . .

    . . .

So when it became totally apparent that she wasn't coming back, I hung up. I hate being the person on the call waiting that people don't come back to. Call-waiting is a terrible invention. I cursed the person who invented Call Waiting with the rage of a thousand suns. Then I went back into the bathroom and stared at my neck in the mirror.

I looked like (a) a battered woman or (b) a freak.

I stared.

At certain angles, it looked kind of . . . interesting. It made me look more interesting. Or something.

Dangerous.

I tried to look dangerous in the mirror, but instead looked deranged. I exhaled and drew a frowning face on the mirror, then wiped it off.

They were still there.

They really were the biggest hickeys that I'd ever seen. (Not that I'd ever had a hickey of my own before.) They were purple. Huge, florid, purple blobs. I looked like I'd been attacked by some sort of exotic and terribly poisonous jellyfish, which in turn had mutated and absorbed itself into my flesh and was perhaps now trying to get out through my neck.

I poked at them to see if it would hurt. Or if it would make them vanish.

Nope.
What is the healing time of hickeys, anyway?

▶ ▶ ▶

Monday, September 16
AKA
The Worst Day of My Life

MOOD	Foul
HAIR	Too short to cover hickeys
HEALTH	Failing, see Note*
HOROSCOPE	Today is the best day of this lunar cycle! You will be the center of attention and will love every minute of it.
JT SIGHTINGS	I

10:17 a.m.
Note: severity of neck bruising suggests hemorrhagic disease. See below.

(from Medline)
Bruising: Definition
Bleeding into the skin, subcutaneous tissues (under the top layer of skin), or mucous membranes ("skin" covering your mouth and lips). Purpura are flat areas where blood has collected under the tissue. A hematoma is a larger collection that forms a lump.
Common Causes
• Local injury or trauma

- Allergic reaction
- Autoimmune disorders
- Viral infection or illness affecting blood coagulation
- Thrombocytopenia
- Medical treatment, including radiation and chemotherapy
- Bruise (ecchymosis)
- Birth (petechiae in the newborn)
- Aging skin (ecchymosis)
- Idiopathic thrombocytopenic purpura (petechiae and purpura)
- Henoch-Schonlein purpura (purpura)
- Leukemia (purpura and ecchymosis)
- Drugs
- Anticoagulants such as warfarin or heparin (ecchymosis)
- Aspirin (ecchymosis)
- Cortisone (ecchymosis)
- Septicemia (petechiae, purpura, ecchymosis)

Dear Junior:

Remind me to ask Dad if we can go to a boarding school, somewhere such as South Carolina where no one would know us. We could learn horseback riding and golf and other sports popular amongst rich southerners. Also, tennis.

Love,

Social Outcast

5:45 p.m.

Things I learned today:

1. Kiki was right: You cannot cover up hickeys with concealor. Or you can, but it doesn't work.

2. Concealor stains clothes.
3. Hickeys are amusing to everyone except the hickee (as in, the recipient of the hickey).
4. Haley Hickey is NOT a nickname that I hope will stick for very long. Or at all. (Like Haley Harmony wasn't bad enough.)
5. Turtlenecks were a great invention. Will wear them until these wretched bruises heal. If they ever do. Likely they will never heal and for the rest of my life I'll be known as the Girl With The Hickeys.

JT Moment of the Day:
On the plus side, I managed to catch JT's perfect blue eye while he was standing and staring vacantly into his locker. He nodded at me. Nodded! I choose to interpret this as a good sign. A sign that he is in love with me. Oh, OK. Even I'm not that stupid. Then his eyes drifted down to my neck, and I swear to God that he flinched. Naturally, this can only mean that he is jealous of the Cute-ish Stranger.

Or at least that's how I've decided to view it.

Wednesday, September 18

MOOD	Irrelevant
HAIR	Irrelevant
HEALTH	Irrelevant
HOROSCOPE	Irrelevant, as horoscopes clearly are all garbage and full of made-up, meaningless lies.
JT SIGHTINGS	Irrelevant

7:12 a.m.

I hate running.

I hate running.

I hate running.

I hate running.

I hate running.

7:34 a.m.

See 7:12 a.m.

7:47 a.m.

It's official: I am never running again. Running is a stupid hobby designed for people who are a) suckers for punishment; b) half robots; c) visitors from other planets; or d) crazy.

In other news, I have possibly broken my nose.

It wasn't my fault, I swear. I honestly did not see that tree. Why do they plant skinny, near-invisible trees on the sidewalk? That's what I want to know. There ought to be a law against it. If I had more energy (i.e., hadn't used it all up while running), I would march down to City Hall and demand the removal of all unnecessary trees.

(If my nose is actually broken, I wonder if I'll be able to get a nose job should they have to reset it. I've never been that crazy about my nose. Would prefer to have a cuter, smaller nose, in the style of Nicole Kidman.)

3:30 p.m.

Student Council Meeting: (or why I shouldn't go to them)

1. Am now officially in charge of this year's "prom." I had

no plans to even GO to the prom. Aren't proms in June? Am I supposed to start planning now?

(*Note to Self*: Devise plan that will result in going to prom with JT.)

How do these things happen to me? Did I volunteer accidentally? Do I have some form of Tourette's that causes me to raise my hand at inopportune moments? (Research Tourette's later, can it begin suddenly? Will find out.)

2. Student Council President Bruce Bartelson AKA Dorkus* Dorkmeister has announced that we are all going on a "Student Council Field Trip" so that we "get to know each other better." (This guy definitely has a future in corporate America.) As a result, I have to spend the better part of next weekend on some back-to-nature-type of group adventure. Which fills me with an overwhelming feeling of . . . dread.

   **Interesting side note*: A whale's penis is technically called a "dork."

3. JT walked by the meeting room and made some kind of muttering sound in the hallway that sounded like, "So that's where all the losers go when the lights go out."

Oh God. JT thinks I'm a loser.

I am a loser.

I can't breathe through my nose.

7:45 p.m.

Dear Junior,

You are my only friend. My real friends find me to be

"funny," by which I mean they laugh AT me. They think it's beyond funny that my nose is swollen. I'm tired of being the "entertaining" friend.

At dinner, Dad asked, "Did you do something different with your makeup?"

Ha.

He's a laugh a minute. I see where I get it from.

Have abandoned watering the garden, as is almost winter, so what's the point.

Love,

Funny (HA) Girl

► ► ►

Thursday, September 19

MOOD	Irked
HAIR	Less of a problem than "eyes" and "neck"
HEALTH	Atrocious
HOROSCOPE	Your creative impulses overtake you today. It's a great day for painting, writing, or music.
JT SIGHTINGS	0

Woke up in the morning with two black eyes. Black. Not pale lavender or slightly yellowish. Not greenish-blue or rainbow-hued. Not prettily bruised. Black.

Does it get any better than this?

"My God," Dad said, when I sat down for breakfast.

"I know," I said. "Please. I don't want to talk about it."

"What happened?" he said.

"I told you yesterday," I said. "I had an accident while running."

He made a strange snorting sound. "What kind of accident can you have while running?"

"Dad," I said. "Please. Give me a break."

"Well," he said, "if you don't want to talk about it, please pass me the Honey Bunches of Oats."

I slid them across the table at him, glaring. I tried to cover up the bruises with make-up, but this clearly didn't work. Short of showing up at school in sunglasses AND a turtleneck (this turtleneck is making me itchy and irritable), I'm going to quickly become famous for being the Bruised Girl.

(from MDAdvice.com)

Symptoms

Frequent bruises. Painful, swollen joints. Excessive bleeding from minor cuts.

Possible Problems

Blood Disorder

What to Do

See Hemophilia.

Hemophilia:

DEFINITION — An inherited deficiency of a blood-clotting factor that results in episodes of dangerous bleeding. Blood normally contains several factors that enable clotting to occur. The factors are designated I through XIII. In hemophilia A, the clotting factor VIII is deficient. Factors I-VII function properly, but the clotting process is then interrupted. Hemophilia B occurs less often and is caused by a deficiency of factor IX. **CAUSES** — The deficiency of a coagulation factor (X-linked recessive gene) is passed by an affected male to all of his daughters, but to none of his sons. These females become carriers of the condition. Some of the sons of female carriers may be affected, and some of the daughters of female carriers may themselves become carriers.

Hmmmf. So it's Dad's fault. I should have known.

Random List of Observations:
- Number of people who asked "What the hell happened to you?": 19
- Number of people who laughed when Kiki said, "She ran into a tree": 19
- Reasons why Kiki is my friend: Can't think of one.
- Reason to live: 0

"How the hell do you run into a tree?" asked Jules. "That's ridiculous."

"I don't know," I said. I do sort of know, but it's embarrassing.

I was daydreaming, OK?

I mean, running can be quite dull. Once you get past the burning pain in your legs and the searing pain in your oxygen-starved lungs, there isn't much to do. And I couldn't make conversation with Kiki, as breathing, talking and running simultaneously seemed impossible.

So I was just thinking about stuff.

OK, I was thinking about JT. We just happened to run by a wedding shop, and I happened to start considering what might happen if we ever started dating. Not that we'd get married or anything. But just that we might fall in love. OK, I was kind of imagining myself in the dress in the window, which was beautiful: white, spaghetti straps, beaded bodice, full skirt. (*NB*: I do not actually ever want to get married. I just liked the dress.)

Anyway, I was side-tracked by this vision of me in a lovely white gown and everyone looking on in awe and jealousy and JT staring lovingly into my eyes and people whispering, "I never would have guessed that they were in love!" . . .

And then . . .

. . . I ran directly into the tree.

I blame the tree. It was a very, very skinny tree. It was the tree equivalent of Jules — too thin for it's own good. Sure, it was pretty. But dangerous.

Somehow a big, huge tree would have seemed like a more normal thing to run into, or at least more easily explainable. And I managed to bang into it directly with my nose. Dead center.

I think I'm having flashbacks. When I close my eyes, I can see that skinny tree directly in the path of my face.

► ► ►

Friday, September 20

MOOD	Grouchy
HAIR	Please, like it matters?
HEALTH	Trying not to dwell on it
HOROSCOPE	Be patient. An eclipse in your 7th house will cause havoc in your relationships. Brace yourself.
JT SIGHTINGS	2

9:14 a.m.
Whenever I pass Kiki in the hall, she doubles over with laughter. She ought to be careful. She's going to get a hernia if she keeps this up.

Am officially no longer talking to Kiki.

3:01 p.m.
Or Jules.

Am determined to bear my new friendless status with good grace.

Monday, September 23

MOOD	Bored & friendless
HAIR	Pfffft.
HEALTH	Bruised & possibly dying
HOROSCOPE	Every day can't be easy. Today is going to bring many challenges. Be patient with yourself.
JT SIGHTINGS	6

11:20 a.m.

List for the Sake of a List:

- Movies watched over the weekend: 14
- Number of times the phone rang: 0
- Reasons to live: 0

Jules apparently did not notice that I wasn't talking to her for the entire weekend. Interesting. Some people are so completely self-involved that they have no idea they are social outcasts.

Attempt to continue to snub Jules failed miserably. First thing this morning, she plunked herself next to me on the floor and said, "Nice shiners. Good weekend?" At first, I thought she was kidding.

"Well?" she said.

"Not really," I said, through gritted teeth. I figured that if I didn't move my lips, then I still wasn't technically talking to her. (It's very difficult to talk without moving your lips, but I had lots of practice last year during a difficult gum operation. It was extremely painful and I had to drink out of straws for two weeks.) (I gained ten pounds drinking milkshakes. Milkshakes are extremely fattening, for the record.)

"I had the worst weekend ever," she said.

"Mmmmfl," I said with my jaw clenched.

"Is something wrong with your mouth again?" she said. "You sound funny."

I gave up. "Nothing is wrong with my mouth," I said as icily as possible. "I did not have a great weekend myself and don't want to talk about it."

"Oh," she said. She looked down and drew something on the sole of her shoe and then scribbled it out.

I stared at her and tapped at Junior as though I was working on something very important, which I would have been if Junior's battery was not dead.

"Your computer isn't even on," she said.

"Yes, it is," I said. Which was stupid, as it clearly wasn't.

"You know," she said. "You used to be such a good friend." She got up slowly and walked away. She looked really sad. For a minute, I felt really bad. I mean, I did. But she hasn't been a good friend to ME, has she?

I thought about chasing her, but then I didn't. I just sat there.

Before Dad "renovated" the downstairs bathroom, there used to be this weird little plaque on the wall that said, "Good friends are the smiles from God." I don't know why I was thinking of that, just then. I guess because I don't believe in God, and apparently I don't believe in good friends either.

Kiki walked by, stepped over my legs, and didn't say anything.

Great.

Everyone hates me.

► ► ►

Wednesday, September 25

MOOD	Saaaaaad
HAIR	Tousled and . . . messy
HEALTH	Who cares? Who notices?

HOROSCOPE	Today is the high point of your month. You will have much success in finances and business.
JT SIGHTINGS	14

2:00 p.m.
Summary of Year So Far Written In Math Class on
Back of Homework Assignment that I Forgot to Do:
It is now Wednesday, of the third week of the best year of my life. I have two shiners. Four hickeys. Bruising seems to be growing and spreading, and not dissipating even slightly. (Possibly also have leukemia or hemophilia.) I have one best friend who is mad at me, and one best friend who is ignoring me. (Possibly also mad, but not sure why.) No boyfriend. (Big surprise there). Cute-ish Stranger (AKA Hickey-Giver and Life-Ruiner) didn't even bother to call. No progress with JT.

Things to Look Forward to:
1. Graduation.
2. Eventually, my hair *will* grow out.
3. One day, will possibly get job and move somewhere interesting and surround myself with fascinating people who like me and don't laugh at me when I accidentally develop bruising ailment.
4. This weekend.
5. Scratch "4." Forgot that this weekend is bound to suck beyond all expectations of suckiness.
6. October. Because it has to be better than September.

10:00 p.m.

Dear Junior:

Tomorrow night I have to set off on "trek" into the wilderness with fifty people to whom I would never normally even bother talking.

I don't know what this "trek" is going to involve, but I'm bringing a first-aid kit. And my tooth strips. While I'm trekking, I might as well be bleaching. Right? Maybe I'll come back ten pounds thinner, a hundred dollars richer, and with teeth like pearls.

Ha.

Hope you recognize me when I get back. I won't bring you along, in case of inclement weather or bear attack. I'm just thinking of you.

Save yourself, Junior.

Love,

Wilderness Girl

▶ ▶ ▶

Thursday, September 26

MOOD	Weary
HAIR	Falling out
HEALTH	Blah
HOROSCOPE	Horoscopes are stupid. No longer believe in stupid horoscopes anyway. Lucky number is 3.
JT SIGHTINGS	5

10:30 a.m.

I've totally forgotten why I thought taking auto mechanics

was a good idea. It was a terrible, awful, horrible idea.

I had to be partners with Kiki because we're the only two girls and that's just the way it happened. It's very hard being partners with your former best friend in the middle of a smelly machine shop while you are supposed to be pulling apart a carburetor to look inside. As far as I could tell, there wasn't anything inside. (OK, there was a bunch of metal bits and black stuff.)

"Stop it," said Kiki, as I tried to pry the thing apart with my wrench, skinning my knuckles in the process. (Which bled profusely, lending credence to the theory that I do, in fact, have hemophilia.) (Or some sort of clotting disorder.)

"I'm bleeding to death," I glowered. "It's not like I can help it. It's a disease."

She laughed. "How is it a disease if you skin your knuckles?"

Me: It just is, all right?

Kiki: Are you going to stay mad at me forever?

Me: Yes. Probably.

Kiki: Don't be stupid. I was bored sick all weekend and you probably did nothing but watch old eighties movies with your dad. That's a sickness, by the way. The eighties weren't a good era for movies.

Me: What are you talking about? *The Breakfast Club* was a classic.

Kiki: I know you think so, and I think that explains a lot about you.

Me: What's that supposed to mean?

Kiki: You KNOW what it means. It means that you aren't

Ally Sheedy and JT isn't Rob Lowe.

Me: (*nastily*) You're getting your movies mixed up.

Kiki: Shut up. You're bleeding on the carburetor.

Me: Oops.

I guess we made up. It's hard to tell from that conversation, but that's what it felt like. Besides, I need friends. I mean, I'm likely going to get mauled by a cougar this weekend in the woods, and I'll need friends to show up at my funeral. I can think of nothing more depressing than having no one show at my funeral. Except my dad. And all the people who are indebted to him.

That would be terrific. A church full of hippie-potheads, bikers, and shady looking "business associates."

Knowing my luck, my funeral would be busted by police and the hippies would all blame me for getting chucked in the slammer. (Maybe my dad's right. Maybe legalizing marijuana is a good idea. At least that way it would reduce the chances of my funeral turning into a showdown between the cops and the morons.)

3:01 p.m.

After school, we decided to go downtown. Me, Jules and Kiki, that is. All was forgiven, or at least we weren't talking about it, which is the same thing.

It was pouring rain. It rains a lot here. I don't know why that is. People associate this place with rain. When I tell people where I live, they always shudder and say, "Oh, it rains a lot there."

Really. It doesn't rain that much. Not enough to keep a garden alive without sprinkling. Not enough to fill the reservoir with enough water to allow people to nurture their organic vegetables.

Anyway, you'd think we'd all carry umbrellas at all times, knowing that it's going to rain at any second pretty much every day. But we don't. At least, I don't. So I didn't have one with me, naturally. (I lose umbrellas constantly. I've lost three this year already, I swear.) I got soaked. Jules had an umbrella (Burberry, naturally), but she isn't inclined to share. I tried to duck under it and she immediately started smoking and effectively smoked me out.

None of us had any money, not even Jules who ALWAYS has money. Her mom has cut off her allowance until Jules apologizes. I can see why Jules resists. Why should SHE apologize for the fact that her mother stole her boyfriend? Really, things were much easier in the olden days when no one got divorced, everyone had two parents, and no one would dream of stealing their kid's boyfriend, no matter how much they wanted to.

Not that I have that problem. My mom, I guess, isn't interested in my boyfriends. (Or me, for that matter.)

In any event, it was pouring rain. BUCKETS of rain. It was sleet. I don't know why we didn't drive somewhere, but we didn't. We just walked up and down the streets for no reason, looking at things in store windows that we couldn't afford to buy. Well, stuff that I would never be able to afford to buy and stuff that Kiki will probably get her dad to buy for her later this week. And stuff that Jules will no doubt be able to afford next week after she makes up with her mom.

I sighed dramatically and kicked a pebble on the pavement. Sadly, the pebble was attached to the pavement and I possibly broke my toe on it. Nothing surprises me anymore. I'm falling apart at the seams.

Note to Self: Check on the internet to see if am too young to have osteoporosis. Seem to be breaking a lot of bones lately, perhaps need more calcium in diet.) (Such as milkshakes.) (Although milkshakes are too fattening to actually consume). (*Question*: is it better to be thin and fit into size 4 or smaller? Or to have bones that don't break while walking down the street?)

Once I was sitting at my desk, just typing something. Not even moving my feet. And my toenail fell off. I swear, it's true. It took me a long time to believe that I didn't actually have leprosy.

"Hey," I said. "Do you guys remember when my toenail fell off?"

"That's so disgusting," said Jules, curling her lip.

"I remember," said Kiki helpfully. "You didn't talk about anything else for an entire week. It was kind of funny. Why?"

"I don't know," I said. "I was just thinking about it."

"It was two years ago," said Jules. "I can't believe I even remember that. Please do not tell us in the future when things like this happen to you."

"Fine," I said grouchily. "I won't."

"Oh, come on," said Kiki. "She has to tell us. Otherwise we won't have anything to laugh at."

We walked along for a bit without saying anything. Then Kiki grabbed my hand. "Oh my God!" she screamed. "Did your nail just fall off again?" Then she laughed hysterically. Honestly, that girl is very wound up. (Suspect she has emotional issues that need to be explored by a professional such as Dr. Phil.)

I ignored them and strolled on purposefully ahead, stopping only when I heard them talking and realized I needed to know what they were saying. In case it was about me, or something important.

We tried some stuff on in a couple of stores (please note, I no longer fit into a size 8 at The Gap and must now stop eating until normalcy is regained), and everyone seemed sort of dejected. If by "dejected" I mean "depressed and annoyed." Or maybe it was just me. Kiki found a great dress that made her look at least 21, which I'm sure she'll own before you can say "Daddy, can you buy me that dress, please." (I'm trying not to be jealous. I am. It's just not working.) Besides, it was hard for me to try stuff on because I kept catching sight of myself in the mirror, bruised and blotchy. Why am I out? I thought. I should go home and hide in my bed until I heal.

Which may be never, at the rate my body heals itself.

We avoided the mall like the plague because we'd recently decided that the mall sucks. It does suck. I mean, at least we were getting fresh air on the sidewalk.

Fresh, wet, wind-blown air.

At least it doesn't rain in the flipping mall.

I'd have been happy to go to the mall, but Jules "The Queen of Cool" had already declared it off limits. I don't know why I listen to Jules.

OK, I listen to her because I secretly suspect that she is cooler than me.

We stopped at MAC and I looked to see if I could find any super-strength cover-up that might cover (a) my hickeys or (b) my black eyes, but there really wasn't any such thing. At least, there wasn't according to the assistant, who didn't even bother trying not to look disgusted with my general appearance.

"I can't help you," she said firmly.

Jules laughed her head off. Really, I like her less every day.

Basically, we were just kicking around (i.e. they were smoking and I was talking about cancer) and getting rained on, when Jules said, "I have an announcement."

So we stopped walking, because Jules' announcements are usually the kinds of things you have to sit down for (we sat) (on the street, which was cold and wet) and she said (a little melodramatically), "I've met Someone."

"Someone," said Kiki. "Someone, who?"

"A boy," she said. "I mean, a Man." (Jules has a way of capitalizing random words in sentences when she talks. It's the way she falls on the word. Not a man, but a Man.)

Uh oh, I thought to myself. But I didn't say anything. I mean, I'm the supportive friend. "Supportive friend," I whispered to myself. "Supportive friend."

"What?" said Jules.

"Nothing," I said. "I was just mentioning that my pants were wet."

"A man?" said Kiki, lighting a cigarette and shivering. She looked up. "This can't be good."

"Well," said Jules craftily, "I figured if mom can date my boyfriends, then I can date hers."

"Shit," I said. As supportively as possible. "I mean, great? Or. No. What do I mean? I think I mean, wow. A man. Uh." I scrambled for something supportive and came up with, "You go, girl."

"You go, girl?" said Jules. "You've been watching too many of those Spike Lee movies again."

"Spike Lee JOINTS," I said.

"Don't," said Kiki. "You probably just meant, 'Don't be an idiot, Jules'."

"Something like that," I said through gritted teeth. "Supportive supportive supportive," I said (but in my head, so no one could hear).

Honestly, it was very hard to be supportive of Jules sometimes. She quite regularly does unsupportable things.

"Who is this Man?" asked Kiki. "Do I even want to know? Let me guess, it's . . . No, I can't even guess." She blew a smoke ring at me and winked. "Who is it?"

Jules waited until she had our full attention. (I hate it when people pause dramatically. What's the point? I was dying to change the subject, just because there was an opening. But I waited.) (Supportively.)

I breathed in the greasy smell of fries and smiled at her, as supportively as possible. She looked very . . . actress-ish.

I can't explain it, but it was generally annoying.

"It's Mr. Jurgen," she said smugly, and stood up. (Her pants were completely dry. How was that possible? Was she fake-sitting on the pavement? Was I sitting on the only wet part?)

"Who?" I said.

"The drama teacher," she said slowly. (Only she said, DRAHma, not dra-mah, like most people.)

"Oh," Kiki said.

When I realized who he was, I swear to God, I swallowed my gum. For one thing, he's a teacher. For another, he's just not . . . Well . . . he isn't someone that . . .

He's middle-aged.

Jules is dating a pudgy, middle-aged teacher? What?

A middle-aged drahma teacher who wears a hairpiece?

Jules took a special summer-school drama (sorry, DRAHma) program. (She's going to college next year to do a theatre major because she is going to be a capital-s Star. Not an actress, but a Star. Figures.) It sort of falls into place. I think she even mentioned that her mother flirted with him at some parent-teacher schmooze-fest.

I remember her saying it was disgusting.

Ugh.

I felt sick. "I feel sick," I said.

"Honestly," said Jules. "Don't be such a drama queen."

Kiki stared at me for a minute and then she burst out laughing. Really laughing. As in, I think she actually laughed so hard she peed her pants. She couldn't even get a word out. And her laughing made me laugh. I hadn't laughed that hard in ages.

We were just lying there, laughing and gasping. Jules stomped off, naturally, but we couldn't stop. We were lying on the sidewalk, hiccoughing with sobs. My sides were killing me. I was wondering if maybe I had a hernia or something, when a pair of feet came into view. And I looked up . . .

And it was . . .

The Cute-ish Stranger. Giver of Hickeys. The Guy Who Didn't Call.

I sat right up.

And that's not the worst of it. As if it could get much worse than being found on the sidewalk downtown in the rain with two black eyes and flat, damp hair, laughing like a drunken monkey with a girl who has wet her pants.

The worst of it is that he was with . . .

JT.

Talk about dramatic pauses.

"Hello, ladies," said the Cute-ish Stranger. "Haley," he said.

And he winked at me.

Oh God, I thought. Please take me out of here right now. Open up the earth and have it swallow me. I don't care. Anything. Please. Amen.

JT stared at me like I was a creature from outer space. If that creature were made of Dog Crap. And had fallen in his path and caused him incredible consternation.

"*This* is the girl?" he said incredulously, looking at the Cute-ish Stranger. "Kiki's friend? The Hippie Girl?"

He doesn't even know my name?

Hippie Girl?

I don't have big hips, I thought irrationally, as I sat there and waited for the sidewalk to crack open and for me to fall through. Come on already, I thought. Hurry it up.

"Hey," said Kiki, standing up and brushing off her wet pants like nothing was at all weird about it. "What's up?"

Honestly. Sometimes she can be so clueless.

"Not much," said the Cute-ish Boy. "Just happy to run into you, Haley."

"Uh huh," I said.

"Haley's happy to run into you, too," said Kiki.

"I didn't know you knew the Hippie Girl," mumbled JT.

"Haley's not a hippie," said Kiki. "Just because her father is a hippie, doesn't mean she is a hippie. I mean, *your* father's a prick, right?"

"Shut up," said JT.

"I guess I was wrong," said Kiki.

"Shall we leave these two to fight?" whispered the Cute-ish Stranger, right into my ear. Which gave me goosebumps, I have to admit.

"Uh," I said.

"Good idea," said Kiki. "Off you go now." And she pushed me into the Cute-ish Stranger.

And so we left.

Oh. My. God.

6:52 p.m.

Dad: You're late!

Me: Dad. I know. Don't worry about it.

Dad: You're late!

Me: Dad, you aren't helping.

Dad: Hurry up!

Me: Oh, THAT helps. Very parental of you.

Dad: You'll miss the bus.

Me: Dad, you aren't helping.

Dad: Pack some cookies, you might get hungry.

Me: You made cookies?

Dad: Yes.

Me: Wow.

Dad: I thought you'd like them.

Me: I do like them. But I'm too fat to eat cookies.

Dad: You aren't fat, you're beautiful.

Me: No, I'm not.

Dad: Yes, you are. How could a daughter of mine be less than beautiful?

Me: Ha ha ha.

Dad: Now you're really late.

Me: Argh!

6:58 p.m.

Ran through the rain to catch the bus that was going to take me to Hell (AKA the Leadership Camp). While running (and being hit in the back repeatedly by overstuffed backpack), I thought about the Cute-ish Stranger. I might have been smiling. (It's difficult to run and smile. The wind kind of hurt my teeth, which are slightly more sensitive than usual due to over use of whitening products.)

I know it sounds stupid, but the Cute-ish Stranger was cuter than I remembered him being. He kind of made my stomach flip-flop.

His name is Brad.

(*NB*: Brad is not a very good name, as names go, but there are worse names. Like Marvin. Or Eugene. Not that anyone names their children Marvin or Eugene anymore.)

He wrote his number on my arm with ballpoint pen.

He kind of kissed me. Again.

But all I could think was, *Uh-oh, I should have brushed my teeth*.

But how could I have known that I was going to bump into him? And that he was going to kiss me? Really, it was quite rude of him to kiss me. ESPECIALLY IN FRONT OF JT**. I wasn't ready. And I don't know him well enough. I mean, sure we've kissed before. But that's different. Or is it?

I was really weighted down with my stupid backpack, so I was trying to concentrate on running (the bus was leaving the school at 7:30 p.m. on the dot for my "wilderness adventure"), when my cell phone rang. I nearly fell over a bench trying to retrieve it while still running. It's a miracle that I didn't trip. I mean, let's face it. My track record with running accidents isn't good.

"What?" I gasped.

"Are you going to call him?" Kiki said.

"Can't talk," I said. "Running. Am late."

"You should call him," she said. "He's cute."

** Unless JT went home and was consumed by jealousy and decided that he now has to have me at all costs and will call me the minute I return from Hell, should I be so lucky as to survive, in which case the whole Brad experience will have been worthwhile, as ultimate goal of seducing JT will have been accomplished.

"Kiki," I said, slumping onto the bench. "Can't talk now."

"Are you sitting down?" she said.

"Yes," I said.

"Then you can talk," she said. "Listen, I was thinking. You should totally go out with him."

"Why?" I said.

"It might make JT jealous," she said. "If nothing else. He was staring at you."

"He was?" I said. Brad may give my stomach flip-flops, but JT literally stops my heart. I thumped on my chest to make sure I wasn't having a cardiac arrest, or the like.

"Well, he was looking," Kiki said. "It might not mean anything. Don't get all hopeful."

"Me? Hopeful?" I said.

"Seriously," said Kiki. "Besides, Brad is as cute as JT."

"Pffft," I said.

"Call him," she said. "He's *cuter* than JT."

"No!" I said, horrified. "He isn't cuter."

"I have to go," she said. "My show is on."

"I'm late!" I said.

I shoved the phone back in my pack and sprinted the rest of the way. If by "sprinted," I mean "hurried." I'm sure I looked like hell when I got there, but really, it's not like there was anyone there worth impressing.

I can't imagine ever calling a boy. I leave that to the confident, pretty girls. Like Jules. And Kiki. Maybe I'll call him, I thought, ducking out of the way of a renegade tree. But what was the point? As far as I was concerned, no one else could possibly even come on to my radar: My radar has been jammed by JT and no matter what I do,

I.

Can't.

Stop.

Thinking.

About.

Him.

► ► ►

Saturday, September 28

MOOD	Petrified and Irritated
HAIR	Disastrous
HEALTH	See "Mood"
HOROSCOPE	There are no newspapers in the middle of nowhere. No horoscope. No future. Blah.
JT SIGHTINGS	0 (potential sightings: 0)

Things I Spent Most of Friday Thinking About:

1. Death. And how I was just about to meet it head on.
2. Falling.
3. Whether I was supposed to be going up the cliff or down it, or if it mattered.
4. What would happen when the rope broke.
5. The fact that the guide for our little adventure weekend was a bit hot. Arguably hotter than JT, but also very taken with the OTHER nature guide. Who is named Amelia and is the perfect combination of sporty and beautiful.
6. How, perhaps, if I angled my body correctly, I could fall

on Amelia (Amelie for short, although is Amelie really *that* much shorter than Amelia? I think not.) and therefore rid the world of both myself and one more perfect woman-who-gets-the-attention-of-all-the-boys-in-sight.

7. Death.
8. Falling.
9. Whether JT would be sad if I fell.
10. Whether JT would hit on Amelia — oh, sorry, AMELIE — if he were here.

In summary, spending a day plastered to the face of a wet cliff is not my idea of a good time. Rappelling apparently is loosely the equivalent of "hanging from a harness attached to some dork you never liked, hoping he doesn't drop you down a sheer cliff." At one point, my right foot found some sort of something to stand on. A tree root? A pebble? A loose piece of clay?

So for at least a second, I was not dangling. It was a high point in the day.

But then it turned out I was standing on a loose piece of clay.

Luckily, the clay fell on Amelie's perfect hair. (God, that made me so happy. I'm starting to believe in the universe again. That had to have been some sort of cosmic karma.)

I quickly decided that going down the cliff was a better option than climbing up it (it was steep, slippery, and pointless, not to mention "really hard work"). Also, when I looked up, someone very fast was coming (i.e., falling) down.

Question: Is there a sign above my head saying, "Bruise me, please"?

It's safe to say that I was completely depressed by nature. I like nature. In pictures. On TV. In movies.

Not in my hair.

Not on my face.

And certainly not for an entire, perfectly good (if rainy) weekend.

Things I Would Have Done if I Had Been at Home Instead of at Camp Hell:

1. Hung out with Kiki and Jules.
2. Hung out with Brad and JT.
3. Lay on my bed, imagining hanging out with Brad and JT. Imagining that Brad suddenly had to leave due to mysterious emergency, such as sudden contracting of Ebola virus, leaving JT and me alone together. On a deserted island. Mmmm.
4. Hung out with Dad watching Tivo'd episodes of "Oprah" and "The View." (He really likes women's shows.)
5. Hanging out on the couch watching romantic comedies featuring The Brat Pack. (Judd Nelson, Allie Sheedy, Molly Ringwald, Rob Lowe, et al.)

Things I Would NOT Have Done if I Had Been at Home:

1. Camped in the rain.
2. Picked mud from behind my nails with a twig.
3. Contemplated running away in hopes of finding a hotel with a bed and a SHOWER.
4. Slogged through wet shrubbery looking for pathetic campsite.

The campsite was, to say the least, horrific. We built it on Friday (on Thursday night, we slept in cabins, miles away, back where the bus is parked) after climbing (for no reason), up and down cliffs for hours. Once we finally finished "rappelling" to the bottom of the mountain, battered and muddy beyond all recognition and really just happy to be alive, we were expected to build tents out of poles and canvas and ropes, none of which seemed to go together. Have you ever seen those tents you just throw in the air, and they erect themselves?

These tents were not like those.

(Normally the word "erect" would make me laugh hysterically, but on Friday night, it just made me want to sob.) A campsite? We had to sleep in tents? (Or, more accurately, "tent-like structures that in no way resembled actual tents.") What's worse was that my tentmate was . . . Izzy Archibaud.

BAARRFFFF.

She is one of those totally intolerable people who maintains an annoying enthusiasm about all things at all times. She makes this a full-time job. Seriously. (Not as in a job that she gets paid for, but as in an interminable, endless barrage of . . . happiness.) It should be no great surprise to find out that she's a cheerleader.

And one of JT's many exes.

I hate her.

Yes, I had to sleep in a tent in the rain with a bonafide cheer leader and vice-president of the Student Council AND the ex of the only boy I'll ever love. Yippee!

If by "yippee," I mean "please, someone, kill me now."

Midnight-ish

Around midnight, I snuck out of the tent with my cell phone to try to call Kiki. I don't know why, it's just that I had to talk to someone who was at least sort of normal.

But of course, there was no signal at Camp Hell.

I crawled back into the tent. (I had to crawl as it was half-fallen down and the doorway had collapsed.)

More bad news (like it could get worse): Izzy snored.

Even her snoring was enthusiastic. I lay awake and pondered if I would be convicted of murder or just manslaughter if I killed her in my sleep. Better not allow myself to fall asleep, in case I do. (I sleepwalk. You never know. Stranger things have happened.)

It was the longest night of my life. She's dated JT, I kept thinking. She's KISSED JT. She is JT's type and I am not. I studied her face in the dim light. Stared at her, really. Got up close and inspected her pores. (She has big pores. Mine are much smaller. How could he like her and not me? I have superior pores. If that sort of thing is important, and I've been led to believe that it is.)

And she was drooling, which was disgusting. No matter how hard I tried, I could not find an angle that she looked pretty from.

If I'd had a glass of warm water, I would definitely have stuck her hand in it. I mean, who wouldn't?

▶ ▶ ▶

Sunday, September 29

MOOD	See Saturday
HAIR	Hair?
HEALTH	See Saturday
HOROSCOPE	See Saturday
JT SIGHTINGS	0

Postcard from Hell:
Dear Dad,
Having a great time. Wish you were here, and that I wasn't. Today's activities include: hiking in the rain, canoeing in the rain, and then finally being allowed to go home. In the rain. This is like summer camp for people who are too old to attend summer camp and not in the summer. There is reason why summer camp is held during the warmer and less rainy months.

There is also a reason why people stop going to summer camp after the age of 12. Just wanted to say "Thanks for never making me go to summer camp." Hope you are eating your greens. And not just smoking them.
Love,
Haley Andromeda
2:00 p.m.
Can we go home now? Please? Please? PLEEEAASSE?

2:02 p.m.
Anytime now would be great.

5:17 p.m.

The bus ride home was torture. Capital t-Torture. I can't even talk about it, it was that awful.

7:31 p.m.

Dear Junior:

I'm home! I'm home! I've never been so happy to have had a shower. And a bath. And another shower. And to see clean (sort of) sheets. And a bed.

And to eat Chinese take-out with Dad.

And to get my pile of phone messages.

Love,

Home Girl.

Why am I here? I kept thinking on the bus (the interminable trip home) as I looked around at all the happy, shiny people.

I am NOT a happy, shiny person.

I am a bruised, morose person.

With a possibly fatal blood disease.

On the plus side, I now know one other person — Izzy — on the Student Council. On the minus side, I hate her. I spent most of the exciting Canoe Adventure this afternoon fantasizing about tipping the canoe on purpose so her perfect hair would get ruined.

I didn't do it. I mean, I don't think my hair could have stood it either, to tell you the truth. The only thing we have in common is that we have both been bitten nearly to death by mosquitoes. Mosquito bites, I assure you, are not attractive on anyone. They look like large, itchy, blotchy welts. Furthermore, we are now all likely to die from West Nile disease.

The last thing in the world I could tolerate right now is being hospitalized with Izzy Archibald. Seriously. I'd rather die of the clotting disease first. At least the mosquito bites pretty much equalized everyone: we all looked similarly awful, except Amelie, who didn't appeared to suffer at all. (Theory: I secretly believe that she is an android. There is something slightly plastic looking about her skin. And her eyes are suspicious. Maybe she is simply visiting here from another planet: a planet where everyone is perfect and has great hair and repels mosquitoes. I wouldn't be surprised. On the other hand, I also look like an alien, but the bad kind. The kind of low-budget alien who did not quite get the human costume right.) (*Additional Theory*: If you ever want people to not notice your black eyes, get a few hickeys. I don't know why I'm worried about the black eyes at all. They seem barely noticeable to people who can't tear their eyes off my neck.)

Note to Self: Find out if anyone has ever actually died of humiliation.

It probably doesn't much matter, as fate probably has already decided to give me the following symptoms within 3-6 days:

(from Medline)

West Nile Virus

Definition

West Nile virus is transmitted by mosquitoes and causes an illness that ranges from mild to severe. Mild, flu-like illness is often called West Nile fever. More severe forms of disease, which can be life-threatening, may be called West Nile encephalitis or West Nile meningitis, depending on where it spreads.

Symptoms

Mild disease, generally called West Nile fever, has some or all of the following symptoms:

- Fever
- Headache
- Back pain
- Muscle aches
- Lack of appetite
- Sore throat
- Nausea
- Vomiting
- Abdominal pain
- Diarrhea — These symptoms usually last for 3 to 6 days. With more severe disease, the following symptoms can also be seen and require prompt attention:
- Muscle weakness
- Stiff neck
- Confusion or change in clarity of thinking
- Loss of consciousness

Great. What next? Ebola?

Conversations That I Endured Over the Course
of the Weekend:

1. Student Council President Bruce, AKA Dorky McDorkperson — two minutes re: "themes for the prom."

   Him: What are you thinking of as the theme for the Prom?

   Me: I'm not thinking about it. (a) It's months away and (b) I don't want to think about it.

   Him: Nice hickeys, by the way.

   Me: (walks away)

   Him: (calling after me) I was thinking maybe a Hawaiian theme?

2. Izzy — ten identical conversations over two day period

   Her: Don't you just love the Student Council?

   Me: No.

   Her: I was so excited to be voted in.

   Me: Being Vice-President must be a huge honour.

   Her: It totally is. I totally love it.

   Me: Huh.

   Her: Don't you just love it?

   Me: Huh.

   Her: What's on your neck?

   Me: (makes noise like strangled person)

3. Amelie — five minutes about my "fatal illness"

   Her: You're doing really well.

   Me: (disentangling myself from ropes) Er, thanks.

   Her: Really, considering . . .

   Me: What?

   Her: Well, you know, your condition.

Me: I have a condition?

Her: You're so brave.

Me: I am?

Her: It must be very difficult (pointing at my neck).

Me: Er.

Her: I knew someone else who had leukemia.

Me: (panicking) Leukemia? (*Does she know something I don't know? What? Maybe she is one of those psychic doctors. Maybe I DO have leukemia*).

Her: I could tell because of the bruising.

Me: (laughing hysterically) They're HICKEYS. And black eyes. Not related.

Her: (blushing) Oh my God. I'm so embarrassed for you.

At that point, I was so desperate to talk to someone normal, I was willing to call Brad (who I can't stop calling "Cute-ish Stranger" in my head).

But of course, there was no signal.

Things I Learned This Weekend That I had Never Previously Cared About, But That Should Get Noted, Just Because:

1. Canoeing is not my best sport. (Not that I have a "best sport." I suspect I'm more cut out for a sport like golf, where the clothes are clean and dry and there is not so much actual exertion. Or bowling. Or billiards. Not that I mind exerting.) (I run, remember?) But canoeing was less than fun. Also, canoeing with Student Council President Bruce "I'm-so-Happy" McFreaky Creep is enough to make anyone try to beat themselves over the

head with a paddle until they blissfully lose consciousness. He — at one point — was actually singing.

But I digress.

2. On a similar note, am now convinced that SCP Bruce
What's-It is the Devil. If the Devil existed. And were
six feet tall and had wild curly hair that sprang out from
his head and actually bounced when he talked.

Well, that's not impossible, is it?

Based on this theory, it stands to reason that it's quite
possible that I did fall off the cliff and perhaps I'm
actually dead and I've gone to hell. This could be hell,
although it strongly resembles my bedroom. (I LOVE
my bedroom. I MISSED this room SO MUCH.) Only
hell would be hotter, I suppose. Although why would
hell be hot? I'd really prefer to be hot than cold. So as
real punishment, hell should be damp, windy, cold and
wet. And everyone would be intolerably itchy from
mosquito bites. And tired from not sleeping. Come to
think of it, hell would be something like the Entire
Weekend.

Oh My God. Am I dead?

8:59 p.m.
Oh. My. God.

WHY DIDN'T I LOOK AT MY PHONE MESSAGES
RIGHT AWAY?

JT called.

I spent a total of eight minutes staring at the phone
message and trying to guess if JT might be shorthand
for something other than JT. Like maybe Dad meant

to write Jules and got a hand cramp. Perhaps he was abbreviating Juvenile Transvestite. Or Juiced Tomato. Or Jack something-or-other. Or . . .

I have no idea. It could mean anything. Remember, Dad is a LIFELONG POTHEAD and can't be trusted to take phone messages.

Furthermore, the number he scrawled on the paper was unrecognizable. Naturally, I looked up JT's number in the phone book. (*Interesting side note:* his dad's name is Chas. Who is named Chas? That's very unusual.)

The unrecognizable chicken scratch was JT's number.

Oh. My. God.

9:00 p.m.

Called Kiki before calling JT. She told me I should wait until at least 9:04 before I called him back. I hung up on her.

She's very weird about numbers.

I dialed the first six digits of JT's number and then hung up. Kiki may be weird about numbers, but she knows more about numerology than I do.

I got up, went into the bathroom and applied a full face of make-up.

And re-did my hair.

9:07 p.m.

Called Kiki back. I missed 9:04. I needed her to give me another time.

"10:15," she said.

"That's kind of late to be calling someone," I said.

"Trust me," she said.

"What will I do in the meantime?" I said. "I'll go crazy."

"We'll go for a run," she said.

"I can't," I said. "I just had a shower."

"I'm on my way," she said. "It's training. Besides, it will keep you away from the phone until 10:15."

I sighed. She was right. And it was important that we train. The mini-marathon is in eight months, after all. Eight months isn't very long, in the big picture, particularly when you can't run down the street without gasping and are carrying ten extra pounds on your buttocks.

I went back downstairs where Dad was eating a bag of health-food chips in front of the TV.

"Are those my chips?" I said.

"Probably," he said. "They taste like sawdust."

"Dad," I said.

"Yes?"

"Forget it," I said. "So."

"So," he said.

"So," I said. "Um, what did he sound like when he called?"

"Who?" he said.

"DAD," I said. "JT, that's who."

"I don't know," he said. "He sounded like a guy."

"DAD," I said. "Come on."

He crunched his chips balefully. "He sounded like a jerk," he said.

OK, then. Great.

I wandered into the kitchen casually and dialed the first

six numbers again to make sure I had them memorized in case the house burned down while I was out and I lost the phone number. Then I went and met Kiki on the corner.

We ran for about ten feet and then I get a wicked cramp in my side so we decided to walk. And by "we," I mean "me." Eventually, Kiki circled the block and walked with me. I knew she would. I walked with my hand pressed into my side and bent over. It wasn't my best look. But hell, the cramp hurt.

"What are you going to say?" she said.

"I don't know," I said. "I'll just say, 'Hi!'"

"'Hi!'" she said dubiously. "I don't know. You need to sound casually busy. Happy and busy."

"Happy and busy?" I said suspiciously. That sounded awfully familiar. "Did you get that from The Rules?"

"No, no," she said. A little too quickly.

"Oh my God," I said. "You're following The Rules."

"No, I'm not," she insisted. "I'm taking a year off from dating, anyway."

"You're a Creature Like No Other," I shrieked. "An Elusive Butterfly!"

"Jules says it works," Kiki said defensively. "It worked on Ben, anyway."

"Ben?" I said. "Who is BEN?"

"Mr. Jurgen," she said.

"Ack," I said. We walked in silence, both picturing Jules with Mr. Jurgen. Balding, paunchy, middle-aged Mr. Jurgen. It wasn't a pretty mental picture. In fact, it's the kind of mental picture that makes you want to shake your head like an Etch-a-sketch until it erases itself. Not to mention that the relationship is illegal. And repulsive.

"The other day?" Kiki said, bending over to tie her shoe.

"What?" I said, dangling my head near hers. (I was already bent over anyway.)

"The other day, he taught an entire class with a booger hanging out of his nose," she said. "I didn't even think it was funny. I just thought, 'Oh God, poor Jules.'"

"Ugh," I said, straightening up as much as I could. (I wondered if maybe I had appendicitis? My stomach really hurt a lot.) "What is she thinking? Besides, isn't he married?"

"IS he?" she said. "I don't know. We should find out."

"I guess," I agreed. But secretly, I didn't/don't care. I mean, it's Jules' thing, right? She's being stupid and she's looking for attention. Or drama. (DRAHma.) Or both. But also, it was 10:07.

"I have to go," I said.

I ran all the way home. I had to. It was pretty far and it would have taken fifteen minutes to walk. But I made it the whole way and wasn't even breathing hard.

Either I'm getting into better shape, or the secret to running is having something (someone) to run to.

10:16 p.m.

I chickened out. I'm a big coward. Now it is really getting late. I should have called before, for example, at 8:21. 8:21 seems like a perfectly casual time to call a person. And if you add the numbers in 8:21 together, 8 and 2 and 1 are 11. And 1+1 is two. And two means "easy" if you follow the Chinese superstitions.

Easy?

I was right to wait. Three ("lively!") is better.

10:18 p.m.

I can't do this.

10:21 p.m.

Four ("death") is definitely bad.

10:22 p.m.

I've forgotten five. What is five? I just looked it up. "Negative." OK. Good thing I didn't call.

10:25 p.m.

OK. The numbers add up to eight. Eight is "prosperous." I decided to go for it.

The phone on the other end rang.

It kept ringing.

Click.

It was an answering machine? All this for an answering machine?

My Brilliant Message to JT, Whom I've Had
Crush on Since the Dawn of Time:

"Hi, uh, it's Haley? From school? You called me? But I couldn't answer. I mean, I wasn't home. I was at a retreat. Well, not a retreat, but with the Student Council. I mean, I'm not really on the Student Council. Well, I am. But I didn't . . ."

And then the machine cut me off.

Reasons to kill myself:

1. See above.
2. Isn't that enough?
3. Doesn't matter, as am likely to die soon from West Nile Disease.

I've decided to lie on my bed and not move until he calls back. (Also, I am very tired.) This way, if he never calls back, I will have effectively killed myself via starvation, if nothing else. Although my dad would eventually bring me food, I'm sure. (This might not be the most pro-active way to kill myself, come to think of it.)

In the other room, I can hear a terrible crashing noise. My dad is actually painting the bathroom now that he's scraped off all the old paint. I must make a mental note to try and remember to ask him where this burst of home decorating passion has come from. It seems odd. Decidedly suspicious.

But I can't ask right now because I am busy Not Killing Myself But Not Exactly Trying to Live Either.

There is a pattern of cracks in the ceiling that looks like Australia. They don't *really* look like Australia, but I imagine that they do. The ceiling at one point must have been white, but it has turned quite yellow.

Note to Self: Ask Dad if he wants to paint it when he's done with the bathroom.

Maybe the cracks look more like Africa. Especially if I lay the other way.

Definitely Africa.

Why is the phone not ringing?

The phone just rang, nearly giving me a heart attack.

It was Jules.

"I'll call you back," I said. "I'm really busy."

"You never have time for me any more," she said. "You know, Ben says . . ."

"I have to go," I said and hung up.

I feel slightly guilty. How long would it take to call the phone company and order Call Waiting? Call Waiting was a brilliant invention. Why have I never liked it before? I should call them. No, I changed my mind. What if JT calls while I'm doing that? Is the phone company even open on Sunday night at . . . 10:51?

I am not going to take the chance.

If you stare at the phone really hard, you can get it to shimmer slightly. This has something to do with not blinking, your contacts slipping, and your eyes crossing.

Imaginary Conversation With JT:
Ring! Ring!
Me: (sounding happy and busy) Hello?
JT: (sounding nervous) Hi, Haley. It's JT.
Me: Well, hello there.

(No, wait. That doesn't sound good. "Well, hello there" sounds too Mae West or Bette Davis or whichever one said, "Why don't you come up and see me sometime" in that weird, drag-queen drawl. Scratch that.)

Me: Hi JT, what's going on?

JT: It's just that I've been wanting to ask you out for months and I haven't been able to work up the courage.

(No, that's not good either. "Work up the courage?" He would never say that. Maybe he would say, "But I was too freaked out." No, he wouldn't say that either.)

Forget it.

If JT and I had kids, they would be blonde and adorable.

I'm 16 years old. I'm not having any kids. Not anytime soon, anyway. What am I thinking? What's wrong with me?

Oh my God.

The phone is ringing.

11:01 p.m.

Actual transcript of conversation I had with JT:

Me: (sounding flustered) Hello?

JT: Uh, yeah. Uh, is Holly there?

Me: It's Haley, actually.

JT: Right, OK, well the thing is that my cousin? Brad? He has the chicken pox? And I just thought that you should know because, you know, we saw you the other day and he was, you know, like his tongue was in your mouth. (Laughs in a rude way.)

Me: Brad's your cousin?

JT: Right, I'll see you around at school. Unless, you're like, sick. Or whatever.

Me: Brad's your cousin?

JT: Bye.

I hung up the phone and wandered into the bathroom. It was bright pink.

"Do you like it?" Dad asked.

I stared at it for a minute. It was really quite blinding, not to mention that it was possibly the ugliest room I'd ever seen.

"It's, er, pretty," I said. "In fact, it looks like Pepto-Bismol. Sort of . . . er, soothing."

"But that's good, right?" he said. "I thought it would be, you know, girly."

"Girly?" I said. I stared at it. When I looked away, I could still see the pink. "Um. Well, it certainly isn't MANLY."

There was also a great deal of paint on the floor. I bent over and touched it. It was dry, so I started picking at it. I mean, it wasn't going to come off by itself, was it?

"Have I ever had the chicken pox?" I asked.

Dad looked up at me and scratched his beard, which was mostly full of pink paint. He'd probably have to cut it off to get the paint out, which wouldn't be a bad thing. It would de-hippify him slightly. I'd never seen my Dad without a beard. I wondered how long it would take him to notice the paint. (Probably six to eight weeks. Dad is not the most observant person I've ever met.)

"No," he said. "I think you had the mumps. The only way to know for sure would be for someone to ask your mother."

"Um," I said. "Right. Next time I'm talking to her. Oh, wait, I don't talk to her, do I?"

Then for some incredibly unknown and stupid reason, I burst into tears.

Possible Reasons for Bursting into Tears:
1. Inevitability of getting chicken pox.
2. Disastrous conversation with JT.
3. Black eyes.
4. Mosquito bites.
5. Inevitability of getting West Nile Virus.
6. Horrible weekend.
7. Hickeys that won't heal.
8. No Mother. (Well, I have a mother, but no relationship with said mother, in fact, no knowledge of who or where said mother might be.)
9. PMS.

I cried for a few minutes. In the mirror, I could see myself crying. I do not cry in the style of Jules (in a pretty, "crystal tears" sort of way). I cry in a blotchy, snotty, wet, ugly way. It was quite surreal. And pink. My face was red and my orange hair clashed horribly with the walls.

"Right then," Dad said. There's a long pause. "Sorry, honey," he added, and hugged me. (He may almost never say the right thing, but he sure knows when a hug is appropriate. I hugged him back and cried into his flannel shirt, which strongly resembled my pyjama top.)

"Dad," I said, pulling away. "That's my PYJAMA TOP."

"Oh," he said. "I thought it was an old rag."

Then The Cat came in and walked straight into the paint pan, so that was the end of that conversation altogether.

Sometime after 1:00 in the morning.
"Someone would have to ask your mother." Ha. Is he freaking crazy? Does he think I talk to her? Or that I know anyone who does?

And . . . does he know where she is?

▶ ▶ ▶

Monday, September 30

MOOD	Flat-lining
HAIR	Reasonably good (a la Meg Ryan)
HEALTH	No chicken pox or WNV. Yet.
HOROSCOPE	Try to be on time for things today as the planets are conspiring to make you late. Lucky number:11.
JT SIGHTINGS	0

10:03 a.m.
Second period. Or it would be, if we had gone to class.

We didn't go to class.

Instead, we decided to cut class to go to the beach. Why did we do that? Well, the weather was nice, for one thing. And the class we were skipping was Life Studies, which is code for Sex Ed. I was frankly quite happy to give it a miss. I think we're all familiar with the basics: penis + vagina = teen pregnancy! The horrors! Not to mention condoms-blah-blah-blah and Planned Parenthood-blah-blah-blah.

Besides, I was in a bleak mood because this morning I said, "Hi JT" from my locker and he said, "Oh, hi, uh . . ." And then trailed off, stared at me blankly, and walked away. As though he hadn't talked to me on the phone the previous night. As though he had no idea who I was.

"I hate JT," I announced, reclining gracefully on (OK, falling over) a small rock.

"Bullshit," said Kiki. "Will the crush never die?"

"I hate him," I said.

"Sure," said Kiki. "If that were true, I'd be thrilled. But I don't believe you."

"It's true," I said stubbornly.

"I'm going to sleep with him," said Jules.

"JT?" I said, moving off the very uncomfortable rock and draping myself more prettily on a log. Well, not actually a log. (OK, I missed the log and sat down in the sand. It hurt. I'd probably broken my tailbone.)

Kiki and Jules sat down beside me.

"Poor clumsy Haley," said Kiki sadly, and patted me on the head.

"I'm not clumsy," I said. "I'm just unlucky."

"Ha," Kiki said, lighting up another cigarette from the one in her mouth. Her face was flushed.

"Mr. Jurgen. Ben," Jules said. "I'm going to sleep with BEN. Not JT. I don't want to sleep with JT, you idiot. Why would you want to sleep with a boy when you can sleep with a man?"

"Ugh," I said. "I can think of a lot of reasons. Think about it. JT? Or . . . Seriously? Mr. *Jurgen*?"

She smiled at me loftily in a way that suggested I couldn't possibly understand her womanly needs. (Oh, barf.) And flipped her hair around. (I really dislike hair flippers.) It whipped into my face. If you've never looked at hair under a microscope, you have no idea what disgusting things it harbours. I opened my mouth to tell her this and then shut it again after I took a look at her. She looked different. Puffier. Sort of . . . bad. Her hair was greasy. She had big bags under her eyes. And she wasn't wearing any make-up.

I didn't think I'd seen her without makeup, like EVER.

"We were out really late last night," she said, lamely, noticing me noticing her.

"Out?" I said. "On Sunday night?"

"Well," she said. "Not *out*, exactly. His wife's away. He wanted to make me dinner. So I went." She was trying to sound casual, I could tell. But she wasn't really pulling it off. I mean, I know Jules. And this wasn't "casual."

"What?" I said. (On the other hand, if she WAS being casual, then honestly, I have no idea who she is anymore.)

She's a total stranger.

Then out of the blue I got this memory of Jules from when we were about twelve and it almost made me cry. That was the summer when her mom was dating this guy whose name was Seth or something like that. And Jules really liked Seth. He was like the dad she never had. (Her own dad is a waste of skin. He's an internet business guy of some sort. I mean, I'm sure he has lots of money, but he has no time for her. He's always travelling and when he comes around, he talks on his cell phone the entire time

and types frantically into a) his Blackberry, b) his laptop
or c) his Palm Pilot.) But this Seth was great. He took
us to the city and we went to see a Broadway show. I've
forgotten what it was: "Les Miserables" or something.
Neither of us liked it, we were too young. But that wasn't
the point. The point was that he treated us like grown-ups
and Jules liked him so much and it seemed so normal. We
stayed in a hotel and he took us to a restaurant for breakfast the next day and the waitress said, "Your daughters
are beautiful, they must be quite a handful." And he didn't
correct her.

Seth told us in the car on the way back into town that
he was going to marry her mom.

Jules was so freaking happy. He gave her a ring and
everything, too.

And then he died. He had something wrong with his
kidneys, apparently, and they quit working and he died.
Just like that. After the funeral, Jules took her ring and we
went on the ferry and she chucked it off the side and said
a prayer. She isn't even religious.

I don't know why I thought of that right then. I ran my
hands through the sand. The wind was pretty cool down
there by the beach (it is almost October, after all), but the
sand was hot. I just sifted through the sand with my hand.
It felt good. Soothing.

And then I sifted through a big piece of plastic.

Which was a condom.

A used condom.

"ARGH!" I screamed.

That was just perfect. I'll probably not only get chicken

pox, but also something worse, something condom related. I started cataloguing the possibilities in my head. I'm not sure what you can get from handling a condom, come to think of it. AIDS? Gonorrhea? The Clap? (Is that the same thing?) Pregnant?

I started paying attention again when Jules said, "At least I won't have to worry about getting an A in drama."

Ugh. That's for sure, I thought meanly.

Kiki laughed and hugged her. She's so nice. I'm lucky to know Kiki. I thought about what a good friend she was to me and how I sometimes forget that she's also such a good friend to Jules, who is really just so hopeless. Are all friendships like this? Groups of three people who are linked by one of them and two of them secretly hating each other?

"Are you serious?" I said finally. I couldn't NOT say it. I mean, Jules is still my friend, so I had to tell her what I thought. "He's middle-aged," I said. "He's perverted and married. What are you doing? What? Can you explain it?"

Jules just stared at me. And blinked. (She has gorgeous eyes. They actually looked better without the inch of black crap around them.) We looked at each other for what felt like an hour, but was probably only a couple of minutes. And then she shook her head, like I'd disappointed her beyond belief. She said, "I'm growing up, little girl, but I guess that's just something you wouldn't understand, is it?"

The way she said *little girl* made my stomach knot up. Then she got up and walked away.

"Shit," said Kiki. "This whole thing is just getting really, really bad." She got up and ran after Jules.

"Sorry," she called over her shoulder. "I can't . . ."

I just sat there on the sand. In the distance, I could see them talking, their heads bent together. Laughing. I guess it wasn't that bad if they could laugh about it. I felt really left out. Totally alone. For a second, I hated them, too. I hate everyone, I said in my head. But I knew even as I thought it that I didn't mean it.

I leaned back against the log and gazed up into the sky. It was blue, but smeared, like someone had put Vaseline on the lens. The waves were rolling in slowly and methodically. It was such a beautiful place. I could live here, I thought. On the beach, just like this. (I must have some of my dad's hippie genes, after all.) There was no one around. I couldn't imagine why there weren't more people at the beach, people living at the beach. I mean, people live on the *streets*. Given the choice, I'd live on a beach.

The sand, the logs, the waves. What's not to like?

I didn't have any sunscreen on and I should have. I knew it. I even thought about it. I mean, it might not have been boiling hot any more, but it was warm enough that I burned. I could feel my face getting redder and redder, but . . . I don't know what happened. It was like I was too tired to move. Also, I kind of half-thought that maybe if I got tanned, my eye bruises and neck welts would be less . . . showy.

And so I stayed.

I was just going to stay for a few minutes. I swear it.

3:30 p.m.

Was woken by some kids screaming and running into the waves. I'd been asleep all day. My face was throbbing. My arms were burned to a crisp — red and itchy.

And blistered.

Blistered?

I looked at the blisters for a minute or more. They looked like little bubbles of water under my skin. Was I having some bizarre allergic reaction to the sun?

Was I an idiot? Oh. My God.

Chicken pox.

Reasons Why Having the Chicken Pox is Bad:

1. It's ugly.
2. It's ugly.
3. It's ugly.
4. It's ITCHY.
5. It's ugly and itchy and even when it's gone, it leaves scars.

Reasons Why Having the Chicken Pox is Good:

1. Won't have to explain why I missed the day of school.
2. Will miss many days of school and won't ever have to finish "What I did on Summer Vacation" essay which is already several days late.
3. Maybe if I get really sick, will lose weight and return to school thinner and prettier than before.
4. Will have lots of time to experiment with tooth bleach.
5. Will have reason to not be at school to witness the Jules/Mr. Jurgen drama that will surely unfold.

OCTOBER

Wednesday, October 2

MOOD	Itchy.
HAIR	Dirty.
HEALTH	Failing miserably.
HOROSCOPE	Get out and enjoy your day! You will accomplish all you set out to do, and then some. Smile!
JT SIGHTINGS	o. There is No Hope.

Dear Junior:
I can't believe I named you Junior. What a stupid name. I'm stupid. And, not only that, I'm going to die. I'm going to die by peeling off all of my own skin. I'm going to die because daytime TV is incredibly annoying when every surface of your skin itches. I have calamine lotion all over me and it doesn't do a thing except make it look like you have calamine lotion all over you for no apparent reason.

It dries and then when you scratch, it leaves a trail of pink dandruff everywhere. Gross. To make matters worse, on some parts of my body I have pox on my mosquito bites. Is this even possible? Could it be any uglier? Could I be in a worse mood?

I don't think so.

Love,

Insanely Grouchy Girl

▶ ▶ ▶

Friday, October 4, 2002

MOOD	Vengeful
HAIR	Who CARES? (Bad roots showing)
HEALTH	Worse than ever
HOROSCOPE	An important message will come to you from a surprising source. Be on the lookout!
JT SIGHTINGS	o . . . o . . . o . . . o . . . o

Even Dad is frightened of me. He was down amongst his crops for hours and then barely came up in time for "Oprah." I thought I was going to have to Tivo it for him, and frankly, I've never figured out how the hell that thing works. It made me itchy thinking about it.

"Oprah."

"Oprah" made me itch.

It was a makeover show.

Makeovers make me itch.

Everything makes me itch.

Typing the word "itch" makes me itch.

ARGHGGHGHGHGHGHGHGHGHGHGHGHGHG-
GHHHH.

Finally, I fell asleep and I dreamed of scratching all my skin off with sandpaper, and not just any sandpaper, but with an electric sander.

Aaaahhhh.

▶ ▶ ▶

Wednesday, October 9

MOOD	Depressed beyond belief
HAIR	Greasy and insupportable
HEALTH	Near death's door; itchy
HOROSCOPE	Am too itchy to care what this stupid column wrongly predicts about my day. OK? OK.
JT SIGHTINGS	—

Useful Things I've Done While NOT Entertaining
So-Called Friends Who Didn't Bother To Visit:

1. Have come up with brilliant invention that involves a brush-like thing with metal things on it and extendible handle that allows you to scratch all the "hard to reach" places without having to stand up or get out of bed.
2. Have scratched entire body raw more than a hundred times.
3. Have had fourteen fever-induced nightmares.
4. Have consumed a hundred glasses of flat ginger ale, which my dad thinks is the cure for everything (marijuana notwithstanding, although I've point-blank refused to even try it as an itch cure). Have learned to

hate ginger ale.

5. Have taken a dozen or more Tylenol.
6. Have developed extraordinary high fever. Quite trippy. Think I just saw The Bird ride by on The Cat's back. This seems wrong. Will go back to sleep.

Don't Know What Day It Is, Sorry

MOOD	?
HAIR	?
HEALTH	?
HOROSCOPE	! ?
JT SIGHTINGS	?

Unnnhhhhhhhh.

Am hungry. And itchy. Have eaten half a loaf of toast. Don't think that chicken pox is a good diet aid after all.

Dad came into the room and put his hand gingerly on my forehead.

"What day is it?" I asked.

"Monday," he said.

Monday? Still? Again?

(From WebMD)

Chicken pox

A very itchy rash that spreads from the torso to the neck, face, and limbs. The rash, lasting seven to 10 days, progresses from red bumps to fluid-filled blisters (vesicles) that drain and scab over. Vesicles may also appear in the mouth, around the eyes, or on the genitals and can be very painful.

This cycle repeats itself in new areas of the body until finally, after about 2 weeks, all of the sores have healed. The disease is transmissible until this time.

Have checked inside mouth and have no evidence of bumps. I guess that's just something else to look forward to.

I am an infectious, transmissible, rashy, bumpy, blistery mess.

Tuesday, October 15

MOOD	I
HAIR	don't
HEALTH	care
HOROSCOPE	about
JT SIGHTINGS	anything anymore

9:00 a.m.
What's the POINT?
Am so itchy.

11:15 a.m.
I'm bored of being sick.
I miss school.

I miss JT.

Isn't this supposed to have passed by now? That's what I want to know. It doesn't make any sense. I've now had chicken pox longer than WebMD predicted. Unless it all spontaneously clears up today, which I find hard to imagine from the state of my skin.

Needless to say, after watching daytime TV for two days straight, my brain feels like IT has the chicken pox, or at least has been replaced by a giant, fluid filled, itchy blister. Who are these people on talk shows? Where do they come from? I have never seen people like this in Real Life. And yet they are supposedly Real People. The people I know actually look and act more like the people from *movies*, which we all know are made up and involve air-brushing, than the people from these shows which aren't air-brushed at all. Or if they are, they aren't air-brushed very well.

I don't mean to be rude, but these are some of the ugliest people on the planet. Not just appearance-wise, but when they open their mouths and scream obscenities at each other, it's almost too much.

OK, so I laughed when that woman on "Springer" drove the tractor through her cheatin' boyfriend's trailer.

I really need to get out more.

2:15 p.m.

"Go outside," Dad said, wandering by with a joint hanging out of his mouth. "The fresh air is good for you, and staring at a computer screen is not."

"A lot of things aren't good for you and you do them

anyway," I said pointedly and glowered at him.

"Yes," he said, missing my point entirely. "Fresh air. It's a nice day. Live a little."

"I can't live," I pointed out. "I have the chicken pox."

"Out," he said, and heaved me off the couch. So he could sit down himself, natch. He immersed himself immediately in "Montel."

I staggered outside, as ordered. It was blindingly bright on the deck. In fact, it was quite nice and sunny and probably more pleasant than being at school. Definitely better than daytime TV. I took several deep breaths of the Fresh Air. This was a good idea. It was very lovely out there on the deck.

Lovely, but slightly boring.

Totally boring.

I lasted outside for exactly twenty-six minutes before going back to the TV.

Summary: I'm the laziest person alive. And quite possibly the ugliest. Giant red blisters have formed on my cheeks and forehead. In combination with the faded-to-yellow-black-eyes, I think I could possibly scare small children in the mall. Of course, I can't go to the mall. I'm infectious. If this lasts much longer, I won't have to worry about a Halloween costume, although I had a good one planned.

3:01 p.m.
God help me, I've never been so bored in my life.

How does Dad do this all day, every day? Albeit without the itching.

"Honey," he said from the doorway, scaring the life out of me. "I'm going out. Are you going to be OK?"

I guess that answers that question. He doesn't do this all day. He goes Out. I want to go Out. Where is Out?

"I'll be fine," I said. "Where are you going?"

"Oh," he said vaguely. "Out."

I'm crazily jealous of people who go Out. The Cat and I stared at each other. The Cat never goes Out. The Bird never goes Out. Normally, The Cat will sit on me for hours and sleep and do cat things, like paw at me until I move or push him away. Now he won't come any closer than the coffee table, where he likes to sit.

Summary, Part Two: I'm itchy, bored, can't go Out, and my face is so horrifying that I frighten cats. What else can possibly go wrong? So much for this being the best freaking year of my life.

Phone Calls Received, Tuesday Evening,
After Nearly TWO WEEKS OF NO CALLS:
1. Jules
Me: Hello?
Jules: OK, I did it. I kissed him.
Me: I'm fine thanks.
Jules: What?
Me: Never mind.
Jules: Just so you know, he's a really good kisser.
Me: Aren't there laws about this?
Jules: Don't be such a prude.

Me: I'm a prude because I don't make out with my teachers?

Jules: (*bursting into tears*) You don't understand anything.

Me: I'm sorry, Jules.

Jules: I don't know what I'm doing! What am I doing? I've made a huge mistake. I don't know how to get out of it.

Me: Um.

Jules: I should just break up with him.

Me: Yes!

Jules: I can't break up with him. What if he flunks me out of drama?

Me: He won't do that. You'd always be able to tell. You could, like, blackmail him.

Jules: I would never do that! I think he's in love with me.

Me: (silence)

Jules: He's not in love with me! He's in love with his wife! He's using me.

Me: Obviously.

Jules: What?

Me: Uh, nothing.

Jules: I have to go. I can't talk to you anymore.

Me: Have you ever had the chicken pox?

Jules: No.

Me: OK then.

I was actually going to tell her to come over. Not because I want to see her. Or deal with her over-the-top-self-created-melodrama. But because I'm so bored I'd be willing to stick flaming sticks in my eyes just for some excitement. Or better yet, use the flaming sticks to burn each and every one of these sodding itchy blisters off my face and ears.

Ears?

Oh no, they're in my ears.

2. Kiki

Kiki: You poor thing, I'm coming over to entertain you.

Me: Have you had the chicken pox?

Kiki: Oh, sure. I mean, I think so. I must have.

Me: OK, come over.

I love Kiki. She is my favourite person in the world. I barely even resent her for being thin and pretty and smart.

OK, I resent it a little bit.

3. Brad

Me: (woken from nap) Hurghlo

Brad: It's Brad

Me: Who?

Brad: Brad

Me: Erghgl?

Brad: I gave you the chicken pox.

Me: Oh.

Brad: Are you still there?

Me: Hate the chicken pox.

Brad: Me, too. Uh, I was thinking.

Me: What?

Brad: I was thinking maybe I could come over. I mean, we
    both have it, right?

Me: No! No!

Brad: I'll be there in an hour.

Hate Brad.

Hate the chicken pox.

I leaped off the couch and ran into the bathroom
to inspect my face. A new batch of poxes had formed
around my mouth. I looked like a leper. No, lepers looked
better than me. All I needed now was for bits of my face
to actually fall off to complete the picture.

There was nothing I could do. No amount of make-up
would cover that.

Still, I had a shower and did my hair. I mean, it was the
least I could do. (The hot shower water made my poxes
itch even more than before, if that's possible. It also made
them redder.) (The shower was a mistake.)

Then I remembered: Kiki was coming over, too. Next
to Kiki, I would look like something that The Cat ate and
then regurgitated. And then ate again. And regurgitated
again (i.e., like a very smelly hairball).

Brad would fall in love with Kiki and they would run
off into the sunset and I'd be left here, scratching my
itchy, ugly, hairy, messy self raw. It is lucky that I don't
even like Brad.

Would calamine lotion be too ugly? Yes. I would
suffer to be beautiful, if by "beautiful" I mean "Nearly
Unrecognizably Heinous."

7:29 p.m.

It's very weird to have friends over when you are crusted over with disease and resemble living plague victim with black eyes. I kept running back and forth to the kitchen and getting them juice and water.

Brad looked good.

Really good.

Note to Self: This may be an illusion brought about by chicken pox, which have possibly infected brain and may be triggering hallucinations, delusions, and other uncontrollable mental phenomena.

It was completely unfair that Brad gave me the wretched chicken pox and he seemed relatively untouched by them. Sure, he had one or two. A handful. And he was scratching uncomfortably. A bit. But he just looked normal-sick, or like he HAD been sick, but was over it.

I, on the other hand, looked bad-sick.

There's a difference.

But I don't like him, so I didn't care.

Really, it was very awkward. I didn't know what to do.

"Uh, we could play a game or something?" I suggested. "Monopoly? Or . . . something." (For some reason, my brain went completely blank at this juncture and I was unable to think of the names of any other games whatsoever except "Farmer in the Dell," which seemed like probably an embarrassing suggestion.) (*NB*: For those who don't know, "Farmer in the Dell," while also being a nursery rhyme, is a game that involves dropping little plastic cherries with hooks on them into very small buckets.) (Very complicated, now that I think of it, but also a game for three year olds.)

"OK," said Kiki. "What games do you have?" She was talking to me very slowly and carefully as though I were a semi-invalid or a senior citizen with Alzheimer's disease. I was tired, but really.

"I don't know," I said. "I'll just go check the games cupboard. Be right back."

"I'll come with you," Brad said.

"No, no," I said. "You can't." For a number of reasons, he couldn't. I wasn't just being weird and standoffish. Reasons for it included the fact that the games cupboard is downstairs and I'm strictly forbidden to let any of my friends see the grow-op in the basement. (As though without that instruction, I'd give them guided tours. Not that they don't know it's there.) And other reasons, which I've forgotten.

Really, it's a silly rule.

"It's forbidden," I said and smiled mysteriously.

Unfortunately, the games cupboard is in the guest room and in order to get into the games cupboard, you have to climb over the bed. Even more unfortunate is the fact that chicken pox makes a person very sleepy. Needless to say, I lay down on the bed for a minute on the way to the games cupboard and I fell asleep.

Sound asleep.

By the time I woke up, both Kiki and Brad were gone and there was a note taped on to the pillow next to me that said, "Have a good sleep."

What does that mean?

Why didn't they wake me up?

Kiki must have designs on Brad. That's the only conclusion I can come to.

The slut.

And after I wake up properly, I'm going to address this situation right away.

Thursday, October 17

MOOD	Well-rested and sort of alert.
HAIR	Scruffy
HEALTH	Ugly beyond belief.
HOROSCOPE	Keep an eye on your health. Be careful not to spread yourself too thin! Be generous with $$$.
JT SIGHTINGS	o. Thank God. If he saw me . . .

11:00 a.m.

Having been asleep since Tuesday night, woke up feeling marginally better. BETTER, but not HAPPIER. I am extremely mad at Kiki. What was she thinking?

What Kiki Must Have Been Thinking:

1. Will take advantage of Haley while she is unconscious and steal her boyfriend! (If he HAD been my boyfriend, which he wasn't.)

2. Will steal Haley's only possible future boyfriend, because I can!

3. Will wait until Haley is asleep and then skulk out of her

house with her boyfriend, who I've practically kid-
napped, but no matter, that's what friends are for!

4. Will just steal Brad because I can and he's cute! Ish.
   Cute-ish.

2:10 p.m.
Something terrible has happened, Brad and Kiki notwithstanding. Here's the thing.

I have accidentally released The Bird into the wild.

I was being generous, as dictated by my horoscope. I
felt sorry for The Bird. In a moment of pity for the poor
creature, who was trapped in the house all day watching
daytime TV (no wonder The Bird is sometimes aggressive
and bites people's ear lobes until they bleed), I set him
in his cage and put the cage outside. I did not know he
knew how to open the door. (The Bird is smarter than I
thought.) (It didn't occur to me that The Bird would take
this as an invitation to escape.)

Dad is going to kill me, I thought. I wondered if indeed
Dad could get angry enough to kill me, and then decided
that he probably couldn't.

My heart was beating very fast, as it tends to do during
a Panic Attack. To calm myself down, I went to the new
Pink Bathroom. (Pink is supposed to be a calming colour.)

It didn't work.

OK, I said to myself. Calm down.

Luckily, Dad was — again — out. (I'm wondering
if he's actually avoiding me because he has never had
chicken pox. Has he? He wouldn't remember. He killed
those brain cells a long time ago. I'm pretty sure that he

would be surprised to find out that he had a childhood at all.) I wouldn't blame him for avoiding me, anyway. Who would want this? Although I'm getting used to the itching. And I've discovered that taking antihistamines quite regularly really cuts down on the itch. Although they make you sleep. A lot.

"Well, The Cat," I said. "Why don't you go find The Bird?" I went back to the living room and gazed outside in a way that I imagined was doleful. I guess there was no reason why I should not venture out and find The Bird myself. How far could The Bird have gone? I reasoned. He's not that big. (Although swallows are not that big either and they manage to fly to San Juan de Capistrano every year to entertain the tourists. The Bird could be in Australia by now for all I know.)

Damn.

And it was raining.

And windy.

Two hours later, I was wandering down the street in my pyjamas (paint-smeared) and there was absolutely no sign of The Bird. I was freezing, no doubt contracting pneumonia and whooping cough simultaneously. (I probably should have put on something other than my pyjamas and my Dad's gardening boots, but I was in a hurry at the time.) At the very least, I should have worn socks. The pox on my feet were rubbing uncomfortably against the rubber. Socks would have been good.

I was also wearing sunglasses. Even though it was cloudy. (Apparently, chicken pox makes you sensitive to bright lights.) So, to summarize, there I was, out on the street: boots, PJs, sunglasses, wild hair, pox. I must have looked quite deranged. (Luckily, I couldn't see myself, so I can't be totally sure of this.) In retrospect, I was probably lucky that no one called and reported to the police that a crazy person was wandering the neighbourhood, wielding a net. (I thought I might need something to catch The Bird with, if he was perched up high.)

I was certainly lucky that a certain someone (JT) did not see me in this state.

With my luck, really, that was just a stroke of good fortune.

Three hours, still nothing.

Three hours and one minute later: still nothing.

I gave up. I went home.

On my way home, it occurred to me that several days had passed and I had not thought about JT (very much). (Or possibly, not at all). Was my crush on JT diminishing?

For a minute, I felt almost sad about all the time I spent thinking about him obsessively. What a waste of time! Now that I'm not thinking about him, I've really filled my time with so many other useful things.

Or not.

I scuffed my feet along the pavement and thought about what an idiot JT was on the phone.

And how he didn't remember my name the next day.

And how his stupid cousin gave me the chicken pox.

And how cute he was. How cute he IS.

And how good we would look together. (*NB*: If I ever look normal again.)

Damn.

7:32 p.m.

I successfully managed to go to the games cupboard without falling asleep on the bed, which is really nothing short of a miracle. (Am still very tired.) But unfortunately, the only game in there was called Ouija, whatever that is, and it looked suspiciously like a hippie game. There were hippies on the box, in any event.

Kiki was waiting upstairs. Both of us were carefully not mentioning Brad. (He hasn't called since Tuesday, for the record. Not that I care.)

OK, I do care. But I don't like him.

I just want him to like me.

"I've seen this in horror movies," said Kiki dubiously, pulling the Ouija board out of the box.

"Doesn't look very scary," I said airily. I mean, really. It's just a board with a bunch of letters on it and numbers and a sun and a moon. What's to be afraid of?

"It's for communicating with the dead," she said. "It creeps me out."

"Oh, come on," I said. "Besides, it's the only game I have. And there's nothing on TV. And if I have to watch the nothing that's on TV for one more minute, I'll probably die. Also, maybe The Dead can help us find The Bird before The Dad comes home and kills me."

"I don't think The Dead will help with that," Kiki said, stretching out her muscled legs. "Or The Undead, for that matter." She ran over here from her place, which is approximately 10 kilometres, or 40000 miles. (I have no idea how many miles, actually. I have no sense of distance.)

Regardless of the unknown distance (trust me, it's far), she barely even broke a sweat.

I remember running. Fondly. (OK, so I ran into a tree that once, which was a negative experience, but not one to necessarily ruin the entire sport for me for all time.) I miss running.

"I miss running," I said.

"Do you?" she said. "It's only been a couple of weeks since you last ran and you said you hated it. You mentioned it about four hundred times, in fact."

"I do hate it," I conceded. "I just miss it. I'm learning to love it. I love the idea of it already. That's the first step. What if I can never run again? Then what?"

"Oh, come on," Kiki said. "It's the chicken pox. It's not fatal or anything. I've had it and I survived."

"Hmmmph," I said. "It can be fatal. I looked it up."

"You shouldn't look at medical sites on the internet," she said. "You're just going to get yourself all worked up."

"I'm not worked up," I said. Although I *was* slightly worried. I mean, I have a fair number of poxes still. More than Brad had, from what I can remember. So if either of us is going to get fatally ill from this, my money would be on me.

"Do you think if I died, JT would come to my funeral?" I asked.

"Oh, shut up," she said. "I'm not even going to answer that."

"Has he asked after me?" I said. "Have you talked to him? What was he wearing today?"

"Uh," she said.

And just then, I realized that something was up. Kiki was quite clearly trying to keep a secret from me. My stomach dropped like a stone. I mean, it wasn't just that she said, "uh," it was the *way* she said, "uh."

"Kiki," I said, frozen in place with the stupid Ouija board on the table and the plastic pointer-thing in my hand, which I'd previously been spinning for no apparent reason. "Tell me."

"Nothing!" she said, in her "I'm totally lying" voice. She flicked her hair (she'd just had it straightened with that Japanese straightening technique and it was the exact colour of . . . I don't know. Something black and shiny) and then twisted it up into a ponytail while I concentrated on giving her the Evil Eye. (Kiki can't stand up very long against the Evil Eye. She's easily frightened.) Then she said, "Uh, what was he *wearing*? He was wearing jeans today, and uh, a white T-shirt, with uh, something on it. No, not something on it. It had buttons. At the neck. You know the one."

"Kiki," I said, horrified. It's obviously something really bad. "Tell me. Has he got a new girlfriend?"

"You're sick," she said. "You aren't up for this." She looked really worried.

"What?" I yelled. "What? What? He's got a boyfriend? Has he turned gay since last week? What's happened? Tell me RIGHT NOW!"

"Hey," she said, looking over my shoulder. "Isn't that The Bird?"

It was.

Really, it was like a sign from The Fates, or God, or Buddha, or someone in a position of power.

We ran — or at least she ran and I stumbled — outside and then spent the better part of an hour chasing The Bird around the garden (it may have been a Sign, but apparently that was all the help the Powers That Be were willing to provide), treading on all my precious (OK, they were dead) organic vegetables. I plucked some withered peas off the vine and ate them raw. (Raw peas are really very delicious. I don't know why more people don't eat them that way more often.)

The Bird did not want to get caught, particularly by us. I suspect that he was actually laughing at us, in a bird style of taunting laughter.

By the time we caught The Bird (as in, "it finally got tired of the game and flew on to my shoulder and sat there as though it doesn't have a care in the world"), I'd nearly forgotten about our conversation. My socks were soaked. I hate having wet socks, so I went into my room and changed them. The only socks I could find were blue-and-pink striped and featured cartoon cats.

I have no idea where socks like this come from. Do people actually pay money for such socks? Did someone give these to me as a gift? If so, why?

Really.

When I got back into the living room, Kiki was looking very serious and upset. For a split second, I thought maybe something terrible had happened to The Bird. But then I remembered that we'd been talking about JT.

Oh, JT.

Was *he* dead? My heart was in my throat. (Literally. It felt that way. I could feel it hammering there, like I couldn't swallow.)

But he wasn't dead. No, no.

Worse.

Worse than anything I could think of.

The Worst Thing Ever.

He was going out with Jules.

JT. Jules.

It was my Worst Nightmare.

"What?" I said numbly. (I must have been in shock. I couldn't even hear my own voice.) "What? What?"

"Are you OK?" she said. "Stop screaming. You're freaking me out."

"No," I said. "What? I'm not OK. No."

"On the plus side, she's stopped seeing Mr. Jurgen," Kiki pointed out helpfully.

"What?" I said. "What?"

Seriously, my brain was ringing like church bells.

I felt sick.

I felt like I might die. More so than I'd felt in the whole two weeks of being sick.

I felt like the Earth had just heaved up a big hairball on top of me. A global sized hairball.

I felt like killing Jules. And JT. And Brad for giving me these goddamn chicken pox. And Kiki for not having the chicken pox, for being pretty, and for telling me about Jules and JT.

"What?" I said again, for good measure. I don't know why I said it. I just had to say something.

"Uh, do you still want to play?" she said.

"No," I said, chucking the Ouija board across the room, where it knocked over my favourite glass vase. Which broke. I would have cried, but I was too worked up. "No, I don't want to play. I'm tired. I have to go to sleep. You should go."

"You can't sleep," she pointed out. "You're all upset. Let's at least try."

"No," I said.

She went and picked the board up from the floor and put it in front of me. She's a good friend. I hate her.

I hate everyone.

"Ask it something," she said. "Ask something of the Universe."

"Why hast thou forsaken me?" I said. "Also, this is a dumb game. What kind of game is this? How do you win this game?"

"You don't win," she explained. "You ask it stuff and it answers."

"It's not doing anything," I said. "Maybe it needs a battery."

"It doesn't need batteries," she said. "Um, we have to put our hands on it."

"On what?" I said. "That's stupid."

"On the pointer," she said, showing me the box. "Come on, Haley. Just try it."

"Fine," I said. I rested my hand on it and concentrated on Not Crying.

"Why Jules? Why?" I said. Nothing happened. Of course. Like the universe could tell me why my so-called

Best Friend was a back stabbing bitch.

Ha.

"Be serious," Kiki said. "Or it won't work. Let's see, I'm going to ask it something. What am I going to be when I grow up?"

"What?" I yelped with laughter. "What kind of question is that? That's seriously lame."

"I'm serious," she said. "I want to know."

So I pushed the thing over the letters so it spelled out "hooker." I know it was cruel. What's wrong with me?

"God," she said, giving me a withering look. "Sometimes you can be really mean."

And she left.

"What's going on?" Dad said, coming into the room nonchalantly and sweeping up the broken glass. "Oh, Ouija! I love that game. Can I play?"

"Dad," I said. Then I burst into tears and ran out of the room. I mean, I hate to be a drama queen, but what else could I do?

Jules.

JT.

Oh God, my life is over.

▶ ▶ ▶

Saturday, October 19

MOOD	In shock.
HAIR	Not bad, considering.
HEALTH	In shock.

HOROSCOPE | Today is a good day to start a new exercise
regime. Pay attention to your body!

Oh, PLEASE.

6:30 a.m.

My body is saying the following: "Your best friend is an
evil cow! Your skin will never heal! Your life as you know
it is over!"

Bloody horoscope. I'd like to start a new exercise
regime that involves running Jules over with my car.

OK, don't have a car.

OK, don't really want to run Jules over.

Sigh.

Good news:

My chicken pox is starting to scab over. This makes me
look (a) worse and (b) disgusting. But it does mean that
it's almost over. Or it is over.

At least, I think it means that I'm no longer contagious
and I can sit back and wait for the scars to form so I can
examine the permanent damage.

Bad news:

Tonight is the big night. According to Kiki, tonight is the
night that Jules and JT are having their first date. I hate Jules.

To distract me from devising ways to kill Jules and sitting
and thinking obsessively about what they are doing at

every moment, Kiki is coming over with movies. It's a very nice thing for her to do. But it's not going to help.

Basically all it means is that I'll have to think up all the possible scenarios before she gets here in case she is successful at distracting me tonight.

Things I Hope Happen to Ruin JT and Jules' Date:
1. Jules breaks out in the chicken pox.
2. JT breaks out in the chicken pox.
3. JT doesn't make it to her house because his car catches fire, although he escapes with no injury.
4. Jules' house burns down with her in it. No, scratch that. It's mean.
5. Jules burns down her house and is arrested for arson.
6. All Jules' hair falls out while she is getting ready to go due to mix up between Nair and shampoo.
7. All Jules' teeth fall out while she is getting ready to go due to mix up between toothpaste and highly corrosive tooth removing substance.

    Jules decides that she's in love with the middle-aged teacher after all and does not go.
8. JT decides he's in love with me after all and does not go.
9. There is a huge earthquake and we are all buried under rubble, but luckily JT was on his way to Jules at the time and happens to be buried in the rubble directly outside my house. We are buried in rubble together but not hurt, just trapped for days on end. With food. And water. And each other.
10. Nuclear War, same scenario, only we end up being the

last two people on Earth and are obligated to propogate the species.

Things That Cannot Happen Under Any Circumstances:
1. JT and Jules have a great time.
2. JT kisses Jules.
3. Jules kisses JT.
4. JT and Jules have any physical contact whatsoever.
5. JT and Jules actually go out on date.

If Jules was any kind of friend, she would not do this to me. How can she do this to me? This is really kicking me while I'm down. It's only 7:00 a.m. It's going to be a long day.

8:14 a.m.
Have come up with a list of over one hundred things that can go wrong on their date. Sure, the shark attack is far-fetched, but it could happen. And the plane crash could only actually occur if they were on a plane.

Oh, #401: Plane could fall from the sky and land on Jules just as she is stepping out of her house to greet JT. A small plane. That doesn't in any way harm JT.

8:36 a.m.
I'm going to call Jules and insist she call the whole thing off.

8:37 a.m.
Jules does not like to be woken up early on Saturday

morning. She will not call anything off. She hates me. Which is fine, because I hate her, too.

8:50 a.m.

Jules phoned to apologize but refused to call date off as she says it doesn't really mean anything and that secretly she has always liked JT herself.

So which is it?

Does it not mean anything? Or has she always liked JT herself?

9:02 a.m.

I called Jules back to clarify but she'd gone to dance practice or rehearsal or whatever it is that she does. Her mother answered. I resisted the temptation to ask her how Danny is. Really, Jules leads a very complicated life. It's sort of sad, if you think about it. I mean, it's really sad.

I have been a bad friend to Jules.

Poor Jules.

I am beginning to get a headache.

9:35 a.m.

Possible Causes of Headache

1. Brain Tumour.
2. Brain Aneurysm.
3. Stroke.
4. Something bad.
5. Stress relating to Jules.
6. Stress relating to JT.

10:48 a.m.

Possible Cures for Headache

1. Sleep.
2. Tylenol.
3. Morphine.
4. Killing Jules.
5. Killing JT.
6. Killing self.
7. Combination of above.

(From MedLine)

Common causes of headaches include the following:

- Common cold
- Fever
- Hangover
- Alcohol withdrawal
- Head injury
- Neck pain from strain or arthritis
- Head or neck infection NOT involving the brain
- Dental disease
- Ear infection
- Mastoiditis
- Pharyngitis
- Sinusitis
- Influenza
- Medications
- Indomethacin
- Nitrates
- Vasodilators

- Premenstrual syndrome (PMS)
- Stress
- Tooth abscess
- Withdrawal from drugs
- Caffeine
- Ergotamine
- Sympathomimetics
- Street drugs

Rare causes include the following:

- Cerebral aneurysm
- Brain tumour
- Stroke
- TIA
- Meningitis
- Encephalitis

Where *is* Dad? Shouldn't he be here, looking after my headache? If he's gone somewhere, I've forgotten where. Actually, I have a vague memory of him saying something about where he was going, now that I think of it. I think he's selling his pathetic drugs, so I try not to listen when he tells me about it. I don't want to be an accessory to the crime. Yes, marijuana should be legal, blah blah blah (not sure if I actually believe it or not), but I still don't want to be a part of it.

I try to assess the situation, but my head hurts too much.

I take three Tylenol and go back to bed.

An hour later.

I couldn't sleep because I kept thinking about Jules. And JT. I wonder what she's going to wear. I wish she was ugly. If she was the Ugly Friend then I could be the Pretty Friend and I would get JT.

I wish it wasn't all about looks.

I wish JT wasn't as shallow as a saucer.

I wish I could sleep.

I wish typing didn't make my head hurt so much.

12:15 p.m.

I was desperate. I did something stupid.

But the pain was like nothing else. I'm not exaggerating. I wove down the hallway. I could hardly walk.

I went into Dad's room and found his stash of joints and lit one. I inhaled tentatively. It wasn't that bad. Cancer patients smoke this, right? It has curing qualities. It's medicinal. I took a bigger drag and held it in. For about three seconds. Before I started choking and coughing.

I coughed so hard that I threw up.

Throwing up tired me out and it did seem to lessen the pain long enough for me to write stuff.

At least now I'll be able to sleep. Vomiting makes me very sleepy. I don't know why this is. Probably very good scientific explanation for it, but can't be bothered to look it up.

Where is Dad?

Headache is terrible.

3:14 p.m.

Kiki is coming to save me. She has aromatherapy. It will cure my headache. Then she is going to distract me.

Ha bloody ha.

4:15 p.m.

Aromatherapy smells good and minty. Kiki has given me a head massage and I think my head feels marginally better. Am cured!

"Maybe you have a sore neck from lying around for days," she said.

"Maybe," I said. "Or maybe I have meningitis. Or encephalitis. Or a blood clot. Or a tumour."

"Or maybe you're a hypochondriac," she said.

"Maybe," I said. Meaning "not." (I mean, I am a hypochondriac, but only if that word means "one who is naturally concerned about her health and interested in her health enough to look things up, just in case.")

"But . . ." I said. Then I did a double take. Right there on Kiki's left cheek.

"Oh My God," I said.

"What?" she said.

"Kiki," I said. "Are you sure that you've had the chicken pox?"

"Sure," she said.

"I don't think so," I said. I dragged her into the bathroom, which was quite a feat considering my throbbing, light head, stiff neck, and rampant nausea.

Right there, on her face, was a pox.

"Oh no!" she said. "Oh no."

We both looked at it in awe. It was quite a pox. I have to say my vision was slightly blurry and I was feeling a bit confused. "A pox," I said dramatically.

"I feel OK," she said. "I mean, I feel really fine. It doesn't even itch."

"Huh," I said, scratching my arm half-heartedly. "Just you wait."

7:00 p.m. exactly

Kiki and I both crashed out on separate couches in the living room, with Tivo frozen on Dawson, from "Dawson's Creek." He's unspeakably hot, and also possibly the perfect boyfriend for me. Not that he would look twice at me in my present condition.

We alternately scratched (her) and complained (me). I love Kiki.

"I love you," I told her.

"Me, you, too," she said and yawned.

"I'm sorry about the hooker thing," I said. "I don't know why I did that. I was trying to be funny. I'm an ass."

"You are an ass," she said agreeably. She's the most agreeable person I know.

"It's 7:00," I said sadly. "He's picking her up now."

"Blargh," she said. Or something like that. I'm not sure if it was a sympathetic "Blargh" or a "Blargh, shut up about it Haley" sort of Blargh. It's hard to tell.

"Blargh?" I said.

"You have to let it go," she said. "I think Jules has liked JT for ages."

"She has NOT," I said. "She would have said so."

"Haley, how could she? You've been rhapsodizing about him since ninth grade."

"Which means I have dibs," I said defensively. My head was squeezing like a vice. Or rather my scalp was. Or something was. I was feeling disoriented.

"I think I have a fever," I said.

"You don't have a fever," she said, scratching her arm vigorously. "Let's do something."

"Like what?" I said. "There's nothing to do." My mouth was as dry as feathers. I made a smacking sound with my lips, but I didn't go get water. The kitchen seemed too far away.

"Let's do that Ouija thing," she said. "We'll ask it what JT and Jules are doing."

"Hmmmm," I said. "I'm skeptical. If I don't believe in it, it probably won't work. Also, my head hurts too much to try."

"We can try," she said. "But first we have to set the mood."

So that's how we came to be sitting in a dark room with candles lit and spooky background music (OK, it's Sarah MacLachlan, but it's as close to spooky as I had) when Dad came barreling through the door.

"What is it?" I said. He looked quite . . . disarrayed.

"Nothing, nothing," he said, coming over to me and kissing me on the forehead. "Do you have a fever?" he said.

"Yes," I said. "No."

He patted my scalp wearily. I'd never seen him look like that. It was seriously non-Dad-like. Frankly, it freaked me out.

"What are you all worried about?" I said.

"Oh, nothing," he lied, scratching at his beard. His beard was still full of pink paint, by the way.

"You're beard is all pink and painty," I told him.

"OK, sweetheart," he said, ignoring me. "I have to go Out."

"You just came in," I said. "I have a headache."

"I know," he said. He handed me a roll of cash. I must have a fever, I decided. And be hallucinating. It wasn't just a roll of cash. It was a ROLL of cash. I mean it must have been a few thousand dollars. Or more. I have no idea. It was heavy.

"Uh," I said.

"Just put it somewhere," he said. "I'm holding it for a friend."

"Uh," I said again.

And then he was gone.

"You know," said Kiki, slowly. "You and Jules have the two most, er, unusual family lives of anyone I've ever met."

"I wish I didn't," I told her. "I really wish I didn't."

I stuffed the money under the sofa. My brain felt like it was rolling around in my head. The Cat immediately went in after the money roll and started batting it around. I took it out and stuffed it into my pocket, where it bulged out a full six inches. And dug into my hip. Very uncomfortable. I took it out of my pocket and threw it on the mantle.

We both looked at it there.

"Decorative," I said.

"Um," said Kiki. "That's a lot of money. Maybe we should hide it."

"I guess," I said.

Which is how we came to bury the roll of money in a Miracle Whip jar in the backyard. This took much longer than you might think. By the time we got back inside, the candles were burned low. By a stroke of luck, we didn't burn the house down. It wouldn't have surprised me. (My brain was on fire. It was only natural that everything else would be, too.)

"OK," I said. "Let's do this." (Please note, in retrospect, I also find this weird. I could hardly move my head, but I wanted to play with the Ouija board?)

But I had this idea in my (inflamed) head: Maybe the Ouija board could tell me where this money came from? And why I had a sinking, sick feeling in the pit of my stomach?

It was cheaper than calling a Psychic Line, at any rate.

We sat.

"You have to put your fingers on it properly this time," said Kiki. "Then we just sit here."

"OK," I said, and balanced my fingers on the plastic pointer thing. It's really quite ridiculous when you think about it.

"Ask it a question," she said.

"Um," I said. "OK." I took a deep breath, which hurt in every part of my head and neck, so I stopped. "Does JT love Jules?" I asked.

Nothing happened. Then the wind blew the curtains in a little bit and Kiki jumped a mile and a half in the air and screamed. I laughed, sort of. As much as I could. I was finding that by holding my head and neck very still, it hurt less.

"This is dead people we're communicating with," Kiki said, taking her hand off to scratch her scalp. "Aren't you freaked out? Ghosts. Spirits."

"Nothing is happening," I pointed out. "We're communicating with nobody. Also, ghosts are dead. You never hear of a ghost hurting someone. Live people hurt you. Not dead ones."

"Well, ask it something else," Kiki said, closing her eyes. "Maybe we just have to concentrate."

"OK," I said. "Um. Who is here? Dead people?"

And the thing moved. Kiki jerked her hand off it like it was a hot iron.

"It was moving!" she said.

"I know," I said, confused. "Isn't that the point?"

But I do have to say that I was a little spooked, too. I mean, it moved, but it didn't move like someone was pushing it. It sort of floated. It slid. Spookily.

"Who is here? You mean, other than us?" she said. "Shit. That's a creepy question. Ask it something normal."

"Oh for God's sake," I said. "You ask it something."

"I can't think of anything," she said.

"My head is killing me," I said. And lay back down on the couch. I was starting to sweat. I must have had a fever. The highest fever you can have without convulsing is like 104. Mine was probably 103.5. I was really starting to feel rotten. I should tell Kiki to go, I thought, but who wants to be alone and feel rotten? Misery loves company. And I had no idea where my Dad was.

"I should go," Kiki said.

"No!" I said. "I've, uh, I've thought of something to ask."

"OK," she said. "But don't ask anything creepy."

"Fine," I said.

We put our hands back on the pointer thing. The CD had now repeated twice and the candles were mostly out. It wasn't that creepy, actually. It was sort of romantic. I mean, if Kiki were, say, JT. And not Kiki.

"Will I ever find true love?" I said.

And we watched as the point skidded over and pointed to YES.

"Hey," I said. "That's cool." It was. I mean, it was wild and totally unbelievable. But cool.

"Ask it something else," Kiki said.

"OK," I said. "Will JT ever ask me out?"

NO.

"Crap," I said. "This thing is a hunk of junk."

NO, it said.

I swear it. And neither of us pushed it.

Then it started to slide towards different letters. My fingers felt like they were stuck to it. But maybe that was just the fever. I mean, the room was starting to look muddy to me.

YOU ARE BEAUTIFUL ON THE INSIDE, it spelled out. YOU WORRY TOO MUCH.

"OK," I whispered. "Now I'm freaked out. Are you doing this, Kiki?"

The thing was going crazy. I swear. It was moving like lightning. It was hard to keep up with the letters.

DON'T BE SCARED, it said. I AM NOT SCARY.

"Uh, who are you?" Kiki said. She was as pale as a ghost herself. I thought she was going to faint.

I thought *I* was going to faint.

NO NAMES.

"Are you a good . . . ghost? Er, spirit?" I said.

YES.

"Can you tell us what JT and Jules are doing?" I asked.

NO.

"Why not?" I said. "I thought you were a ghost/spirit."

I AM HERE WITH YOU.

"Er, are you alone?" I asked.

NO.

Then the thing started to move strangely. Not like the previous movement wasn't strange, but now it got jerky and bizarre. I was scared, but too feverish to care. I was both fully freaked out and really interested.

RIDDLE.

"Riddle?" I said. "You want us to ask you a riddle?"

NO, it said. Then it turned and pointed back to NO again and again.

"This is a different one," Kiki said, like she could hardly breathe. Her lips were barely moving. She looked totally terrified. "It feels different."

The hairs on my neck stood straight up. I had goose-bumps all over my arms.

"Are you a different one?" I said.

YES, it said. YES YES YES I WILL NOT LEAVE YOU YES YES YES.

"Are you good or evil?" said Kiki.

I WILL NOT LEAVE YOU. YOU CANNOT MAKE ME LEAVE. CANNOT. YOU. CANNOT. RIDDLE.

"Uh," I said. "If we answer your riddle, will you leave?"

And it stopped moving.

"Let's put it away," said Kiki.

"We can't put it away," I said, panicking. "There is some creepy evil spirit in here. I don't want to put it away until it leaves. Look," I pointed at the board. "It has to say goodbye."

Across the bottom of the board was a big GOODBYE.

"OK," she said, using the pointer to scratch her back. "OK."

We put the pointer back and asked, "How can we get you to go?"

It started moving right away.

HE IS GONE. It said. GONE ALREADY. IT IS HARD FOR ME TO STAY LONG. I WANT TO TALK TO HALEY.

"OK," I said. Suddenly I wasn't scared. I can't explain it. Even the candle flames stop flickering. I wasn't thinking about anything else but this "voice," which wasn't a voice, just a bunch of words. It sounded almost like a voice in my aching head. It makes no sense, but I felt almost, like, euphoric.

HALEY, it said. HALEY.

"It's just wasting time," said Kiki. "We both know your name already."

IF I HAD NOT DIED, it said. I LOVE YOU.

"What?" I said. "Who are you?"

NO, it said.

HALEY, it said.

Then it stopped. "That's freaking crazy," said Kiki, who hardly ever swears.

"It was fun," I said.

"Fun?" she said.

"It was," I said. Then all of a sudden my stomach clenched up in knots. I threw up. (It surprised me, too.)

Then I passed out.

Or so Kiki told me, later.

Note to Dad Written in Emergency
Room on Back of Admission Form:
Dear Dad,

Have meningitis.

Am going to die.

Where are you?

Love,

Your Daughter, Haley Andromeda Harmony

Summary of What Must have Happened:
1. Kiki called 911.
2. 911 call was responded to by police and ambulance.
3. Oh no. Oh no. Oh no. Police were in the house.
4. Ambulance guys took me to ambulance.
5. Ambulance took me to hospital.

Random Collection of Notes to Self:
1. *Note to Self:* find out where Kiki is.
2. *Note to Self:* find out where Dad is.
3. *Note to Self:* find out if there is internet terminal where

can go to Web MD to find out about meningitis.

4. *Note to Self*: stay awake long enough to find out answers to 1-3.
5. *Note to Self*: find out what is in IV bag.
6. *Note to Self*: IV bag is full of morphine. Morphine is very good. Headache feels much better.
7. *Note to Self*: Ouija board is neat. And complimentary. Must find out more about complimentary Ouija Ghost who loves me. (Is ghost a boy? Or is it my mother, even though she isn't dead? As far as I know. Maybe mother has died? Must find out for absolute sure.)
8. *Note to Self*: can convince nurse to allow me to apply tooth-whitening strips before passing out.
9. *Note to Self*: Must. Find. Dad.
10. *Note to Self*: Ask someon . . .

▶ ▶ ▶

Sunday, October 20

Dear Junior:

I am so happy to see you. Kiki is a terrific friend for arranging to have you brought to me, even though she isn't allowed in the hospital herself because of her contagious pox. Am so bored. But I'm alive.

Lucky me.

I'm in a special room that expels all the air outside, so that it doesn't vent back into the hospital. I'm in this room because of the meningitis. Which is apparently highly contagious. And can cause death. Hah.

Death!

Here's what happens. The lining of the brain swells up and pushes down on the spinal cord. Which is where your breathing center is. I'm hooked up to all these machines that make sure I'm still breathing. I'm afraid to ask what happens if I stop. OK, I asked.

Me: What happens if I stop breathing?

Nurse: You die.

Me: Wow. That's comforting.

Her: We'd try to save you.

Me: Gosh. Thanks.

Her: Save your questions for the doctor, honey.

Me: Will I see the doctor soon?

Her: I have no idea.

Me: Great. Thanks.

Her: You're welcome.

Me: You don't happen to have today's paper, do you? I'd like to read my horoscope.

Her: No. We're very busy here. We don't have time to read the paper.

Junior, was she implying that I was a lazy person with nothing better to do than read the paper? Honestly, it's hardly my fault that I'm at death's door and quite stoned from the morphine drip.

Me: Can I have more morphine?

Her: No.

Love,

Sick Girl

Dear Junior (again):

Am bored out of my mind. If people want to visit me, they have to wear full surgical scrubs and a mask so my germs don't get on them. Lovely.

On the plus side, the hickey bruises are gone! Yippee! When did they go? I don't know. It doesn't matter. Black eyes are also mostly gone, just shadowy. Look almost normal, except for millions of chicken-pox scabs, wild unwashed hair, incredible pastiness (from pain and vomiting) and . . . drum roll please! . . . itchy rash all over body.

Apparently, I'm allergic to morphine.

La la la. It's not like I want any visitors, anyway. I mean, think about it. I'm happy to be here with you, Junior.

Love,

Lonely Girl

Later (there are no clocks in here)

"Hey, ghost," I whispered. "Are you here?"

I mean, obviously he/she couldn't answer. But there wasn't exactly anyone else to talk to in here. And it was noisy, due to the fan system that got rid of my germy air.

I couldn't go out into the hallways. I couldn't do anything.

Not that I'd want to. Not with this headache.

I puked into the bed pan. (Truly one of the more disgusting experiences of my life, so far.)

Things really, really couldn't have been much worse.

Later still

Dear Junior,

Remind me never to say the words "things couldn't get

much worse". It tempts fate. Fate shouldn't be tempted.

Where is Dad? I'm starting to get scared now. No one seems to know.

Oh, help.

Love,

HAH

Later still, or possibly the Next Day

Dear Junior:

I'm sorry to write so often. But some lady came to see me. I think it was a lady. I mean, obviously, it was a lady. She was all in scrubs though, so it was hard to say for sure. Maybe it was a man with a woman's voice.

She was a Social Worker.

(See how things got worse?)

Apparently Dad has been arrested for possession with intent to sell, and for the grow-op. She told me what he was charged with, but my head was very painful. (They stopped the morphine and switched it for something less good, but also less itchy.) It was hard for me to concentrate.

Also, I was stoned on allergy stuff plus this new pain killer.

Stoned. Me.

Ironic, isn't it?

Ooops, sorry. Not concentrating. I have to write this down. Let me think.

First thing she asked me about was my black eyes. I tried to explain it, but really, it sounds like a lie. They aren't even really black any more.

"Look," I said. "Just call Kiki and ask her. We were running and then there was the tree. I can't explain it." My tongue felt all thick, like I couldn't talk properly.

"I only want to help," she said. "You can talk to me."

She had one of those syrupy sweet voices that rings with false sincerity. I had a strong, burning desire to leap out of the bed and punch her in the nose.

"Crapsticks," I said out loud. I didn't actually mean to. Crapsticks is one of those words that sometimes comes into my head that I don't use.

"Sorry?" she said.

"It's all right," I said. "I forgive you." I felt drunk.

"For what?" she said.

Naturally, I found this to be hugely funny, so I started laughing. I have no idea what drug I was on, but it's a good one. I tried to explain this (I think) (I can't actually remember), but instead, I fell asleep.

What's going on, Junior? We need someone to tell us something. Am so confused. Will read this later and perhaps all will fall into place. In the meantime, am very sleepy and need to rest.

Love,

Sleeping Girl

Reasons Why I Thought That Woman Was Funny:

1. It's hard to take a woman in scrubs and a surgical mask seriously.
2. The drugs.
3. The drugs.
4. OK, it wasn't even funny.

5. Where's my dad?

Night Time
Am very confused.
Where is my dad?
What's going on?

Day Time (again?)
I forced myself to open my eyes. The woman was there again, staring at me. (I hate it when people watch me while I sleep. It's very weird. Sleeping is private.)

"What about your neck?" she said.

"My neck," I said, worried. I mean, what was she trying to say? Was there something wrong with my neck? Was it broken? Had I been in an accident? I reached up and touched it. It felt all right to me. Neck like. (You know, the neck is a part of your body that isn't touched very often. It's just there. Supporting the head. My neck feels kind of veiny.)

"You have bruises," she said.

"Bruises?" I repeated. "I have bruises?" (I was feeling quite thick and stupid.)

"On your neck," she said. "What is the nature of your bruises?"

"They're hickeys!" I said, suddenly understanding her. "Old hickeys! They're almost totally gone. How can you see them? You have very good bruise-seeking abilities."

"Who gave you these . . . er, hickeys?"

"Oh," I said. "Um." And I couldn't for the life of me remember his name.

"Uh," I said, stalling for time. "Do you speak any other languages?"

"What?" she said.

"I was just curious," I said.

"Where did the bruises come from?" she said in a voice that indicated that straying from the topic was not permitted. (She could easily get a job at SHH. She has the right Strict And Cruel Aura.)

I could picture the hickey-giver. JT's cousin. The Cute-ish Stranger.

"He gave me the chicken pox," I told her. "This is all really his fault."

Then, I remembered. "Brad," I said. "Ha!"

And he walked through the door.

The social worker looked quite taken aback. Like I'd planned it. But I hadn't. There Brad was, looking . . . cute-ish. (Albeit covered with chicken-pox scabs. Well, not really covered. But sprinkled with them.*)

"Hi Haley," he said. "I brought you these." He whipped out a dozen red roses from nowhere. It was like magic! Where did they come from? He made me laugh. (At some point, I'm going to read this and think, "What the hell was so funny?" And "Why didn't I ask about my dad?" But I was stoned. I was. Really.) (I don't think my body does well with drugs. It's a drug-repelling sort of body.)

"Crapsticks," I said, when I stopped laughing.

Then . . .

Well, I don't know what else happened. If anything. I

---

* From what I could see of him. That is, the two inches of face skin that are revealed above his surgical mask.

must have passed out. When I woke up, they were both gone. But the flowers were still there. And the drugs had worn off enough for me to seriously panic.

A Social Worker? Does this mean that Dad's in jail?

Oh. My. God.

I'm so screwed.

I wish I could think properly.

Night Time

Immediate Problems:

1. Spring Dad from jail.
2. Spring self from hospital.
3. Get someone to bring makeup (cover up for eyes and hickeys and pox marks) in case other boys visit.
4. Get head examined: what other boys might visit?
5. Get phone in room.
6. Get TV in room.
7. Get more drugs.
8. Get sick. Again.
9. Get weighed. All this sickness must have resulted in miraculous ten-pound weight loss. So, apart from bad, dirty hair, no make-up, and no access to tooth-bleaching strips, may be on the road to great beauty. Through suffering. You do have to suffer to be beautiful, after all.
10. Get lawyer.
11. Get Kiki to bring in Ouija board to see if we can make further contact with the "I would have loved you" dead boy/dead mother ghost.

It's at times like these that I wish I had a mother.

"Hey, ghost," I said aloud to the room. "It would be

great if you could tell me where my mother is, if she isn't you and you aren't her. If you could find her and get her ass back here then maybe I could avoid a lifetime of foster care while Dad languishes in jail. I mean, if you don't have anything else to do."

I've been lying here in the dark for a while. The moon is full, I guess, because I can see all the way to the ocean. It's all lit up and pretty. The room is full of vaguely frightening shadows from all the equipment and the dim flashing of the green light above the bed on the monitor. I'm staring at the drip drip drip of the IV and wondering if it is someone trying to communicate from the other side. I'd feel better if I could at least read my horoscope.

I really need something (or someone) to tell me that everything is OK.

I have no idea what time it is. When I look around my weird reverse-air-flow room, I feel a bit like one of those experimental monkeys in that Dustin Hoffman movie where the monkeys get out and infect everyone in the world with their terrible virus and Rene Russo has to save the day.

Low Point Of The Day:
Realizing that the fact I'm treated like a virus-ridden experimental monkey is actually the high point of my life right now.

High Point Of The Day:
Realizing that I have not wasted any time thinking about and/or obsessing about JT.

Which makes me think about JT. I wonder how his date with Jules went.

Why hasn't Jules visited me? What a bitch. She's proba- bly run off with JT to California or the like, where they'll live happily ever after.

How long have I been here for?

On the bright side, my headache actually felt less . . . painful.

A bit.

Maybe I'm getting better, after all.

Or maybe I'm dying. I understand that you usually feel better for a few minutes before you actually die. It's like the eye of the storm.

A few minutes later
Nope, not dead

Later still
Still not dead.

► ► ►

Tuesday, October 22

MOOD	blank
HAIR	blank
HEALTH	blank
HOROSCOPE	blank
JT SIGHTINGS	blank

Today I feel blank.

"Blank" is one of those words which, when repeated, starts to sound hilarious. On its own, it isn't the least bit funny. That's true of a lot of things.

I know it's Tuesday, October 22 because I asked my doctor, who is the tallest man I've ever seen, and bald as a baby. A bald baby. Some babies have a lot of hair, granted. This doctor doesn't. Somewhere along the way, I've apparently lost a couple of days. The doctor said that it was the drugs.

He also said that the danger has passed.

The danger!

I think it's very surreal that I was in danger. To be honest, I've always felt like I was in danger, but never really was.

Anyway, he said that I could probably go home eventually after I've gone off the IV antibiotics, which I have to have for a certain amount of time, just to be safe. And after I've had solid food for a couple of days. To "see how I do".

I am a bit curious to see what might happen. How could solid food be somehow disastrous?

But home!

The problem is that I apparently can't be discharged, because I'm a minor, and my dad is in jail.

Right. I'd forgotten.

Oh God, Oh God, Oh God.

Come on, Fates. Make this better.

Goddamn it. Stupid marijuana.

After the doctor left, I concentrated very hard on not

crying. Instead, I wiggled the IV thing on the back of my hand until it came out and a bit of blood came from the opening, and the nurse had to come and put it right.

"Do you have any questions about . . . er, anything?" the doctor had asked. He looked nervous, or like he pitied me. Or like he really wanted to leave at that very moment. (I can't say that I blame him.)

"How long do hickeys usually take to disappear?" I asked.

"Oh," he said. "I don't really know. It would depend on the degree of the hematoma. A couple of weeks, I should think. Not longer."

"Thanks," I said.

Later

Dear Junior:

Am worried sick about Dad. And everyone. And me. I could really get into a funk if I'm trapped in here for much longer.

A viral monkey funk.

It was nice to be given roses. No one has ever given me roses before. Or any kind of flower, come to think of it. No, that isn't true. Kiki once gave me roses. I've forgotten why. Oh, when I got my first period. Hahahaha. Must still be stoned because that strikes me as very funny in an *Are You There God, It's Me Margaret?* sort of way.

Kiki is the best. I wonder why Kiki does not have a boyfriend. She is really the most beautiful and kind person that I know.

Wish I had phone, so could phone Kiki.

Have cell phone in purse! Will call.

More later,

xo, H.

PS — Had great conversation with Kiki and she will send Ouija board up with Jules, who is coming to visit later. She obviously can't come herself because she is still contagious and wouldn't be allowed into the hospital. Jules is coming! Yippee! A visitor. And even Jules can't look good in scrubs and a mask.

Note to Self: Using cell phone in hospital causes machines to go haywire and team of nurses have just rushed in with crash cart. It's good to know that (a) I would be saved if in fact I did stop breathing, and (b) nurses respond so quickly to haywire machines. Am very reassured by fantastic nursing care in this hospital. Although I did talk to Kiki for at least ten minutes. So if I had stopped breathing ten minutes ago, would I not now be dead? How long can you be not breathing and still be alive?

Am very alarmed by lax nursing care in this hospital.

Visitors to Bizarre Reverse-Air-Cage Viral Monkey Hospital Room Today:

1. Social Worker (Dad's bail has been set and am allowed to stay with Dad if he makes bail.)

Note to Self: Find money for bail. Where? Ask Kiki.

2. Wish that I knew lawyer or proper adult person who knows how these things work and who could help out with the situation.

3. Doctor who specializes in Infectious Disease who examined me like I am frightening experimental lab animal. He does not know how long it takes hickeys to heal, but suggests that is the least of my problems as he can't actually see any hickeys and I am just "lucky to be alive."

4. Other Doctor with team of medical students who stared at me (over their masks) disdainfully, like I am contaminated lab waste. Mostly, they were staring at my eyes. And my hickeys, which aren't even there. (Why is everyone so obsessed with my neck?) They were told they could ask questions, but none of them did. Realized that I looked like Linda Blair in The Exorcist right after her head spun around and she spewed green vomit.

5. Nurse One — took temperature, blood pressure, and advised me to eat green Jell-O.

6. Nurse Two — took temperature, blood pressure, and advised me to eat green Jell-O.

7. Nurse Three — took temperature, blood pressure, and asked if I would prefer orange Jell-O (I would), but then came back to report that there was only green Jell-O available.

Accomplished So Far Today:
1. Ate three bowls of green Jell-O cubes.
2. Did not throw up.

3. Stayed awake during most conversations.
4. Established that having a shower was out of the question because although I was "out of the woods," I still could not go down the hall to the shower room because I might "infect other patients" with "weak immune systems."

   Observation: Hospitals are very dangerous places for sick people.
5. A whole lot of nothing.
6. Conjured up ten or a thousand fantasy segments in which JT comes to visit with Jules, sets eyes on me, and falls madly in love in spite of vile appearance, greasy flat hair and revolting skin.

Dear Junior,
Me again.

What are we going to do?

This is so crazy. My head hurts, but not in the same way as it did before. More in a stressed-to-the-max sort of way. And possibly a hungry-as-hell sort of way.

Would kill for a veggie burger and fries. Did you ever wonder why they make so much vegetarian stuff that resembles and/or tastes like meat? If you wanted meat, why wouldn't you just eat meat?

Unless it's a political decision. Maybe there are droves of vegetarians in the world who secretly love the taste of meat but refuse to kill sacred animals.

Or I could love a salad. Honestly, I never thought I'd crave salad, but I do. Anything fresh that is not Jell-O would be ideal.

Fresh and/or salty.

Should I ring for nurse and ask for salt? No, that would probably be construed as "rude" or "demanding." The nurses here hate me. I'm sure of it. Well, not Nurse Three, but she is gone for the day. But I know from experience that Nurses One, Two and Four aren't entirely receptive to food orders.

If I can't find bail money for Dad, what's going to happen?

More importantly, even if I come up with the money and bail him out, what if he ends up going to jail? I could go into foster care. There are a handful of kids at school who are in foster care. At least, there must be. Statistically, odds are good that there are. I wonder who they are. I wonder if JT's parents do fostering. Hmmmm. Could be fostered by JT's parents and end up having to live with JT. During which time, he would realize that Jules was not his ideal girlfriend and that he'd secretly loved me all along, only didn't ask me out because he didn't want to step on Brad's toes. That must be it.

Wish I had an internet connection. I'm dying to go to Web MD to find out more information about meningitis.
Love,
Cured Girl
p.s. — I can feel my hip bones. They are definitely more pointy than before. Must have lost at least ten pounds on this bizarre green Jell-O diet. Good.

Uh oh. Am going to be sick. Thought I was "out of the woods"! What's happening?

Early Evening, I guess
Brief relapse into meningitis-type illness seems to be passing. But now have to be subjected to some kind of horrible test where fluid is extracted from my spinal cord. This strikes me as a terrible idea.

Things that Could Go Wrong During Test:
1. Needle could slip and spinal cord could be severed, causing paralysis.
2. Spinal fluid could all leak out, causing . . . death?
3. Likely will hurt.
4. Any number of bad things.

I also have to have an MRI, which I'm not worried about. I mean, it's not like it's invasive. It's not like it's a GIANT NEEDLE IN MY BACK.

This is a horrible nightmare.

I want my dad. I miss Kiki. I'd be happy to see *Brad* at this point.

Why don't I have a mother?

And where the hell is Jules? Where?

Night Time
Jules was here. I love Jules. Why did I hate Jules for so long? She is a very sweet, thoughtful girl. She brought me a new tooth-bleaching system, which I can't use because I keep throwing up.

Still, it was very thoughtful.

And she did not mention JT. So I did not mention JT.

Also, I'm on a valium drip, so the details are hazy. I'm

not really sure what we talked about, come to think of it. We may have talked about JT.

Spinal tap was relatively painless. No, that's not right. It was very painful, but valium made it quite relaxing and nice in a strange passing-of-time sort of way. Reminded me of that time I went on a road trip with Dad and spent three days throwing up until he gave me so much Gravol, I just drifted away from the whole thing.

Felt nice.

Now feel like a crazy person who has been plucked up by aliens and is undergoing some kind of alien experimentation but am too relaxed to care.

Come to think of it, what proof do I have that these people are doctors and not aliens?

Help.

Hmmmm. It probably was not even Jules who was just here, but an alien made to look like Jules to trick me into allowing aliens to take fluid samples from my spine. Will sleep now, but will address this grave situation in the morning, first thing.

▶ ▶ ▶

Wednesday, October 23

Aliens! Ha ha ha.

I guess from this bit of nonsense we can conclude that:

a) spending a long time (a week? How long have I been here?) in a room alone makes people crazy.

b) Valium makes crazy people crazier.

c) I am crazy.

This morning, I went into The Tube, which apparently is a rare privilege. There are people on wait-lists for The Tube!

The Tube is an MRI.

Lucky me.

I was first subjected to a pop quiz that featured such questions as *Have you ever been impaled in the eye by a metal object?* And *Do you have artificial ears?*

It was hilarious. I wished that I had someone to share it with.

If Jules comes back this afternoon, will not be all strung out on Valium and I'll be able to get the scoop on her and JT. And, more importantly, will be able to get her to help me find out more about Dad.

And maybe she can get me a phone for my room. And a TV. And fries.

Can't wait to see Jules.

In the meantime, will write clever essay, as follows:

The Tube, A Short Story
Once upon a time, there was a tube. People (or "patients") were put into the tube and incredibly awful loud noises were made and the tube closed in around the people until they repeatedly squeezed their "emergency exit" ball and had to be pulled out four or seven times. After the fourth (or seventh) time, people ("patients") were given Valium and put back into the tube where they no longer cared about the loud noises and the closing-in feeling. And even though they wanted to squeeze the

"emergency exit" ball, they couldn't be bothered, due to the Valium.

The End.

If I ever get out of here, I will use that in place of the "What I Did on my Summer Holidays" essay that I never handed in. Overall, I think it is much more interesting. Have shown it to Nurse Four, but she laughed (nastily, in the style of Kathy Bates in "Misery") and said it looked like something that a paranoid six-year-old might have written.

Suspect that Nurse Four is a frustrated writer herself with bitterness issues.

Will just rest a bit and then when I wake up, will re-read short story and congratulate myself on cleverness of short-story writing while under the influence of Valium.

► ► ►

Thursday, October 24

What happened to Wednesday? I lost Wednesday.

I have lost a lot of time in here.

When I'm not stoned, I'm scared.

How come my dad hasn't even called?

I am suddenly crushed under a huge wave of anxiety.

Huge.

Like all the breath has been sucked out of me.

I can't breathe.

Breathe, Haley, I keep telling myself.

Earlier, I tried plugging my nose to see if my body would instinctively then TRY to breathe, but apparently my body lacks instincts. The room got hazy.

Oh my God.

OK, I admit it, I rang the bell. I thought that maybe my breathing center was being crushed by my swollen brain. I rang the bell several times. And then I waited 47 minutes for Nurse One to respond. She laughed when I told her that I couldn't breathe. And then pointed out, quite rightly, that I was breathing.

"See?" she said, tapping the monitor. "Breathing. Besides, your MRI came back and the swelling in your brain has gone down. This time, you are definitely out of the woods. In fact, the doctors say you should be out of here in a few days."

"Huh," I said, still trying to breathe.

"You're hyperventilating," Nurse One said condescendingly. She went and got me a paper bag.

I did feel better after I'd breathed into the bag. A bit.

"If I'm out of the woods, does that mean that I'm not contagious?" I asked.

"Yes," she said. "Would you like to go take a shower?"

Would I? Do pigs like mud? Do caged birds sing? Is there anything I'd rather do?

12:45 p.m.
That was singularly the best shower of my life. The hospital soaps and shampoos are very bizarre antiseptic-smelling lumps of goo, but I don't care. I'm clean! I'm clean! I have CLEAN HAIR.

I have never been happier to have clean hair, although was distressed to find that there are no hair dryers in the hospital. Now I'll get terrible flat fluffy bed-head.

I feel so much better. Still anxious. Paralyzed with anxiety, really. But clean! I'm clean!

When I fainted on the way back to my room, this apparently meant only that I was hungry and not that I was on death's door. So I was given a Full Breakfast. It sounds good, but trust me, it wasn't.

Full Breakfast: Bowl of something that may or may not be Cream of Wheat. Hard nugget of something that may or may not be toast. Boiled egg. (Hate eggs and am trying to be vegan, so obviously did not eat it.) Brown substance that may or may not be coffee.

Yuck.

2:15 p.m.
I hate it here.
I miss Dad.
I miss Kiki.
I miss my room.
I miss JT.
I miss JT.
I miss JT.

7:02 p.m.
I hate JT.
I hate JT.
I hate JT.

Jules was here.

Me: Hi! I'm so glad to see you.

Her: You look better. Cleaner. Last time I saw you, you were grotesque.

Me: Thanks a lot. I'm sick, remember?

Her: Are you? You don't look that sick any more. Just sort of scabby and . . . bruised. That's amazing that I can still see hickey marks. He must have sucked the living crap out of your neck.

Me: Nice. Thanks.

Her: I'm just saying. Are you doing something to make them worse? (*squinting suspiciously at my neck*)

Me: What? Like what?

Her: I don't know. I wouldn't put it past you. You've always liked attention.

Me: What? (Does she think I'm giving MYSELF HICKEYS to GET ATTENTION? Is she INSANE?) Are you INSANE?

Her: Oh, you know what I mean.

Me: No, I really don't.

Her: Ugrhghgh.

Me: Tell me what you mean, drama queen.

Her: I'm a drama queen? Me? You're one to talk, Princess Self-Centered girl.

Me: Princess Self-Centered girl? That doesn't even make sense.

Her: Who are the roses from anyway?

Me: Er, what's-his-name.

Her: Ha! I told you. He really likes you. And you don't even know his name.

Me: He likes me? How do you know?

Her: JT said so.

So there it was. Right there, between us. Like a ghost. Or something bigger — a brick wall. JT.

"JT," I said slowly, drawing out the letters.

"Don't be like that!" Jules said.

"Like someone whose best friend betrayed her?" I said, glowering at her.

"You can't make someone like you if they don't," she said, quite logically. Flipping her perfect flippy blonde hair.

"You can," I said, resisting the urge to strangle her with her lovely locks. (Why does she always look like she was just in a shampoo commercial?) (Honestly, it's disgusting.) "It's easy for you."

"What is that supposed to mean?" she snapped, putting her feet up on my bed. She was wearing new shoes. (Black and strappy). (A little inappropriate for the season, but attention getting.)

(I would kill for those shoes.)

"Nice shoes," I said. Out of habit more than anything else. I mean, someone gets new shoes, you point it out.

"Thanks," she said. "Jimmy Choos."

"Really?" I said. (Those things are about $700.) "Huh." I myself will own $700 shoes the day after hell turns into a hockey rink and fills up with tiny flying pigs.

There was a big silence and we both looked around the room. OK, she looked around the room, and I stared at her neck, looking for JT hickeys. She doesn't have any. Of course. JT wouldn't be so . . . crude.

The walls of this room are a really sickly green colour.
(Who chose this colour? Is it supposed to be restful? It's
seriously ugly.) (It made me think of the bilious pink bathroom and all of a sudden, I got a bit teary.)

"Haley, I'm sorry," Jules said suddenly. "He's just a boy.
It's not worth it."

"That's not it," I tried to say, but it came out more like,
"Thgjkgj sjk blkjfgh."

"What?" she said.

I just shook my head and cried for a few minutes.

"Can I tell you something?" Jules said finally.

"What?" I said.

"I never made out with Ben," she said. "I just said that
to shock you."

"What?" I said.

"I don't know," she shrugged. "I thought it would be
funny, and then it wasn't. And then there I was at his
house, sitting on his couch, watching his TV, and he was
pouring me drinks, and all I could think of was, who
would buy a couch this ugly? What am I doing here? And
he was nervous. And it just made me feel sick. So I left.
And that was all that happened."

"Huh," I said.

"And," she said.

"What?" I said.

"I don't know," she said. "I just thought it might be kind
of fun if you were going out with Brad. And then we
could all do stuff. You and me. Brad and JT. If I see him
again. I mean, after last night, I don't know."

"Why?" I said, getting interested. "What happened last night?"

"Oh," she said, "I don't want to talk about it. Can I smoke in here?" She pulled out her cigarettes.

"Jules," I said. "It's a HOSPITAL."

She stared at me.

I sighed. "No, you can't."

And then she started laughing. For a few minutes, I forgot that I hated her. I don't hate her. I love her. OK, I both hate her and love her. But that's normal, right?

▶ ▶ ▶

Friday, October 25

MOOD	Frantic!
HAIR	Well, at least it's clean.
HEALTH	Improving!
HOROSCOPE	WHY WILL NO ONE BRING ME MY HOROSCOPE? Am going crazy without regular daily updates. Gah.
JT SIGHTINGS	Zip.

I was finally allowed to talk to my dad on the phone. I can't believe it. Everyone was all apologetic that it didn't happen sooner, blah blah blah. (Really, I am furious about this, but will delay my furious outburst until after I talk to him.) (I never thought I'd be so happy to talk to Dad.) (Ever.)

Me: Dad!

Dad*:Honey! How are you? I've been worried sick. The social worker said that she saw you and that you were fine. Are you fine?

Me: I'm fine. Why are you there? When can you go home?

Dad: Oh, honey. I'm sorry this happened. I got mixed up with something I shouldn't have got mixed up with. I'm so sorry. And I think the fact that I'm an activist is making it worse.

Me: Oh, Dad.

Dad: I'm really sorry.

Me: You should be.

Dad: I am.

Me: Dad, I miss you.

Dad: I miss you, too, honey.

Me: It's horrible in here.

Dad: It's not so great here either. No Tivo.

Me: Yeah, I know what you mean.

Dad: I love you, sweetheart.

Me: Yeah, me too.

Must figure out some way to get Dad a) out of jail and b) a good lawyer.

12:14 p.m.

The door swung open dramatically. (It always does in this

---

* *Note:* His voice sounded weird and hoarse. Presumably he hasn't been able to smoke marijuana since going to jail. Wonder if he has taken up regular smoking. Hope not. Smoking causes lung cancer. Don't want my dad to die of lung cancer while languishing in jail, leaving me alone to raise myself.

room because it's a special double door that prevents my germs from leaking into the hallway, although I'm allowed to walk around in the hallway now so it seems perfectly ridiculous to continue to lie around in the Experimental Monkey Room.)

In walked Kiki. She was not looking so good. If by that I mean she looked perfect, like always, but if you looked very very closely she was totally covered with chicken pox scabs.

"I know, I know," she said, rolling her eyes. "I look like crap."

"It's all relative," I said helpfully.(I didn't want to tell her that she actually looked perfectly fine. It might have gone to her head.)

"But I have some news that will make you feel better," she said.

"What?" I asked. Thinking, *JT JT JT.*

"I've figured out how to bail out your dad," she said dramatically.

"How?" I say. "Did you borrow money from your parents?"

"No," Kiki said. "I just remembered. You know. The MONEY."

"What money?" I said. "What?"

"Duh," she said. "I knew you forgot."

"What money?" I asked again.

"THE ROLL OF MONEY," she said. "Remember?"

I remembered. The money in the jar! It all seems like so long ago, mostly because I've been nearly dead in the interim, and frankly I wasn't sure if that afternoon with the roll of money had actually happened or if it was part of a dream I'd once had. A fever dream. (You know how that happens, how something weird goes on and you aren't quite sure, later, when you look back on it, if it was real or not.) (Come to think of it, how do you know if anything is real? So I pinched my own arm. It hurt. This was clearly real.)

"What the hell are you doing?" Kiki asked.

"Nothing," I said quickly. "The money. Of course. But can we use it? Isn't it . . ." I hesitated.

"What?" she said.

"Dirty money," I hissed.

"Dirty money?" she repeated. "Haley, it's not like your dad is the kingpin of the mob. He sometimes sells pot. I think you've seen too many movies."

"Maybe so," I said. "But he's in jail, isn't he? So that proves it's as bad as I thought it was."

"Maybe," she said. "I still think we should use it."

"OK," I said. I was very tired. I feel better, but sometimes I get sleepy. I just can't help it.

Dear Junior:

Am going to bail Dad out of jail but am worried about using crime money. What if we get fingered for having crime money? What if using the money makes it worse?

Why does Dad have to be involved in selling marijuana?

If he gets out, I'm going to kill him.

Junior, I'm so tired. I don't know if I can do this. Why do I have to be the grown-up?

It isn't fair.
Love,
Haley

► ► ►

Saturday, October 26 — Wednesday, October 30

The weird thing (well, one of the weird things) about being in the hospital is that all the time you spend inside blurs together. I wonder if that's what it's like for Dad. I've been so tired that I think I slept for the whole week.

Activities of this Week So Far:
1. Worry.
2. Sleep.
3. Eat Jell-O.
4. Worry.
5. Entertain smattering of guests, if by "entertain," I mean "stress out all my guests by making them worry about the same things I'm worrying about, such as my dad and why he's in jail." Apparently, he hired a lawyer who is one of his "friends" (read: "clients") which probably explains a lot.
6. Sleep.
7. Have long conversations with Dad on the phone. He says jail is actually pretty nice, what with the satellite TV and regular meals featuring meat. Try to convince Dad that meat is bad for him until he admits that he'd much rather be at home eating tofu and "unusual soy

products" with me, but that he doesn't want me to worry.

8. Worry.
9. Sleep more.
10. Contemplate Jell-O.
11. Watch I.V. tube drip.

Thursday, October 31

MOOD	Spooky
HAIR	Appropriately horrible as is Halloween.
HEALTH	Super tired
HOROSCOPE	You will receive news from far away that will change your life, your income, or your way of thinking.*
JT SIGHTINGS	still nada

Halloween in the hospital is weirder than you would expect. There are armed guards at the doors. It's really very off-putting.

Of course, everything in the hospital is weird.

9:42 a.m.
Bad news. Dad's bail release was somehow delayed. I don't understand it, but that's the way it is.

I feel weird. I wonder if I'm suffering from brain dam-

---

* *Note:* Have found nurses' break room and now have access to daily newspaper! Yippee!

age as a result of meningitis resulting from chicken pox.

Would kill for an internet connection.

Noon

Have inadvertently deleted ward clerk's file system and am forbidden to touch hospital computer ever again.

Will try again later when no one is around, which seems surprisingly often considering this is a hospital and should be overflowing with medical personnel at all times.

After all, you never know what might happen.

Armed guards are making me nervous. I asked them why they were there and they vaguely mentioned that on Halloween sometimes people get weird.

Which people? Outside people? Or the people inside?

Have nap and have bizarre zombie dream sequence in which nurses turn into brain-sucking monsters. May never sleep again.

5:31 p.m.

Kiki has my hospital room all decked out for the Ouija "date" tonight. It's so stupid and lame, I will pretty much kill myself if anyone found out about it.

She went a little crazy, what with the candles and stuff. I'm pretty sure candles will set off the fire alarms, but she says that they are just tea lights and therefore won't hurt anyone.

I let her do it. I gave up. The thing was, I kept thinking about how it said, "I would have loved you if I hadn't died," or whatever. Granted, it was slightly creepy. But maybe it was my mom, if my mom has died. (*Note to Self*: Stop forgetting to ask Dad what he knows.)

Or maybe it was a boy I would have loved if he'd lived.

Either way, I wanted to know more. Who wouldn't?

OK, I'll admit it. Last night I had a dream that I met the ghost-spirit-Ouija thing and it was a cute boy. Very cute. He was so . . . I can't explain. I was going to say "hot," but that just sounds lame. It's not that he was hot, which he was. It's just that he was hot in a familiar way. In my dream, when we were talking, I felt so . . . safe.

"Safe" is something I haven't felt for a long time.

I might as well admit that I all but forced Kiki to come up tonight to do this because even though so much other stuff is going on, I just can't get the Ouija board experience out of my head.

(Kiki didn't want to do the Ouija board again because she's been having nightmares ever since about letting in evil spirits from the Other Side and having them possess her and turn her into a crazed chainsaw killer.)

Note to Self: Don't let Kiki watch any more horror movies if at all possible.

7:45 p.m.
I think it may be possible that there IS such a thing as too much tooth bleach. Teeth are extremely painful and glow strangely in the dark.

Anyway, they are really white.

Things That Could Happen When We Play Ouija:

1. Nothing.
2. Get stuck making riddles with evil spirits.
3. Could all turn out to be a joke — maybe Kiki was pushing it?
4. Could get saddled with a boring dead person who has nothing to say.
5. Could be completely uneventful and pointless.
6. It might not work in hospitals (which I imagine are full of dead people anyway, right?).
7. The "I love you" boy might not know where to find us.
8. Might not be boy at all, but may be mom communicating from the other side, if mom is dead and dad has been lying all this time, which is implausible but you never know. And dream about Ouija board may, after all, have just been a dream and not a communication at all.
9. Kiki could be right, and an evil spirit could possess her, thereby causing her to become a female Jason from Friday the 13th and turning this into a different sort of diary altogether.
10. Kiki might not show up.
11. Someone else might show up and ruin our plans.
12. The nurses might freak out about the candles.
13. The candles might set off the smoke alarms and cause massive hospital evacuation.

Note to Self: Do not light candles. They may be "just tea lights" but suspect that flames may be more trouble than they are worth.

I took the Ouija board out of its box and set it up on the table-like thing that they serve their delicious meals on here. (If by "delicious," I mean "truly horrifying." Kiki is hopefully bringing me some vegetarian fries.) (Not fries fried in beef tallow, like most fast food fries. Which is disgusting, for the record. Think about it: fried in the fat sucked out of a cow. Nice.)

I bet if you asked people who were trapped on a desert island (a la "Survivor") for weeks without access to food what they wanted to eat, they would choose fries. There is just something about them. Grease + Salt = Heaven. As far as I'm concerned, at any rate, fries are the perfect food.

Later

Kiki was late.

For a while, I pushed the pointer thing around the board to different letters by myself. It felt much different than when Kiki and I were doing it together. When I did it alone, it just kind of dragged across the board. Also, I had to push it. It didn't take on a life of its own or anything.

I drank some ginger ale and lay back down on the bed. It was dark outside. The shadows dropped spookily across the parking lot. Halloween gives me the creeps at the best of times.

It must be awful to be in jail on Halloween. I wonder what kind of jail my dad is in? I hope he's OK. He's not really Jail Material. He isn't tough. I mean, he probably still has pink paint in his beard.

I hope no one beats him up, like in the movies.

I know how it must feel to be in jail now, to have to

watch out the window while everyone else gets in their car and drives away. It must be like being here, but worse.

I got up and wandered down to the nurse's station. There was no one at the computer, and I figured it couldn't hurt. After all, the files I shouldn't delete are the ones I'd already accidentally deleted. What harm could it do now? I went to webmd.com, which is one of my favourites. I punched up meningitis.

(from Web MD)

> Meningitis is almost always caused by another bacterial or viral infection that began elsewhere in the body, like the ears, sinuses or upper respiratory tract.
>
> The bacterial form of meningitis is an extremely serious illness that requires immediate medical care. If not treated quickly, it can lead to death within hours or to permanent brain damage in about 30% of people.

Permanent brain damage?

Greeaaaaattttt.

I went back to the room to wait for Kiki.

On the plus side, my hickeys are all but gone. They just look like fingerprints now. Like someone tried to grab my neck and strangle me. Which is arguably better than what they looked like before, which was more like an alien life form had tried to suck my internal organs out through the skin in my neck.

Permanent brain damage?

The thing with being a hypochondriac is that while you think everything is going to happen to you, like you'll get skin cancer from sitting in the sun, or you'll get food poisoning from some bad seafood, or you'll suddenly develop a life-threatening allergy to shrimp and drop dead at the dinner table, you never *really* think it will actually happen to you. Almost by imagining it happening, you ward it off.

What if I get permanent brain damage? What if I do? I have pins and needles in my legs. This could be permanent brain damage.

I have to learn how to stop thinking about things. How to shut it off. Likely what is wrong with me is closer to "obsessive-compulsive disorder" than actual brain damage.

I hope.

Things that Are Wrong With Me:
1. I'm obsessive.
2. I'm compulsive.
3. I think too much about myself.
4. I'm tired of being here and driving myself crazy.
5. I'm nuts.
6. I think too much about what's wrong with me.

I got bored waiting around for Kiki and took my IV pole for a walk. It's like walking with a pet. Only the pet is more likely to run away, and less likely to fall over and cause a commotion in the hallway.

Not that this happened to me.

By the time I got back to my room, Kiki was there.

"Where were you?" she said. "I was about to leave." She was wearing a slip with the word "Freud" written on it with magic marker. Of course, she looked perfect in this ridiculous ensemble, like she'd just fallen off a catwalk in Milan.

"What are you wearing?" I said, stunned.

"It's a costume," she said, looking down at herself. "Freudian SLIP, get it?"

"Meg Ryan did that in DOA," I said. "That's where she met Dennis Quaid."

"I thought she met Dennis Quaid on that movie where he got shrunk into the size of a pea and had to run around inside someone else's body."

"Was that him?" I said. "Or was someone else shrunk down and put in his body?"

"I don't know," she said. "You're the movie person. So where were you?"

I shrugged half-heartedly. "Oh, just fooling around on the internet," I said.

"Oh no," she said. "Not . . . medical stuff?"

I nodded.

She laughed. "Honestly, Haley," she said. "When will you learn?"

"I don't know," I said. "I don't know if I feel like doing this, after all."

"Of course you do," she said. "It'll be fun. Just think of all the people who died in this very room!"

"I thought you were scared," I said.

"I'm not scared," Kiki lied. "I want to talk to this mysterious dead kid, anyway. We have to find out who he is."

I wish I could say this part of the story is really interesting, but it isn't. We just sat there for ages with our hands on the pointer. But nothing happened.

No, that's not true.

Something happened.

But it turned out just that Kiki sort of drifted off and pushed the pointer when she almost fell asleep.

"Is there anyone there?" I asked. Nothing.

"Hello?" Nothing.

"We'd like to talk to dead people," Kiki said politely.

"Ha ha ha," I laughed. "That's too much like that movie. You know. 'I see dead people.'"

"Ha ha," she said. "OK, you make it come out and play."

"Can any dead people come out and play?" I asked. But the mood was ruined. We just started laughing and laughing and laughing.

"I see dead people!" she shouted.

And off we went again. I laughed so hard that I got the hiccups. Really bad hiccups. I was lying there, trying to hold my breath and not hiccup and she was knocking on the table saying, "Hello, dead people!" when the door swung open.

And it was Brad.

"Er, hi," he said. And Kiki stopped laughing and kind of stared at him. I tried to stop hiccoughing, but I couldn't.

"You know what the best cure for that is," he said.

"Ha," I said. Not laughing. And gritting my teeth together to stop from hiccoughing. (Honestly, the guy doesn't give up. I guess he is reasonably cute, in a "not JT" sort of way.) I touched my neck self-consciously. I still have the Mark of Brad, sort of.

A shadow of it, anyway.

"Uh, what's going on?" I said, hiccoughing loudly.

"Not much," he said. "I heard you were getting sprung tomorrow, so I thought I'd come by one More time. You know. To say sorry-I-gave-you-the-chicken-pox-and-nearly-killed-you."

"Oh," I said. "That."

"I have to go," said Kiki abruptly. It was almost sort of rude, come to think of it. She just grabbed her bag and marched out of the room.

"Hey," I said after she was gone. "She was supposed to bring me fries."

"I'll go get you some," Brad offered.

"No, no," I said. I looked at him. He's very cute-ish, I thought. He has nice eyes.

"You're healing nicely," I said. What? I'm so inane. I shouldn't be allowed to talk at all.

"Thanks," he grinned. "Uh, so . . ."

"So . . ." I said. We looked at each other some more. He sat down on the edge of the bed, so I moved over. He was too close. It kind of freaked me out. Although his blue eyes pulled me in. They were sort of . . . friendly. All the same, I felt weird with all this "looking" back and forth that was going on. Staring, really.

I felt like I should either kiss him or push him.

"You look really good," he said.

"Uh," I said. (I don't think I'm very good at accepting compliments, especially compliments that are clearly blatant lies.)

"Want to try the Ouija board?" I said, to break the silence.

"Um, sure," he said. "Does it work?"

"I don't know," I said. "I mean, it worked once. With Kiki. But according to the box it works even better between two people of the opposite sex. So . . ." Then I blushed, because of the word "sex." (This probably explains why I've never had a boyfriend.) I'm a prude. A prude who blushes easily.

"Sounds great," he said, avoiding my eyes. (Did he stop looking at me because I'm repulsive or because he couldn't stand to watch me blush and hiccup?) I took a big gulp of ginger ale and nearly choked to death on it. Naturally, that broke the awkwardness up a bit, as he had to slap me on my back.

My bare back, in my lovely back-revealing hospital gown. Will the humiliation ever end?

"OK, thanks," I said brightly and tried to ignore the fact that he was still resting his hand on my bare back. It's a hospital, for the love of God! It's the least romantic place on the planet! I kind of shrugged and stretched vigorously and his hand fell off. (Or he took it off, probably because my back skin is still scabby and gross.)

I got busy setting up the board again. (Kiki and I had kind of flung it aside when we got hysterical.)

"OK, what do I do?" he said.

"Well," I said. "You sit there," and I pushed him off the

bed and into the chair beside it, "and we put our hands on this thing and ask it questions."

We sat for a few minutes with our hands on the thing before I started to hiccough again. (Why do I get the hiccoughs? Why can't I stop?)

Note to Self: Check to see if hiccoughs are symptomatic of any disease.

"Cute," Brad said.

"What?" I said.

"The hiccoughs," he said, staring at me.

"Ask it a question," I said, frantically trying to change the subject.

"Will Haley ever go out with me?" he said. And the thing started to move. (OK, I pushed the thing.)

(I confess.)

(I'm a Ouija-pointer-pusher.)

I pushed it to No. I don't know why I did that. I think I sort of panicked.

And he got up and said, sort of sadly, "I guess I should have known better. I mean, guys like me never get girls like you."

"Wait," I said leaning forward a bit. "Brad!"

That's when my hair caught fire. I didn't even feel it. I just saw his eyes open wider, like he was surprised or like there was something behind me. "Holy shit!" he yelled.

"What? What?" I said. I could smell it. It smelled terrible. It took forever, or a few seconds, but that's when he started whacking me in the head with a pillow to put out the flames right at the same time as the sprinklers went off and my room filled with nurses and armed guards.

Oops.

Naturally, there was a bunch of excitement after that. Me lying in bed with half a charred head and Brad getting in trouble from everyone for having candles and me trying to explain that it wasn't him, and him saying it was all his fault, and all the while me selfishly thinking, "Oh God, I've gone and done it and now I have half a head of hair and will have to get a terrible haircut to cut the lump of burned hair off my head and will look ugly for a minimum of six months and possibly no one, least of all Brad, will ever love me, because why would he? I'm mean and I have no hair."

I'll admit to crying a bit, not that people noticed with all the ruckus. My bed was soaked from the sprinklers and before I knew what was what, I was being moved into a different room dragging my IV behind me.

A room with other people in it, all of whom were staring at me, probably because the fire alarm woke them up. There was one very elderly lady who looked almost like a zombie herself and one young lady with wild long hair and a hysterical expression on her face. And I thought I saw someone else, a funny looking girl with weird hair, and then I realized it was me in the mirror.

I got out of bed and went into the bathroom and stared at myself. My hair had sort of melted. Under the sink, I found some scissors. Blunt scissors, but scissors just the same. I don't know what I was doing, but it seemed like a good idea at the time.

I cut my hair.

When I was done, it was pretty short all over. And messy. It almost looked tousled and cute, a bit like Colleen's hair from "Survivor". That girl had good hair. (I wonder what happened to her after the show ended? Must check on the internet if I'm ever near a computer again.)

Computer! I ran back into the room, nearly ripping the IV from my arm in the process. Junior! Where was Junior?

I tried to get back to my other room, but it was still full of people.

Oh God, I thought. If I lose Junior, I've lost everything.

Then I realized that Brad was gone. He didn't say good-bye. Clearly, he hates me. I deserve to be hated. I'm a bad person who isn't kind to boys with beautiful eyes who like me.

I went back to my new room. The wild-haired girl was snoring with her mouth wide open. I went into the bathroom and stared at myself for a long time. I couldn't see any trace of the hickeys at all.

None.

Reasons Why I Ruined the Evening:
1. I'm in the hospital. Give me a break.
2. I'm not sure that doing Ouija with Brad was a good idea. What if ghost/spirit type thing came back and found me with a man? I didn't want to ruin that.
3. I knew the candles were a bad idea from the get go. Therefore, I'm an idiot.
4. I'm an idiot.

5. I'm an idiot.
6. In conclusion, it's safe to say that I'm an idiot.

At 11:42 p.m. (I know because there is a clock on the old lady's bedside table.) Nurse Two brought me Junior!

Junior!

Am happy. Ish.

Dear Junior,

I'm an idiot. Brad likes me, and he's cute and has great blue eyes. And he said, "Guys like me never get girls like you."

That's a really complimentary thing to say. I mean, I never thought of myself as a girl like me either. Well, not like the actual me. But like the girls that he meant when he said it.

You know what I mean.

Love,

A Girl Like Me

I've just climbed into bed and pushed the Ouija board away and turned off the light. In the moonlight, I am watching the antibiotics dripping down the IV and into my hand. I am about to fall asleep. I won't dream of anything. What I need is a big blank sleep, OK?

Like the sleep of the dead.

NOVEMBER

Friday, November 1

MOOD	Ecstatic
HAIR	Charred and unusually short
HEALTH	Fantastic
HOROSCOPE	Today will be uneventful. Use the time you are given to look inside yourself for answers.
JT SIGHTINGS	Zippety zip

I've never been so happy to see The Cat!

And The Bird!

And the ugly bathroom!

And my DAD!

My dad was sprung!

I love Kiki. I love my dad.

First thing I did when we got home was go downstairs. The grow-op was totally gone. (I have no idea how they do that, but they do. It's all completely dismantled.)

"Sorry, Dad," I told him.

"It's not your fault," he said. "It's the cops."

"Damn cops," I echoed.

But the truth is, a part of me was relieved. (A huge part of me.) (OK, all of me.) I was completely and totally relieved. And also a little dizzy.

OK, very dizzy.

I sat down on the bottom step and leaned my head against the wall.

"It's been quite a month, huh princess?" Dad said, laying his hand on my shoulder.

"Yup," I said. "Sure has."

We just sat there quietly for a while and stared at the empty basement and thought our own thoughts. OK, I admit it, I wasn't thinking anything deep. I was pretty much just thinking:

a) I get to sleep in my own bed tonight. Yay!

b) I need to go to sleep soon.

c) Must remember to apply bleach strips to teeth before bed.

d) I'm sure as hell not going back to school this week.

e) I'm so tired, I could sleep right here.

The point is that I was so tired, I could hardly keep my eyes open. Maybe one-tenth of one percent of me was thinking, "This isn't over." I mean, Dad is out on bail, right? He hasn't had a court date yet. But he says he might not get one for years.

It might not ever happen. But I'm still scared. But right

then, what I needed was flannel sheets, my stuffed rabbit named Nub, and a whole lotta sleep.

So that's what I did.

I love The Cat.
   I love The Bird.
   I love this bed.
   I love Nub.

► ► ►

Saturday, November 2

MOOD	Home!
HAIR	Not that bad! OK, very bad, but didn't want to spoil otherwise upbeat mood.
HEALTH	Healthy!
HOROSCOPE	If only you had more time in the day, you could get it all done. Consider taking a dance class.
JT SIGHTINGS	Who cares!

The phone started ringing fairly early. If by "early," I mean "before noon." (There should be a rule about calling anyone on a Saturday before noon. As in, it should not be allowed.) I could hear Dad talking in a hushed voice in the other room. He isn't ordinarily up before noon, much less on the phone. This was serious.

Everything was serious suddenly.

I got a sinking feeling in the pit of my stomach, but that

could have been hunger. (I'd become seriously thin in the last couple of weeks.) (OK, not that thin, but thin enough that my clothes actually fit instead of just about fitting or about-to-fit-if-I-lost-ten-pounds.)

My pants hung off me. "Hey, skinny," I said to myself in the mirror.

I turned sideways. But the thing was, it didn't look good. It didn't make me look like a ballerina, like Jules. Or a model, like Kiki. I just looked . . . tired.

Maybe I ought to take a dance class. For the posture, if nothing else.

"Yuck," I said to myself. At least my teeth looked good. And my hair looked . . . better. It had acquired a certain messy-cute quality almost. Although I could have been imagining that.

I did a few push-ups on the bathroom floor, just to see if I could.

I couldn't.

I mean, I never could. I thought maybe now that I was lighter, it would be easier. I guess I'm not that much lighter. Also, my arms feel like string cheese.

Note to Self: Join gym. Get muscles in arms. Consider taking a dance class! Nah.

I went down for breakfast, and Dad was sitting there with a big long list of stuff in front of him, writing madly.

"What are you doing, Daddy?" I asked. (I never call him Daddy. Don't really know where that came from, it just slipped out.) I dumped some food in the cat's bowl and poured a huge bowl of cereal. I was very hungry, and clearly my body needed food to heal and to regain all that lost strength.

Without "permanent brain damage."

I crunched my cereal noisily. I love cereal. (Cereal is the next best thing to fries.) (Current favourite: Frosted Mini-Wheats, the brown sugar ones.)

"I'm making lists," Dad said. "Lots to do, sweetheart."

"You're not going to have to go back to jail, are you?" I asked, as casually as I could. As though I didn't care. But my voice was shaking a bit.

Then I started to feel weird. Like I couldn't breathe. I gasped for a minute and put my head down on the table. Hard. (I hope I didn't bruise myself.) (The last thing I need is another giant bruise, this time on my forehead.) I closed my eyes and tried to breathe normally.

"I don't think I'll go to jail, no," my dad said. "I don't think so. It will probably get dismissed out of court, my lawyer says. But we have to make arrangements for you, just in case."

"Just in case?" I repeated. I breathed in through my nose, out through my mouth. In nose, out mouth. "What's going to happen to me?"

"Well," he said. "Probably nothing. I don't want you to get upset, sweetheart. But I was thinking maybe we should track down your mother."

"OK," I said. And then I fainted.

Bruise Count from Fainting in the Kitchen and
Hitting Head, Elbow, and Arm on the Way Down:
1. Giant bruise on forehead.
2. Entire elbow = bruise.
3. Forearm = bruised in three places.
4. Small finger of left hand slightly discoloured.

Dear Junior and/or Ghost (if you exist) (not my mother)
(who isn't dead, although I knew that, I just wasn't totally
sure),

School is starting to sound like a less stressful option
than being at home. I'm definitely going back on Monday.
I'm sure the Student Council needs me. And then I won't
have to think about all this.

It's all too much. I'm so worried.

Find my mother?

Love,
Scared Girl

▶ ▶ ▶

Saturday, November 9

MOOD	Festive, fatigued, fat
HAIR	Uh, can't talk about it
HEALTH	Bloated (too much cereal?)
HOROSCOPE	Animals play an important part in your day today. Maybe you will save someone or something from a dangerous situation. You are in the right place at the right time.
JT SIGHTINGS	5

Why did I go to a party? I was not in a party mood.

I was crazy to go to that party.

Reasons Why I Shouldn't Go to Parties. Ever.

1. Am no longer the Hickey Girl, which drunk people at parties forget.
2. Am very clumsy and break things.
3. Tend to kiss strangers randomly.
4. Tend to bump into Brad and kiss him for no reason and allow him to give me MORE HICKEYS on my neck.
5. Get hiccoughs when I drink.
6. Allow the sight of JT kissing other girls (i.e., Jules) to give me excuse/reason to drink which gives me hiccups which apparently gives me excuse/reason to end up kissing Brad.

"Why am I here?" I shouted at Kiki, who smiled and waved in response. The music was really loud.

"Why are any of us here?" she yelled.

"Good question," I said, and looked around. It was crazy. Someone was going to get into serious trouble when their parents got home, that was for sure. I wondered whose house it was. On the coffee table, there was a really ugly arrangement of dried flowers that was about three feet tall. (How would you see the TV around such a thing? I imagined someone's mother going and choosing those huge magenta paper roses. I imagined her matching it to the wallpaper.)

To tell you the truth, those ugly flowers made me feel kind of sorry for myself.

"Hey, Hickey Girl," someone said, tugging on my arm. I turned around and was just about to say, "I'm not Hickey Girl anymore," when I realized who it was.

And naturally what came out of my mouth was more like "Agglllll, blblblbl."

"What?" JT said. He was so close, I could smell his breath. And his whole ocean-y smell. Oh God, oh God, oh God, oh God.

I swear, all other thoughts left my brain. It's happening, I thought. It's JT. This is TGYML after all.

The Fates are giving me JT to make up for all the other stuff.

Thank you fate, I said to myself.

I concentrated on breathing so that I didn't hyperventilate. He was soooo close to me. It was all I could do not to lean in and kiss him. (Hello? What's wrong with me? Am I crazy?)

Then I remembered so suddenly it was like there was a crashing sound in my brain. (There was a crashing sound, but it came from the kitchen, not from in my brain. Although it felt like it came from me.)

"Jules?" I said.

"She's in the other room," he said, leaning in to me. I could smell the beer on his skin. It wasn't pretty, but hey, it's JT. I cut him all sorts of slack. I guess I always have.

"Where have you been?" he said. He was looking at me. JT's eyes were on my mouth. Which made my mouth feel weird and paralyzed. For a heart-stopping second, I forgot how to talk.

"Me?" I said. "Oh, I was . . . sick."

"We're out of weed," he said.

"Oh," I said. "Um."

"Get me some weed," he said. "I've heard you're . . . connected."

"What?" I said. I was breathing funny. I almost felt like punching him. I felt sick and wobbly. "I don't have connections," I said.

"Oh," he said. And then he stumbled off.

JT! JT! JT! I thought.

But it was more out of habit than anything.

JT?

Weed? (Who SAYS "weed"?)

The thing is, I didn't feel as bad as I thought I would have. I mean, I felt . . . nothing.

I guess a near-death experience will do that to you.

Not that I was really near death.

I mean, I could have been.

Suddenly, I was desperate to go home and get the Ouija board to work. I had to talk to that dead person. I don't know why. It doesn't make sense to me, either. I just felt like if I didn't, I was going to die. For real.

I got up and knocked over an incredibly ugly lava lamp, which naturally crashed on to the coffee table and broke into about a thousand pieces. (Who are these people and who advised them on their home decorating? Seriously. It made our house look almost like Better Homes and Gardens.) Everyone stopped what they were doing to stare at me.

"Um," I said.

Question: How much liquid is in a lava lamp? They seem quite small, and yet approximately one gallon of putrid fuschia ink was spreading into someone's parents' ivory coloured throw rug.

"Er," I said. "Whose house is this?"

A couple of people shrugged and laughed at me. "I'll be right back," I announced. As though I was about to go into the kitchen and find something to clean it all up with.

As if.

I was on my way to the kitchen to (a) escape or (b) find cleaning products when I happened to accidentally catch a glimpse of Jules leaning on JT and laughing, her hair flicking over his face. Just the look on her face made me feel like gagging or retching or just throwing up all over her Jimmy Choos.

I thought, "Oh my God, she really really likes him." And it made me feel sick and weird and . . . good.

Good because I was sort of happy for her.

I mean, I still hate her for it. But it was nice to see her happy instead of all weirdly puffy and sad. But sick, because JT is *mine*. It's *my* name that he doesn't remember. *I'm* the one who knows which socks he wears with which shoes. *I'm* the one who has memorized his phone number. It's *me* who accidentally on purpose goes for runs by his house on the off chance that he might come out and say hi.

Anyway.

That was over.

I felt all emptied out. I was standing there, kind of staring in a possibly psycho-stalkerish way, when someone put a beer into my hand.

Which I drank.

Beer is actually a very delicious drink. I'd never really noticed that before. It was really very good. And then, next thing I knew, I was hiccoughing. (It's a short walk for me from perfectly-sober-and-not-hiccoughing to hiccoughing-like-an-idiot.)

Somehow, whenever I get the hiccups, that damn Brad appears out of nowhere. And there he was, looking kind of grumpy and forlorn, so naturally I said, "What's wrong with you?"

And he said, "I'm just feeling sorry for myself."

And I kissed him.

Sunday, November 10

MOOD	Confused
HAIR	Tousled and cute
HEALTH	Seems OK
HOROSCOPE	If you are expecting legal activities, watch your back today. A partner will be anxious about your actions in a formal setting. Avoid financial dealings.
JT SIGHTINGS	0

Inventory of Ugly Marks:

1. Chicken pox scabs are mostly gone, but skin is still red and blotchy and possibly forming giant keloid scars as we speak.
2. Black eyes have faded to weird, pale yellowness which gives vague appearance of jaundice, which, in conjunction with skinniness and weird red blotchiness, makes me look like Death Warmed Over.
3. Old hickeys have nearly vanished altogether.
4. NEW HICKEY, THE SIZE OF RHODE ISLAND, IS PRESENT ON LEFT SIDE OF NECK.

Dear Junior,

No longer have need for Ouija Ghost Boy who loves me, or for JT. Have a real boyfriend of my own. A boyfriend with lovely blue eyes.

A boyfriend who gives me hickeys. But no one's perfect, right?

I'm so happy. I love everyone. Specifically Kiki and Jules and Brad and Dad and the Student Council geeks and even JT.

OK, not JT.

And not the Student Council geeks either. (Particularly those involved with The Ice Ball. More on that later.)

Love,

Haley A.,

Official Girlfriend of Brad

▶ ▶ ▶

Sunday, November 24

MOOD	Happy
HAIR	Shiny
HEALTH	Perfect
HOROSCOPE	Try to listen more than you talk: someone is going to give you a clue that you've been waiting for your whole life. You will know how to proceed.
JT SIGHTINGS	Who?

Sunday Dinner at the Vegetarian
Chinese Food Place on the Corner

Me: Let's have tan-tan noodles.

Dad: Whatever you want.

Me: Are you OK? You hate tan-tan.

Dad: No, I don't.

Me: OK, we'll get that bean curd stuff that you love if you're going to be that way.

Dad: What way? I want you to have what you want to have.

Me: You're making me nervous. What's going on?

Dad: I found her.

Me: Who?

Dad: Your mother.

Me: Who?

Dad: Come on, Haley.

Me: You found her?

Dad: Yup.

Me: Where is she?

Dad: She lives here in town.

Me: What? Who is she? What?

Dad: She is who she is, honey.

Me: That doesn't make sense!

Dad: You're in shock. You sound weird.

Me: I'm not hungry. Let's go home.

Home, Eating Toast at the Kitchen Table:

Dad: Are you OK?

Me: (Staring at him in silence).

Dad: I'll make you more toast.

Me: (Still staring at him in silence).

He found her.

She *lives* here.

What am I supposed to do with that information? What? Am I supposed to go visit her? Go live with her? Meet her?

I felt sick. And yet hungry. And yet furious. And sick.

She *lives* here? Maybe I've seen her before.

Maybe she's seen me. Maybe she walks by the house. Maybe she knows who I am.

But if she does, why hasn't she ever introduced herself?

I bit into another piece of toast. Toast is one of my favourite food groups. There is no occasion where toast is not welcomed. I love toast.

But thoughts of my mother were ruining my toast. (The words "my" + "mother" don't even match up properly in my head. Like orange and purple. They just don't go.)

I wonder if She loved toast. Did I get my love of toast from her?

Do I care?

Why is this so hard?

"I have to call Kiki," I said. I got up from the table. The chair made a terrible squeaking sound on the floor and The Cat, startled, rushed past me out of the room. I stared after him.

The Bird twittered on my plate. Like he was laughing at The Cat.

I went upstairs. It felt like it took a long time, like the air was thicker than usual and that gravity was stronger. I sat down in the hallway on the floor with my feet up against the wall. Phone in my lap. But instead of calling Kiki, I decided to go see her. Kiki would make it all make sense.

I got changed and threw the Ouija board (*NB*: The Ouija board was slightly warped from the hospital sprinklers, but still appeared to be functional, if you can describe a board with letters written on it and a plastic pointer as something that could be "functional" to begin with) into a bag and took it with me.

I don't know why I did that.

I guess I thought that maybe the universe might have some answers. Also, it made me feel safe.

I had this huge desire to run as soon as I got outside and the cold air slapped me in the face. So I started running.

And running.

And running.

OK, I'll admit that I only made it about three blocks before I almost died from heart failure. (Perhaps my heart was weakened due to my extended illness. Must ask doctor.) My legs felt wobbly, like wet pasta or pipe cleaners. The point was, my body was still too weak and crippled to go for a long run.

Or a short run.

Or really any run.

I lay down on a bench (that was covered in frost; I kind of stuck to it) and tried to breathe. It was cold. My own breath hung in front of me like little puffy sailing ships and my lips were chapped and dry. I chewed on them for a minute and thought about nothing. I tried to catch my breath. The air was almost too cold to pull into my lungs. The stars were amazing. Winter stars are the best. I could see the outline of the constellations.

What am I going to do? I asked.

The stars didn't answer.

They never do.

After about half an hour, I limped to Kiki's house. (It would have sounded better if I'd run the whole way, but I didn't.) (*Note to Self*: Must make gym a priority if I ever go back to school again.)

I staggered down Kiki's driveway and started throwing pebbles at her window until she finally came out. She has the greatest house. It's not huge or modern-looking, it just looks like the most normal, tidy house. OK, it's pretty big. She has her own little balcony thing.

I felt kind of like we were Romeo and Juliet. She was in her nightgown and looking down on me from above.

"Juliet," I called, in a falsetto. Only I didn't need to use a falsetto, I guess I needed the opposite if I was going to be

Romeo. I tried again with a deep voice, "Juliet!"

She howled with laughter. "What are you doing here?" she shrieked. "I'm coming down. It's late. Just a sec."

A couple of minutes later, she appeared in her night-gown with her jean jacket over the top. (On her, it looked like a million dollar outfit that ought to be featured on the pages of *Vogue*. Or at least, *Jane*. Or maybe just *Seventeen*.) (Not that I read *Seventeen*. OK, sometimes I do read it, but just to look at pictures of haircuts that I might get if my hair ever grows out of its current crop.)

Question: Why do I have such glamorous friends? I'm such a schlump.

"What's going on?" she said.

"He found her," I said. She knew exactly what I was talking about. (That's the great thing about Kiki. She can know what I'm saying before I say it.)

"Uh oh," she said. "What are you going to do?"

"I don't know," I said. "I thought I'd just cry for a while."

"Go ahead," she said.

Only I didn't. Because I couldn't. I didn't even feel sad. I just felt hollow and empty and weird and confused.

"What's in the bag?" she said.

"Ouija," I said.

"You're hopeless," she said, shaking her head at me. "But let's try it."

We set it up right there on the lawn, which was crunchy with frost. It was freezing cold and damp also, but that didn't stop us.

Actually, it was kind of . . . ethereal. There we were, fingers in place, waiting for the universe to tell us what to do.

"Should I meet my mom?" I asked.

YES, it said. Right away. Without hesitating.

"Is that you?" I asked.

YES, it says. ME.

My heart started beating really fast, like it used to when JT came into sight. I swear to God, I have a crush on the Ouija board.

Note to Self: Seek psychiatric help at earliest opportunity.

Weirdly, I felt . . . guilty. What about Brad? Was I *cheating* on Brad with a dead guy?

Was I crazy?

"Can you tell us more about yourself?" Kiki asked quietly.

YES.

"Like what?" I said.

I LOVE YOU, it said.

"Why?" I said, blushing.

WHY NOT, it said.

"But who are you?" I said.

I DIED, it said. DIED DIED DIED DIED. It got quite frantic at this point.

"Should Haley date Brad?" Kiki said.

And the thing stopped dead.

It just sat there. We stared at it for a full five minutes before we gave up.

"Way to make him mad," I said, angrily. "Why'd you have to say that?" Then I realized how weird that sounded. I mean, it's just a *ghost*, right? Or some kind of joke the cosmos is playing. Or more likely just some kind of weird physical manifestation of my thoughts and Kiki's thoughts. Our energies. I don't know.

But maybe, just maybe, it was for real.

And it made me feel . . . special. Stupid, huh? I mean, Brad made me feel special. I don't know why I thought I needed validation from a dead guy who I probably just made up.

I'm so screwed up.

I got up to leave. My clothes were all wet and stuck to me and I was shivering.

"Bye," I said to Kiki. "Sorry. I'm being weird. I know it. I'm sorry."

Kiki shrugged. "Whatever," she said. "I'm tired, too."

"Bye," I said again.

"Bye," she replied. "Take this with you." She grabbed the board and shoved it into my hands. "Take your boyfriend-in-a-box." She sounded mad. I hate it when Kiki gets mad.

"You keep it," I said. "I don't want it." But I did.

"Take it," she said. "It's too creepy for me to have around. I don't even want to look at it. It's just . . . weird."

I knew that she was right. I knew that I was messing something up. It made my knees wobble.

"I have to go," I said. I was shaking. I walked home slowly. My legs didn't seem like they wanted to take me that far. I had to keep stopping and leaning on things. I kept imagining falling over and freezing to death on the sidewalk and how mad my dad would be if he figured out that I was a) out at this time of night and b) wet and cold and c) being such a . . . child.

I thought about everything that had happened. I wondered why, for a while, I had kind of thought that the Ouija board WAS my mother. That SHE was talking to me. That it wasn't a weird dead boy at all, but just my mom. Telling me what to do. What to think. What the right things are. What's wrong with my life.

That's what moms do, right?

Then I started crying. And I didn't stop for a long, long time.

▶ ▶ ▶

Monday, November 25: Back to School

MOOD	Anxious
HAIR	Needs to be coloured. Badly needs it.
HEALTH	Sore throat, cough, stuffed up
HOROSCOPE	Feelings you aren't sure you should be having creep up on you today. Try to not act without thinking.
JT SIGHTINGS	0

I knew I was going to have to go back to school eventually. But my immune system was (apparently) still compromised. Also, the fact that I have had a cold bought me a bit more time.

Then my dad said enough is enough.

In fact, he said, "If you're well enough to go out with boys and see your friends and go to parties, there's no reason in the world why you should get to lie around here all day, hogging the remote control."

I think he was kidding.

I think he wanted me out of the house because he's been looking for work and pretending not to. I'm not sure why he's ashamed of it. (Because he doesn't want to admit that I was right all along? That drugs weren't a life?)

Ha.

I like being right.

Things I have Missed by not Going to School:
1. Everything

Things that I Care About Missing:
1. Nothing

Weirdest Things About Today:
1. Seeing JT and Jules together at school. Seeing JT with his arm draped around Jules. Seeing Jules laughing into JT's face. It's just . . . wrong.
2. Not being able to obsess about JT.
3. Not caring that much about JT, but caring about not caring about JT.
4. Weird new reputation as The Girl Who Almost Died.
5. Weird new reputation as The Girl Whose Father Might Go To Jail.
6. Weird old reputation as the Hickey Girl.
7. The feeling that everyone in school knows too much about me.
8. The feeling that I can no longer just disappear.

"I just want to disappear," I told Jules on our way from one classroom to the next. "What's so hard about that? Why is everyone staring at me?"

"They aren't staring at you," she said. "They're staring at your damn hickey. What is it with you and hickeys?"

"Oh, God," I said. "I feel like I should start smoking or something. Then I could hide behind a veil of smoke."

"Nah," she said. "You don't want to do that. Cancer, remember?"

I smiled a bit. "Oh, yeah. Cancer. I forgot."

"And it yellows the hell out of your teeth," she added.

"Right," I said. "Yellow teeth."

I got sucked into another classroom without saying goodbye. (The flow of traffic is so weird in schools, don't you think? You can just get swept along in the current.) I stared at the back of JT's head for a full fifty minutes. The weird thing was that my mind kept wandering.

It just wasn't the same.

In a way, it made me sad. I've spent a lot of years staring at the back of JT's head. Looking for something. I don't know what. Now, it's just the back of some guy's head.

Some guy who is dating my best friend.

I started wondering about my mother. (OK, also doodling in black ink on my desk. I might have carved my initials, HA. And Brad's initials. BS. HA + BS.) (That's kind of funny, no?)

This is going to sound completely crazy, I know. Don't think I don't know. But the thing is, now that JT is NOT occupying all my thoughts, it's like I can't stop thinking about Brad.

My boyfriend, Brad.

But also about my mom.

Wondering.

What's she like? What does she LOOK like?

What does she do?

Who is she?

Does she think about me?

And I guess the big one: Why?

Questions She Has to Answer:
1. Why?
2. Why?
3. WHY?

I don't want to meet her, and yet I'm obsessed with it. I can't stop thinking about it. I want to just see her, without having to talk to her. I want to watch her talking, or hear her talking, but I don't want to have to talk back. Like maybe she could be in some kind of human-type zoo where she wouldn't be able to see me, but I could see her.

That would be ideal.

I spent the rest of the class drawing a Mom Zoo in my notebook.

I'm three weeks behind now in everything. I have no hope of catching up.

GOD, I hope I don't have to repeat twelfth grade.

Worst Case Scenario: I flunk out of Grade Twelve and have to live The Greatest Year Of My Life (!!!!!) all over again. TGYML. Ha. If this is supposed to be The Best Year, I want my money back.

Not that I paid anything. It's just a figure of speech.

And it has been kind of great. I mean, Brad has been great.

But it's also been the worst year ever.

Summary of TGYML, so far:
Things that have been lost:
most of my hair, all of my dignity, my love for JT.

Things that have been found:
my mother, a boy who is willing to kiss my neck and doesn't think I'm repulsive, a ghost who said the 'l' word.

Things that have been saved, however temporarily:
my life, my friendship with Jules, my Dad (from jail).

Immediate problems:
am too behind in everything to catch up, have non-healing hickeys on my neck, feel like I need some kind of . . . advice.

► ► ►

Thursday, November 28

Dear Junior,
No time to write. Just wanted to say that I had the best date ever with Brad. Brad, Brad, Brad.

I might be in love. Don't tell anyone.

He held my hand.

He said, "I've never felt this way about anyone ever before."

I swear, when I look into his eyes, it's like the floor drops out from under me. Do I sound crazy? Like I'm in a romance novel? I feel crazy.

I feel like I'm in a romance novel.

I'm so scared. And happy. And scared.

Sometimes, when he's kissing me, I'm thinking, "Oh my God. I'm just not ready for this yet." Other times, I'm thinking . . . well, I'm not thinking that I'm not ready. I'm just right there. Weird, huh?

Thanks for listening,

Love,

Girl-in-Love

Friday, November 29

MOOD	Vague
HAIR	Needs cutting.
HEALTH	Light-headed and anxious
HOROSCOPE	It would be easy to forget about other people today and do your own thing. An invitation will bring good news.
JT SIGHTINGS	No idea, didn't count

2:14 p.m.

"Come over later for Ouija board?" I whispered to Kiki in Computer Lab.

She grinned at me. "No way!"

"Come on," I said. "Why not?"

"Shhh," she said, typing something on her keyboard as Mr. Zak wandered by, glaring at us.

"Please?" I whispered.

"Shhh," she said. "Maybe."

I know it's stupid. But I can't help thinking that the whole reason why we started fooling around with the Ouija board to begin with, was that it has something important to say. Some piece of advice that I need to hear.

Something that will make everything make sense.

I mean if the ghost/spirit loves me (as creepy as that sounds), maybe he'll have some good, cosmic advice for me. A message from the Fates (or whatever).

Why not? I have no one else to ask. No one else can help me.

At least, I don't think they can.

Kiki e-mailed me: "I think you are getting obsessive about this I-Love-You ghost."

"No, no," I wrote back. "Not obsessive, just curious. One more time, please?"

"OK," she typed. "One more time. But that's it. You have to deal with real people. Like Brad, for example. Your BOYFRIEND."

"My boyfriend," I whispered. It still seemed so weird to me. Is he my boyfriend? I guess he is. He's the boy I hang out with. The boy I kiss. The boy who makes me feel all melty and stupid.

If that's my boyfriend, then he's it.

I'm so lucky.

I didn't actually respond to that note. I mean, Brad is

all very . . . Brad. But call him my boyfriend? I do. I mean, I guess he is. I just feel so strange about it, like I'm not quite ready to take that step. Besides, I am an ELUSIVE BUTTERFLY! I am a CREATURE LIKE NO OTHER.

OK, I'll admit it. I'm scared.

9:42 p.m.
"This is getting boring," Kiki said, lying back and sipping her herbal tea. "We have to stop doing this and start going out or something. Where's Brad?"

"I'm starting to think YOU should date Brad," I said. "You're always asking about him."

She looked at me sideways and rolled her eyes. "Yeah, right," she said. "I'm just worried that you're throwing away something great."

"Well, don't sweat it," I said. "He's working tonight. He's helping his dad out at his restaurant. Sweeping the floors or pouring water or something."

"Huh," said Kiki. "Want to go down there later and hang out?"

"Kiki," I said. "Don't be crazy. It's a really expensive restaurant! We can't just show up. Besides, we're doing this. And it's good for Brad and me to spend time apart."

"Why?" she said. "You've never had a boyfriend before. I'd have thought you'd want to spend all your time with him."

"Well, I don't. OK?" I snapped. "I want to spend time with YOU because you bug me so much. Why wouldn't I want to? THIS is soooo much fun."

"OK," she laughed. "Don't get all bitch-o-rama on me."

"I'm not," I said. "Look, let's just do this."

"OK," she said. "But I still don't know why you want to. It's creepy." She shuddered.

"No, it's not," I said. "Besides, we'll all be dead one day. How would you feel if you came back to impart some little gem of wisdom and the person you chose to communicate with thought you were creepy? That's rude."

"I'm being RUDE to a ghost," she said. "Seriously, dear, I think your brain is still inflamed."

I stuck out my tongue. "OK," I said. "Point taken. This is the last time. OK? Then we'll burn it. Or something. Stop the evil spirits from finding the, er, portal."

"Portal?" she said. "Jesus. It's like 'Buffy the Vampire Slayer' in here. Only we're not demons or slayers or witches. Or really anything interesting. The Big Evil is going to come for us . . ." She crossed her eyes.

"Come on," I said. "Let's just get going."

I hunched over the table like a maniac.

"You know what this is like?" Kiki said suddenly.

"What?" I said.

"It's like the internet. Instant Messenger. But the thing is that you never really know who you are talking to. They might claim to be a really hot, young guy and turn out to be an old, toothless pervert."

"I guess," I said dubiously. Instantly, my image of the Ghost as a JT-meets-Mel Gibson lookalike was shattered. (Why do I assume my ghost is hot? That really is insane.)

"We've never really asked what he looks like," Kiki said. "I'm going to." She grabbed my hand and plunked it onto the pointer.

"What do you look like?" she said.

DEAD, it said. Right away, without hesitating. Like he'd just been there waiting for us to get on with it. The hair on my arms rose.

"What DID you look like?" she said.

LIKE A BOY, he said. NOTHING SPECIAL.

"Look," I said. "I just wanted to ask you, you know, if there is something that you wanted to tell us."

I WANTED TO TELL YOU THAT YOU ARE CUTE, he said.

"Um, thanks," I said.

"What about me?" said Kiki, rolling her eyes.

YOU TOO, he said.

"I don't think this thing is going to tell you anything," said Kiki. "He's some kind of dead player. He's toying with you."

"Are you toying with us?" I asked.

NO, he said.

"Um," I said. "Can you tell me anything about my mom?"

Kiki looked up at me sharply. I could feel her eyes on me, but I chose to stare at the letters instead. I lifted one hand off the pointer and took a big drink of diet Coke, which I almost choked on.

NO, he said.

"No?" I asked, dazed. I don't know why I thought he would (or could) know my mom. I don't know why I thought that was the point. Like he was tapped into something. Not that he was some kind of weird cosmic . . . joke.

GOODBYE, he said.

And that was it.

Big finish, huh?

"Will it burn?" I flipped the board over. It's some sort of wood, I thought. I grabbed it and took it into the living room and crammed it into the fireplace, which hadn't been used in like, forever. I tried to light it on fire. But it wouldn't light.

"Stop it," Kiki said finally and grabbed it out. "Just stop it."

I hadn't realized it, but I was crying like crazy. "Just stop," she said again and grabbed me. She hugged me so hard, I couldn't breathe. "Just stop," she said. "And you'll be OK."

My hands were shaking like mad. I felt completely nuts.

Hello, therapy? Come in, therapy.

"I need therapy," I said finally, when I could stop sobbing. "I'm so fucked up."

"Everyone is fucked up," Kiki said.

"Not you," I said. "You're not."

"Sure I am," she said, making a face. "Everyone is. I promise you."

"We could bury it," I said after a few minutes. "Like in the garden. Then it would be like burying the dead."

"Too creepy," she said. "Look, let's just put it away."

"OK," I said. I fished it out of the fireplace and brushed all the dust and crap off it and dropped it into the box. It looked really innocuous lying there. I wondered a bit if the ghost guy was hot and if he would have had a crush on me when he was alive. If he was ever alive. If he wasn't just a manifestation of whatever vibes were in the air.

I took the box down the stairs and stuffed it in the cupboard.

"You have to walk me home," Kiki said. "I'm all freaked out. And this was all your stupid idea."

"OK," I said.

I'm not totally cured of my obsession with JT. On the way home, I admit that I may have walked about ten miles (*NB*: distance is totally made up as I have no sense of distance) out of my way to walk by JT's house. Just in case.

In case of what?

I have no idea.

Possible Reasons for Walking By JT's House
1. Can't break old habits?
2. Still have crush on JT?
3. Enjoying walking and need the exercise?
4. Brad might have gone there after work?

OK, am I now stalking Brad? What is wrong with me? Ugh. I am an ass. Must not think about Brad. Or JT. Must solve immediate problems first.

Immediate Problems:
1. Dad: will he go to jail?
2. Mom: should I meet her?

I sighed and tried to jog home. It was freezing and the rain that was falling felt an awful lot like snow. It hit me in the face and stung, no doubt leaving irreversible pock marks.

It took me ages to get home, and by the time I did, I was both sweating and freezing. I settled into the couch with The Cat and some hot chocolate and watched late night talk shows.

Note to Self: Late night talk shows are no better than daytime talk shows.

A bit later, Dad came in and sat with me for a minute and then fell asleep. He can fall asleep faster than anyone I've ever met. AND he snores like no one else on earth. I swear, the pictures on the wall shook. While he was sleeping, I carefully and quietly cut all the pink paint out of his beard using the hair-cutting scissors I bought when I got home from the hospital so I could cut my own hair. (Will never trust Dad's druggy hairdresser friends again, and am getting quite good at doing my own.)

I mean, he has to appear in front of a judge one of these days, and having pink paint in his beard will not bode well for him.

I don't think.

When I was done getting rid of the pink, his beard looked kind of weird and patchy, so I trimmed it a bit.

OK, I cut it all off. I admit it. I don't know how he slept through it. He must have been very tired. Or else he was faking it.

But who can fake that kind of snoring?

At one point, he lurched his head wildly and I was so startled (if by "startled," I mean "terrified") that I almost gouged his face with the scissors. I didn't though.

Nothing went wrong. (Which is a miracle, if you think about it. I'm not generally that lucky.)

When I was done, I swept up the hair and threw it out. That seemed wrong, to throw hair in the garbage, but I couldn't leave it on the couch, either. Dad would think he suddenly developed alopecia while he was sleeping and he'd freak out. Understandably.

Not that he won't freak out when he wakes up to find his beard mostly gone, but he'll forgive me.

I think.

Things I Think About Instead of Sleeping:

1. School and how behind I am in everything.
2. If Brad will call tomorrow.
3. What to get Brad for Christmas.
4. What to wear to meet Mom.
5. What to wear to court with Dad.
6. Whether or not double-dating with JT and Jules is a good idea.
7. Why I wonder about shallow, pointless things when big life issues are waving in front of my face like GIANT RED FLAGS.
8. Whether my roots are showing and whether I should dye my hair dark brown to cover up the roots.
9. The Ouija board.
10. Fate.
11. The meaning of life.

Which is why a few hours later, I woke up screaming my

head off and imagining a stalker-esque ghost standing at the foot of my bed, staring at me, but without eyes. Just with big white eye sockets that were all full of light.

And why my dad leapt up off the couch and tried to run up the stairs to see what was wrong and ended up tripping on The Cat and falling down the stairs instead of up, and putting his back out.

Oh, no.

What else can go wrong?

Wait, I wasn't going to ask that anymore, was I? Scratch that last question. I mean it. I officially un-ask it.

DECEMBER

Friday, December 6

MOOD	Incredibly tense
HAIR	Hmmm. More on this later.
HEALTH	Dizzy? High blood pressure?
HOROSCOPE	Today is a good day for making major purchases. Get your shopping done early! Watch for urges to overspend.
JT SIGHTINGS	No idea

Major, Life Changing Events of Today:
1. Dad goes to court.
2. I'm having lunch with Mom.
3. Shopping for dress for the winter dance.
4. Going to the Ice Ball. With Brad.

I figure I should get it all over with at once. If nothing else, I'll be able to write this off as the Worst Day of My

Life. At least I get to cut class with good reason.

9:00 a.m. exactly

Why is it that court is not as dramatic and interesting as on television? For some reason (because I'm an ass?), I half-expected Dad's lawyer to look like Ally McBeal and the Judge to look like Judge Amy Grey from Judging Amy. Just so you know, in real life the judges are not bizarrely beautiful. And the lawyers? Ugh. Dad's lawyer is a short, glasses-wearing guy who looks about twelve years old and keeps staring at my neck. I don't even HAVE a hickey any more (well, not much of one), so staring at my neck is just rude.

I'm starting to believe that, in fact, I have an unusually ugly neck, which is why people are always looking at it.

I glared at the lawyer with my best stop-looking-at-me-you-worthless-jackass look. And then I tried to take it back, because after all, he is on our side. And I don't want to screw with karma.

As it turned out, though, it didn't much matter.

The judge is either (a) bored sick with marijuana cases (this is totally a hippie town) or (b) a smoker himself or (c) having one of those days where he just doesn't give a damn.

Really, it was very anticlimactic. But in a good way.

Dad was given some sort of suspended sentence that involves community service. I have no idea why. (I'll admit that I did sort of drift off partway through the proceedings, which weren't nearly as interesting or lively as on TV.) (I didn't get very much sleep last night.) (I was worried.)

(And excited.)

I know it's really important, what happens here, and I do care. I was really proud of Dad, with his newly shaved face. It's not like he was wearing a suit or anything but at least he wasn't wearing any of the following:

1. My pyjamas.
2. A T-shirt with writing on it.
3. Any kind of colourful pants.
4. Unmatched socks.
5. Hippie sandals.

"It's going to be OK," he said, hugging me so hard that if I'd been choking on something, he most certainly would have saved me.

"Hurrah!" I said. "Ouch." And I hugged him back.

And that was that.

(Oh, and his lawyer tried to hug me, but I elbowed him really hard in the sternum "accidentally" as he came in for the hug. "Ouch," he said, and doubled over.)

I laughed.

And he laughed too, but I could tell he didn't mean it. But who cares? Not me, that's for sure.

We walked out of there like we are walking on air. At least, I did. Dad was really limping because of his back. I felt sorry for him, I did. But I'm also really, incredibly happy.

Of course, this means he'll have to get a real job.

And so will I.

But that's OK. I want to. I want to do it right this time around.

New List of Things to Worry About:
1. Employment.
2. Money.
3. How we will pay rent.
4. Social Services, who still are "assessing whether Dad is a fit parent."
5. Money.
6. Money.
7. Dad's back.
   Who will hire Dad with a bad back?
8. Money.

12:00 approximately

I called Kiki from the corner. It was freezing and it was just starting to snow. It would have been pretty if I weren't so afraid.

Me: I'm going to be sick.

Kiki: No you're not.

Me: Yes, I am. I need a cigarette.

Kiki: You don't smoke.

Me: I'm starting.

Kiki: Liar.

Me: OK. Just tell me it's going to be OK.

Kiki: It's going to be OK. I promise. Call me the minute you're done.

Me: I'll call you during. I'll call you from the bathroom.

Kiki: Breathe, sweetie.

Me: I am breathing.

Kiki: You're hyperventilating. Breathe like this.

In.

Out.

In.

Out.

Me: (*breathing*) I'll call you when I'm done.

I hung up the phone and put it in my pocket, then took it out again and dialed Brad's number. He answered right away.

Brad: Haley?

Me: Yeah, it's me.

Brad: I'm so glad you called. How was your dad's thing?

Me: Great. It was great. He's off the hook.

Brad: Where are you?

Me: I'm . . . um . . . on the corner. I don't know what street. Hey . . .

Brad: Yeah?

Me: It's snowing.

Brad: It'll be OK, you know.

Me: I know.

Brad: I'll see you later. Have a good time. Don't be nervous.

He hung up. He was on his cell phone, so it made that little bloop sound that cell phones make when you flip them shut without disconnecting. I kept listening in case I could hear him talking to someone else or something, but the connection was broken.

I traced my boot through the dusting of snow on the sidewalk. I wished there was more snow, so that I could do something great. Like make a snowman or snow angels or snowballs or something.

Anything.

But I was already late. A bit late, not a lot late. I could see the restaurant from where I was standing. It was a cute little place. Already, the windows were steamed up from whatever they were cooking. Soup, I thought. Or maybe just the coffee. It looked homey and safe.

My heart was beating like crazy. I took my gloves off and held my hands out in the falling snow. It was falling thicker and faster. I thought for a second about all the snow I'd ever seen. All the snowmen I'd built with my dad. Snow forts. All the times he zipped me into my snowsuit and took me out to shovel the driveway and all that other stuff.

All the stuff my mom missed. For a minute, I was really pissed off, and then it passed. I lay the fingers of my left hand on my right wrist and listened for a bit. OK, I timed it. It's a habit. It makes me feel like I'm OK. I counted up to seventy-five in one minute. Lub-dub. OK, I said to myself. No matter what happens, this will still be here. It will still be snowing. My heart will still be beating. It will be OK.

I checked the time.

12:11. I was eleven minutes late. I straightened up and ran across the street. I figured if I went really fast, I wouldn't be able to stop.

And I wouldn't be able to turn around and run the other way.

I kind of burst into the restaurant and pushed my way past the tables right to the washroom. I didn't look at anyone. I couldn't breathe. I felt like I was going to faint. I'd never been so nervous in my life. I splashed some water on my face (which totally smeared my make-up). (I don't know how women always do that in movies and manage not to smear any make-up and to come up looking dewy and fresh.)

Other than the smearing, I looked OK. Jules dyed my hair dark brown last night when I went to her place to find something to wear. Sure, there is a bit of hair dye on my face that I can't seem to remove, but my hair, at least, was shiny. It looked healthy.

"Your hair is amazing," Jules said. "Really. It looks awesome."

She was lying on my bed amongst a pile of clothes that I'd tried on and rejected. "It looks like Ashley Judd's hair in that movie she did with the good-looking Australian guy."

"It does?" I said dubiously. "I don't think so. I think her hair was really short in that movie."

"OK," she said. "It looks like a darker version of Rene Russo's hair from that movie that had James Bond in it but wasn't a James Bond movie. The one where she had all the good clothes."

"Hmm," I said, wanting to believe her. Rene Russo had really good hair in that movie. "I have nothing to wear."

"She isn't going to care what you're wearing," Jules

said. "She's probably more nervous than you are. After all, she's the one who left."

"True," I said. Jules flopped over and knocked a pile of sweaters on the ground.

"It's not like it's a date," she said, eyeing my sweater speculatively. "That's a date sweater. Not a meeting-your-mom sweater."

Which for some reason made me cry.

"Don't cry," she said. And hugged me. Which made me cry harder. Jules never hugs me. At least, she hasn't for a long time. Not since we were little kids.

"But what am I supposed to wear?" I wailed. "I have nothing to wear."

"I don't know," she shrugged. "This?" She reached into the pile and extracted a black turtleneck sweater. "Not that you need it," she added, staring at my neck speculatively. "Haven't seen Brad lately, have you?"

"Ha ha," I said, touching my neck self-consciously. My neck felt weirdly hickey-less and naked. "Maybe we should call Kiki. She'll know what I should wear."

"OK," said Jules, reaching for the phone. "Emergency summit at my place!" she yelled when Kiki answered. And so Kiki ran over. Literally ran. (Without breaking a sweat. As usual.)

I think I hate Kiki. How could she not sweat? I was sweating just from trying on and discarding so many outfits.

Kiki was great, though. She marched right to the closet and found:

1. Black pants (removed all cat hair later).

2. Dark blue top that makes me look (a) blue eyed and (b) pretty.
3. Black boots with low heels.
4. Leather jacket.

Which was exactly what I was wearing as I leaned against the bathroom counter of the restaurant and counted my pulse again. Ninety-two. I breathed slowly and tried to calm down. In my head, I made a list of all the things my mother might be:

1. Old
2. Fat
3. Ugly
4. Young
5. Tiny
6. Beautiful
7. Strange
8. Psycho
9. Weird
10. Scary
11. Happy
12. Sad
13. Bizarre
14. Annoying
15. Someone that I know?
16. Someone that I've seen?
17. A hippie? (this is a good possibility)
18. A street person
19. A hooker
20. An entirely dislikable person

21. Just like me
22. Nothing like me
23. Not even here

I took a deep breath, pushed open the door and stepped into the dining area.

In spite of all the steam, the restaurant was all but empty. There was a young couple with a baby at one table. A nun at one table. An old man at the next table. And two young women at the next. Was she one of the young women? I examined them. They didn't look that much older than me. And they were really pretty. I couldn't imagine either one of them dating my dad. Or marrying him.

Just then, someone tapped me on the shoulder.

Oh. My. God.

Oh.

My.

God.

My mom is a nun.

See what I mean? It's always the one scenario that you don't imagine. That's the one thing that wasn't on my list.

I recognized her right away. Well, not right away, because like she says, people see the habit first and don't see her face. But as soon as I saw her face, I knew it was her.

I'd like to say that we flung ourselves into each other's arms, but that totally isn't what happened.

THIS is what happened:

Her: Are you Haley?

Me: Yes?

Her: I'm, er, your mother.

Me: Like Mother Superior you mean?

Her: No, your actual mother.

Me: Is that a costume?

Her: No, I'm a nun.

Me: Oh.

Her: Can I sit down?

Me: Uh, OK.

Her: This must be very confusing for you.

Me: Um, yes.

Silence. While we stared at each other. She was pretty ordinary looking, my mother the nun.

Me: So I guess you believe in God, huh?

Her: Yes.

Me: You know, Dad isn't much into that.

Her: I know.

Me: I guess I wasn't raised that way.

Her: I guess not. I mean, I thought you wouldn't have been.

Silence, while we read the menu. All the food looked the same to me. I couldn't concentrate on it. Suddenly, I was hit with an overwhelming desire to laugh. The laugh hovered just at the back of my throat and came out like a really big cough.

Her: Are you OK?

Me: (in strangled voice) Yes.

Her: Is there anything you'd like to talk about?

Me: . . .

Well, I mean, there's lots I want to talk about, but somehow it doesn't seem right to talk about these things with a nun.

Things I will Never Have a Heart-to-Heart Conversation with My Mom About:
1. Boys
2. Sex
3. Anything

I mean, who is she? What do I have to say to a nun? I felt like I should confess. Or something.

Me: It must be interesting being a nun.

Her: It's peaceful.

Me: That's good.

Her: It's a vocation.

Me: A vacation?

Her: No, a vocation.

Me: Right. I know what you mean.

Her: Is there anything you want to ask me?

Me: Yes. No. I don't know. I need a minute.

I drank a glass of water. And then we ordered.

And then we ate. (Me: egg salad sandwich with a side of salad and another side of mashed potato; Her: bowl of soup, dry bread — I kid you not, she eats "nun food.")

We didn't really talk about much of anything. I watched her eat. She was a small woman with dark brown hair and straggly eyebrows. She really needed to do something about those. Her lips trembled a little bit while she ate. Like she was really afraid. Or really sad.

Or both.

Or maybe she had some sort of palsy, such as Parkinson's Disease. (I could look it up when I got home, I thought. It occurred to me that I hadn't looked at my medical sites very much lately. Not since October. Weird.)

Her teeth were perfect: even and white.

I really liked her teeth. I wondered if she bleached them. Well, duh. She's a nun. Of course she doesn't bleach her teeth.

The waiter took our plates away and we sat there for a few more minutes. I wanted to ask her why. I did. I just couldn't do it. It was like every time I opened up my mouth to ask her, my throat just closed up and I couldn't talk.

"I have to go back," she said. And for a minute, it felt weird, like she was going to get swallowed back up into whatever movie she had stepped out of. Like it was all going to turn out to be fake.

"Back," I said.

"Back home," she said. "That's all. Maybe we can . . ."

"I'd like to see you again," I said. I must have been crying a little bit, because she reached over and wiped a tear away. It was weird. Like a mom kind of thing to do, but being done by a stranger. "I wanted to ask you . . ."

"I know what you want to ask," she said. "I might be a nun, but I'm a human being. I know what you need to know. I just can't answer it."

"You can't?" I said.

"No," she said. "I wish I could. It was just something that happened."

"Something that happened," I repeated.

"I know it's not enough," she said. "I'm sorry. I want you to understand, but I don't understand myself. I guess what I want to say is that it's God's will."

"I don't believe in God," I said, so quietly I wasn't even sure she heard.

"No," she said. "I guess you wouldn't."

I wanted to tell her what my horoscope had said for today. That it said that the universe had great things in store for me today. That everything would be set right. That I'd get the answers I'd been seeking.

That the universe was wrong. That everything wasn't set right. That it was just shaken up. That nothing was answered.

I went past her, out into the snow, and on my way by I kind of patted her on the arm. She just isn't the kind of person who looks huggable. I wondered if she had ever hugged me. She kind of raised her hand. I think she looked sad. Like she knew what she'd given me wasn't enough.

I left. I didn't call anyone. It was getting dark outside and it wasn't even three o'clock yet. I walked for a while, past stores selling Christmas stuff. I kept my hands deep in my pockets so that they wouldn't freeze. So that no one would notice how much I was shaking. Eventually, I remembered that I had to get a dress. That I had to go home and get ready for the dance.

I walked into the first shop with dresses in the window.

They were all pretty. It felt surreal. I couldn't imagine myself in any of them. I just bought the first one that fit. I couldn't even really see what it looked like. It was like there was a blur between me and the mirror. The sales-lady kept asking if I was all right and I kept saying, "Yes." Which meant "No."

I know it's stupid, but I'd had this weird fantasy about my mom coming with me to get the dress. I'd made it a big imaginary deal. And here I was alone, wet hair flat-tened to my skull, shaking hands, trying to pull enough money out of my wallet to pay for it while the sales people watched me suspiciously, as though I might be about to bolt out of the store with all their lacy, beaded gowns.

The dress I bought was black, that's all I noticed. It was probably a bit bleak, but I didn't care. It was a black-and-white ball. All the other girls probably bought white, thinking they'd be different, but I didn't want to be differ-ent. I just wanted to be exactly the same as everyone else for once.

I took the shopping bag and instead of getting on the first bus, I decided to walk. I don't really know what I was thinking. I walked until I got to the school, which was really a fair distance. It took over an hour. I sat on the play-ing field for as long as I could (which wasn't very long). It was way too cold for that kind of drama.

If I'd stayed longer, I would have got pneumonia for sure. And one near-death experience was plenty for the year, thanks anyway. There were lights on inside the school, so I went up to the window, thinking that maybe I'd go in and use the washroom before going home. And I realized, of course, that the lights were on because all the other little Student Council geeks were running around decorating the place.

"What the heck," I said. And went inside.

Don't tell anyone. I just felt like I ought to do my part. That's all.   •

It wasn't a big deal.

On the way home, I called Kiki. She was in the shower, her mom said. Did I want to leave a message?

"No," I said. "I'll see her tonight."

I was kind of disappointed. I was sort of ready to talk about my mom. I tried Jules, but her mom said she was already gone. I looked at my watch. 7:02 p.m. I was going to be late, if I didn't really hurry.

Brad was picking me up at 8:00.

How I feel Now That I've Met My Mother:

1. Same as before
2. Different than before
3. Sad
4. Happy
5. Relieved
6. Empty

Very, very late.
Dear Junior:
The ball was great. I'd write a big long paragraph about it, but it would sound stupid. It would sound sappy. And God knows I wouldn't want to sound sappy. I was wearing the weirdest dress there. It was black and long and had

feathers sewn into the bodice. Tiny little feathers.

I felt kind of like a big crow, to be honest with you.

Brad said that I looked great. He said I was prettier than anyone else there, which is stupid, because Jules and Kiki both looked like princesses. Like swans. In beautiful, white beaded dresses.

They were amazing.

I was like the ugly duckling. But that was OK.

I had fun.

Love,

Haley Andromeda

or HA, for short.

EPILOGUE

New Year's Day!!!
(OK, I've been too lazy to write this stuff down every day.
I've been busy.

  You know how it is, right?)

At Christmas, I told Brad that when he said, "Guys like
me never get girls like you," that's when I knew that he
was The One.

  That he would be my Boyfriend. Ha. Boyfriend. Sounds
funny when you say it out loud.

  I don't think I'm going to have much time to write too
much in here for a while. I'm super busy. You know,
school and stuff. Life. It gets in the way of all this typing.

  So.

TGYML (so far):
Accomplishments:
1. Drugs are gone from the basement.

2. Lost ten pounds.
3. Got teeth to peak of whiteness.
4. Got boyfriend.
5. Got good hair cut.
6. Met mom.
7. Got dad to quit eating meat (!) (Or so he says.)
8. Made up with Jules.
9. Found out exact healing time of hickeys. (Varies according to strength and size of hickey: from seven to sixteen days, depending.)
10. Survived chicken pox, meningitis, and Student Council meetings.

Still to Do:
1. Write essay re: what I did on my summer vacation.
2. Stop obsessing about boyfriend Brad and get some homework done.
3. Get job.
4. Save up money.
5. Get into college.
6. Graduate.
7. Plan prom? Ugh. Someone save me from this. How did I get involved? Someone remind me. Please. And get Dork McDork-a-lot to stop leaving me notes on my locker asking me how the Prom planning is coming along. I beg you.
8. Plan after-prom Party, officially called The Best Party of The Best Year of Our Lives, So Far.

Final Analysis:

Hair	Excellent, in style of Winona Ryder in that movie where she dies while dating Richard Gere.
Mood	Excellent.
Health	You know what they say, right? That which doesn't kill you, makes you stronger. If that's true, I'm practically a super-hero.
Horoscope	Excellent (Today is the first day of the rest of your life, Gemini, get out there and enjoy yourself! Consider taking up a new hobby or sport or just enjoy doing something that you love.)
Things I love	Brad, my hair, running. I can now run five kilometres without having to stop to either (a) throw up or (b) pass out. (OK, I hate running, but don't tell.) (Still love the idea of running.)
Possible Ideas for New Hobbies	Needlework? Have hilarious idea to needlepoint "Guys like me never get girls like you" into pillow to give to Brad for graduation present. (How long could that take? I'm sure I could do that. It would make him laugh.) (I think. Must call the girls and ask for their opinions.) (I'll be seeing them both in an

	hour or so anyway. We've hired a psychic. She's coming over to read our palms. To tell us what it's all about. And what's going to happen next.)
Outlook	Excellent.
Hickeys	One.
Approximate time to healing	Four more days.

ACKNOWLEDGEMENTS

I've never done acknowledgements before, but now I feel like I must. A lot of people inspired me, encouraged me, and listened to me go on and on during the writing and editing process of this book. So here I go: A big "whoot" to the following, for being there at the proverbial water cooler whenever I started to have a meltdown and became convinced I couldn't do this after all: Pamela, Kandi, Carolyn, Lisa, Nancy, Lela, Tina, Aileen, Adrien, Heather W., Heather H., Melissa Rock, Melissa LP, Jacquelyn, Kim, Amy, Cate, Kate, Rebecca, Karri, Meghan, Lori, Deb, Jill, Deirdre, Alison, Danielle, Lynn, Denise, Jennifer, Lauren, Lyndsey, Marianne . . . if I've forgotten anyone, it's just because my brain is too tiny to retain information. (It's true. I had an MRI once and it said I had an atrophied brain. I can't be held responsible.) (And if anyone knows what brain atrophy is, please contact me immediately! I need to know if I should worry.)

Also, thanks to everyone who said, "You should write a

funny book! It would be so easy for you!" (To them, I'd just like to say "HA . . .") This list includes, but is not limited to, my mum and dad, Sonja, Diane, and everyone who ever laughed at any one of my stories.

For selling it and believing in it, my agent, the superlative Carolyn Swayze (superagent to the stars). For her magical editing and guidance, Lynn Henry.

For attending to all my ills, real and imagined, my dad and the dozens of other doctors I've badgered over the years. For the hours of Ouija and subsequent fear and hilarity, Helen B. and Tamara B. (Sure, it was a long time ago, but I'll never forget it.) For actually lighting her hair on fire and for letting me steal the story, Kate LeVann. (Buy her books. She's really the funny one.)

For the late night poetry sessions that kept me sane and made me crazy, Evan, who is the only other person awake and online at 4:00 a.m. To my therapist (OK, he isn't really my therapist, but he's the closest thing I have to one) K(h)en, who one of these days is going to write something amazing himself other than technical documents. For Jim Stewart, because he was around at the beginning of this one and built a house in the time it took me to get it down on paper. For Deb Stinson, who will one day be a character in a future novel, I promise. For Tim, who took me to the hospital and read to me while I waited for the pain and itching to stop during my run-in with meningitis and chicken pox. For Cheryl and Diane, who were there on the night out that led to the infamous line that started the whole thing: "Guys like me never get girls like you." For everyone who has ever been there and called 9-1-1 when I've ridden off the edge, or run into a tree, or fallen into a hole and broken, bruised or maimed myself, and for the paramedics who have picked me up and brushed me off and set me straight. And of course, to everyone who ever gave me a hickey. Thanks a LOT.

I also owe a huge debt of gratitude to all the online medical websites, whose powers should only be used for good and not necessarily to fertilize the active imaginations of hypochondriacs the world over: they are a great source of information. Use it wisely. (And always, always, go to your doctor instead of sitting at your desk worrying yourself into a frenzy over the remote possibility that you have contracted monkeypox, even though you've never even seen a prairie dog.)

ABOUT THE AUTHOR

Karen Rivers has published five books for teens, including *Dream Water* and *The Gold Digger's Club*, which were short-listed for the Sheila Egoff Children's Literature Prize, and *Surviving Sam*, which was shortlisted for the White Pine Award. Karen lives in Victoria, British Columbia, Canada.